Stealing the Glass Slipper

Rachel Anne Jones

I dedicate this book to my mom, Connie (my other mom), Michelle, Marie, Aunt Mary, Aunt Lois, NiNi, and all of you brave, beautiful women who have the courage to stay strong in your faith and devoted to the greatest and truest love that can only come from above. May we always remember whose Crown we wear.

"Someone stole the glass slipper, and now it's shattered to pieces."

1

Sheri Mallo sits in an unforgiving chair in the basement of the church she grew up in, willing herself to focus solely on embroidering a pinpoint, chocolate-brown sunflower seed just like the twenty-two others beside it. But who's counting?

"Are you counting, Sheri? They have to be exactly the same."

Sheri turns toward Gladys Knight and her sharp tone. Gladys may as well be Weezer from *Steel Magnolias*, which is the church lady's favorite movie despite its release date and borderline sacrilegious language. *The movie's only redemption is Dolly Parton*, Sheri figures. After all, if you can't love Dolly, who can you love?

"Yes, Gladys, I'm counting," Sheri answers while trying to hold in a smirk at the thought of Gladys going over their quilt squares with her bifocals and counting every single stinking sunflower seed in the center of every single sunflower to ensure its conformity to uniformity.

Gladys clicks her tongue. "Well, we certainly can't have a repeat of last year. That would be a travesty."

"What happened last year?" Raine, the only teenager in the group, asks in an innocent, naïve tone that's about to be destroyed.

Gladys lays down her embroidery, does an extremely dramatic eye roll, and sets her laser-beam stare on Raine, who, to her credit, does not flinch in the line of fire. "Our quilting group was disqualified for unknowingly using a semi-professional to apply their quilt backing to a quilt they worked two years on." Her voice breaks.

Sheri ducks her face to cover her embarrassment.

"It was the first time we had ever entered the Flying Bees Quilt Competition in Kentucky," Gladys states as solemn and sacred as the Declaration of Independence, "because some shirttail relative of Rosie's," she practically shouts, "who lives down South," she mutters beneath her breath like it's a dirty word before clearing her throat, "told Rosie we were a sure win."

Gladys sticks her almost nonexistent nose in the air. "It was nothing short of a disgrace. I've never been so mortified in all my life. We are from Wisconsin, a northern state. We had *no business* entering a Kentucky quilting competition." Gladys eyeballs everyone in the circle as if daring anyone to object.

Sheri follows her challenging glare as it circles the room, aiming at every ducked head, except for one smiling face.

Rosie shows no shame. "It was just a snafu, Gladys. No need to get your girdle in a twist," Rosie pops off and giggles while the rest of the circle holds their breath.

Gladys shifts in her seat.

Rosie continues. "We have all made a pact to do our very best to enter another quilt into the same contest as soon, and as correctly, as possible. We will clear the tarnish on our good name and put the dreadful debacle behind us. It'll all come out in the wash. You'll see."

"Well, I wasn't aware this decision was officially made. After all, I'm not on the quilting committee. Was it put to a vote?" Sherlene questions as she stands up so fast that no one can answer. "Excuse me," Sherlene announces as she walks out.

"You wash your hands when you get back," Gladys calls.

The outside door slams in answer.

Rosie gives Gladys the stink eye over the top of her bifocals. "Must you say that every time?"

Gladys's chin lifts even higher. Sheri didn't think that was possible.

"I will not have our prize-winning quilt smellin' like cigarettes and havin' yellow stains from her tainted fingertips."

Rosie's gaze falls on Sheri, who doesn't duck fast enough. "Anything new with you, Sheri? How's your love life? Are you still as dusty as a library bookshelf?" Rosie shoots Sheri an earnest smile, the only thing that keeps Sheri from despising Rosie and her nosy ways.

Gladys clears her throat, and Sheri wishes she would have said something—anything.

"Purity is a virtue, Rosie, but I don't expect you to understand that," Gladys states.

"I'm fine, thank you," Sheri manages to get out, but it's barely above a whisper and certainly not loud enough for two old women with hearing aids to hear or acknowledge.

Sheri supposes there are things more humiliating than sitting on a metal chair in the middle of her quilting hobby and being recognized as probably the only virgin in the room, but she doesn't know what. She opens her mouth to speak up and shut Rosie down, but Rosie's already started on her favorite subject: a sickeningly sweet, barely appropriate trip down memory lane of her marriage to Walter, a former war veteran who apparently picked up more skills than just firing a gun as a young marine in Italy. Sheri bites her tongue to keep from giving Rosie a smart retort.

"I hear you, Rosie," Leslie interjects in a firm, but kind, manner.

Sheri breathes a sigh of relief. Rosie's descriptions of her and Walter's fun times border on soft porn, something Sheri would rather not hear from an eighty-five-year-old woman in TED hose and bifocals.

"I don't know what I'd do without my dear Frank," Leslie croons.

Deb catches Sheri's gaze in her crosshairs. "I agree." Deb's eyes light up. "Sheri, how do you not feel so terribly lonely?"

Her question is an honest one, and Sheri knows Deb thinks she's being kind, but Sheri has had enough.

Sheri glances over at her best friend, Jenni, whose eyes scream, "Proceed with caution." Sheri clears her throat and addresses the would-be compliment from Rosie regarding Sheri's chastity. She didn't know her virtue was going to be on display like a lit-up neon sign hanging over her head shouting, "No Business Here—Keep It Moving." She could have done without Deb's not-so-subtle pity of her being single.

"You know what they say," Sheri mutters as she skims

her phone screen and shares the latest post by the local football coach. "'It is not happy people who are thankful. It is thankful people who are happy.'" Sheri reads these words aloud as a healthy reminder to curb her bad attitude as of late and her sense of restlessness.

Sheri wonders if it is because she is basically past the age of bearing her own children or if it is the fact that she hasn't had a serious boyfriend in literally twelve years. Rom-coms, bags of pretzels, and hot cocoa can only do so much to fill the emptiness of her living room couch cushion. "How's the baby?" Sheri asks Jenni with a forced *Rainbow Brite* tone as she begs Jenni with her eyes to save her from further awkwardness.

Jenni pats her ever-growing stomach. "Do you mean this one or my three lovelies at home?"

Sheri gives her a wry smile. "Either," she responds.

Jenni sighs. "Well, my feet aren't swelling quite as bad this time. I think it's because my other three were born in the summer, but this time we managed to get that part right. I'm so relieved this baby is due in February. We may even get a Valentine's Day baby. Wouldn't that be adorable?"

Sheri returns a smile to her best friend and pushes away her envy, which is somewhat new and ridiculous. It's not Jenni's fault Sheri hasn't met Mr. Right. Or that ever since she turned forty-two years ago, she feels like she's standing closer and closer to a fault line attached to a pit of loneliness that's going to open up and swallow her whole any day now. Sheri shakes her head at the thought of being forever cursed to remain the town librarian whose only date on a Saturday night is a good book.

"Yes. A Valentine's Day baby would be the cutest thing ever," she responds.

Jenni's slightly swollen fingers struggle with the needle. "It'll be nice to have my last baby right after I turn thirty. That has always been our family plan."

Her words linger in Sheri's covetous ears. She chokes on her bitterness as she pastes on a smile and meets her best friend's eye. So what if Jenni is living the dream while Sheri is stuck being the imaginary, chaste twin sister of Bridget Jones who seems all too happy to let life happen? At least one of them is content. *Maybe that's my problem*, Sheri thinks to herself before coming to the conclusion that she's not much of a planner. She kind of goes with the flow, which seems to work most of the time. It's just lately she feels as if she's a canoe with one oar in the lake of life, turning in circles that lead to nowhere.

Lettie sits beside her. She grabs a hold of Sheri's wrist with her gnarled hands, which are a wonder. Lettie may have the most crooked knuckles in the quilting group, but she sews the straightest stitches.

"It's a shame you don't have a sister or brother, dear. I never married either, but I always had my sister, Clara. She and I were both teachers. We loved to talk about our students. I miss Clara every day, but I've got lots of great memories to keep me company until I see her again."

Sheri glances over at little Lettie, who grows shorter by the day, no thanks to her losing battle with osteoporosis. Sheri loves Lettie's floral dresses, little stocking-clad legs, and tan Eccos. Lettie's bright blue eyes sparkle and shine behind her spectacles. Lettie may be ninety-two, but her youthful spirit suggests otherwise.

"I've always had so much respect for teachers. It takes a

special person to love each child for who they are," Sheri tells her.

Lettie laughs a little. "Back in my day, if you had a little whippersnapper who got out of line, you just straightened them up with a good knuckle rap. You can't do that today. That's for darn sure. Someone's liable to call the cops. But some kids *need* a little tough love."

Sheri holds in her laughter as she catches Raine's eyes widen, followed by a strange sound before she hunches over her embroidering even more as if to shield herself from Lettie's barbs. Sheri has a sneaking suspicion Raine did some fast talking with the local Judge Jones and talked him into letting her serve her community service with the quilting women instead of picking up cans on the side of the highway under the supervision of the local sheriff's department. Raine had the misfortune to be the only one in a group of kids who got caught down at the local park setting fires in the bathroom trash cans.

Sheri glances in Raine's direction again. She thinks Raine's just a kid who got caught up in the wrong crowd. Sheri hopes she starts heading in the right direction soon.

Lettie leans in toward Sheri and points a bent finger at Raine. "That little missy over there, she could use a good knuckle rap."

Sheri coughs a little too loudly. She wonders if Lettie knows how loud she's speaking. Sheri notices Raine has the good sense to duck and keep her eyes on her stitching.

Sheri sighs as she sits in her chair and looks around the room. She knows she has a lot to be thankful for: a wonderful family, a great group of friends, her dream job as a librarian in her hometown, and her most recent coveted position of backup alto in the church choir.

"It's a shame, dear, that they took you away from singing solos. I thought maybe some man might notice you standing front and center," Kathy, ever the hopeless romantic, shouts out from across the room at Sheri.

Sheri manages a smile. "Thank you, Kathy, but I love singing backup. It takes the pressure off. I've never been a fan of singing solos."

"How are you going to catch a man, dear, if you're too happy being a wallflower?" Rosie saucily shouts at Sheri, seconding Kathy's unwanted advice.

Sheri tries to think of a polite way to tell Rosie she shines enough for the whole quilting group with her new fashion statement, which happens to be sparkles everywhere, a theme inspired by her favorite grandchild's bedazzler.

Sheri clams up while wondering how the conversation that she didn't start turned on her so fast. First, they were praising her for holding strong to her virtue, and now they're accusing her of not putting herself out there.

Jenni clears her throat. "I'll certainly miss your solos, Sheri, but you make a wonderful backup singer. You're such a great encourager, and you have a wonderful listening ear."

Sheri gives Jenni a small smile and a silent blessing. Jenni may be twelve years younger than Sheri, but she's been a fantastic friend. At least she understands why Sheri was never so relieved when they took her off front—and center—in front of the mic after seven months of pure torture. Sheri's anxiety over being on the main mic got so bad she felt like she was about to start popping Xanax—with the approval of the local doctor, of course.

Sheri wasn't about to start purchasing them from her

over-the-road, truck-driving neighbor, whose gutters get more in-and-out action than a coffee shop drive-through on a Monday morning. His rooftop may as well be the North Pole for all the mysterious packages that appear—and disappear—from his roof, which has as much traffic as the Panama Canal Zone at 5:30 a.m. Sheri wouldn't have noticed this strange phenomenon if she weren't such an early riser, but insomnia seems to be another after-forty perk she's acquired.

"Did you hear Daniel Post passed away?" Sally, the doomsdayer of the group, calls out from her corner of the circle.

Sheri drops her quilt square on the floor. Suddenly, there's not enough air in the room. She leans over and attempts to put her head between her knees. A half second later, she slowly sits up and tries to hold back her unexpected tears. Daniel Post was her best friend all through high school and college, not to mention her standby husband. She and Daniel once had a few too many bottles of wine together on a rare occasion in college, as Sheri's always been a "boring girl," and tipsy is all she's ever been. She and Daniel agreed that if neither of them found happiness by the age of forty, they would marry each other.

"I'm sorry," Jenni mouths at Sheri right before Sheri lays down her quilt square and heads for the bathroom.

Just before Sheri flips the lock on the single-toilet bathroom, Jenni throws the door open wide. "I'm sorry, Sheri. I was going to tell you. I just haven't found the right words to say. It all happened so fast. He had cancer, and they didn't find it until it was too late. They only gave him weeks."

Sheri slides down the wall. She feels ridiculous, but

she's unable to stop her own pity party. She hasn't heard from Daniel in years—she can't explain the sense of loss that has come over her. Sheri didn't exactly try to keep in touch, but knowing her default marriage choice is no longer a choice feels so hopeless.

"I didn't know, Jenni. I had no idea. If I had known, I would have called him up. I would've gone to see him," Sheri laments.

Jenni leans against the wall of the bathroom. "I know, Sheri. I know you would have. These things happen for a reason you know."

Sheri looks up at Jenni from the floor. "Is this your way of telling me I'll definitely never have a husband—like ever?"

Jenni rolls her eyes. "You heard me say Daniel passed, right?"

Sheri buries her head in her hands. "Yes. I wonder why he didn't tell me he was sick."

Jenni side-eyes her best friend. "Maybe he was afraid you would make him hold up his end of the marriage deal from his deathbed."

Sheri ducks her head in embarrassment. "I suppose that's fair." She looks up at her best friend. "I'm so glad you know me so well and love me anyway."

Jenni gives Sheri a wink. "Remember that if you ever decide to sell your beautiful monstrosity of a house that's just begging to have my children's handprints all over its pristine walls."

Sheri studies Jenni a second too long. She considers her best friend's words. She snaps her fingers. "I think you're on to something. You need a bigger house, and I need a change of scenery." Sheri nods her head. "I need it like yesterday." She closes her eyes again. "I can't take another Christmas alone."

Jenni coughs. "You have me."

Sheri looks up at her. "You know what I mean." Sheri slaps the floor. "I'm forty-two years old. Forty-two! It's time for me to start taking control of my life. If I don't make a change now, I never will."

Jenni closes her eyes and tilts her head to the side. "Where are you going to hypothetically go this time? Just tell me so I can start researching another place on the map. It gives me something to do while I'm awake at 2:30 a.m., *wishing* I could live vicariously through my unattached best friend who has the freedom to be adventurous but limits her excitement to words on a page in the action-adventure section at work."

Sheri gives a little-kid foot stomp. "First of all, don't knock C.J. Box and his fantastic way with words, which is the only reason I'll ever get to be a park ranger in Montana who hunts down murderers beneath the wide-open sky or discovers inner-woman empowerment and a few hot kisses with mysterious men via Nora Roberts, the queen of romance and suspense. And secondly, I got a little lost in your tirade, but basically you're saying I say I'll go some-where, but I never do because I'm too chicken to follow my dreams."

Jenni crosses her arms on her very full stomach. "Crap or get off the pot, sister. That's what I'm saying."

Sheri taps her fingers on the wall. "Well, if I'm going to even think about going husband-hunting, I need to pick a place that has good odds."

Jenni taps the side of her nose. "They say the farther South you live, the more likely you are to be married."

Sheri sniffs. "This may be true, but I'm not moving to some backwoods hick town to marry an inbred Jed."

Jenni waves her hands around. "Okay, okay, Wis-con-sin snob." She claps her hands. "What about Texas? There are some pretty cute wranglers down there, I hear."

Sheri shakes her head back and forth. "Uh-huh. Nope. Texas is on its own energy grid, and that's just the start of its problems. I'm not about to support their views on capital punishment, not to mention their crazy gun laws."

Jenni puts a hand to her head. "Geez. You're not exactly making this easy on me." She studies Sheri. "What about Maine or one of those northern states?"

Sheri frowns. "The cost of living is too high, and I hear the crime rate is not that great either."

Jenni puts a hand on her chin. "So you're thinking of moving to a low crime rate state that has a decent cost of living, where the men might outnumber the women, and it's relatively quiet and low-key."

Sheri gives an affirmative nod. "Sounds good to me."

Jenni grins. "Then why not stay just where you are?"

Sheri side-eyes her best friend. "Because I can't. I want to get out and see the world. I need to have a little adventure."

Jenni raises an eyebrow. "How about Alaska?"

Sheri swallows hard. "Excuse me?"

Jenni lays a hand on her hip. "Yep. That's my vote. It has all the characteristics you're looking for, and it will *definitely* be an adventure."

Sheri has butterflies at the thought. What does that mean? "I don't know."

Jenni flips the latch on the door. "You're already used to the cold. And you're used to the quiet. I'll miss you, you know that, but you're right. If you're going to go do something, you'd better do it while you're still relatively young and healthy. You'd better go now. Alaska may not want you otherwise. Time isn't slowing down for any of us." Jenni winks at her best friend. "Go get that glass slipper, girl. It's waiting for you."

Sheri peels herself off the floor. "You think so?" she asks, wincing at the insecurity in her voice.

Jenni gives her a big hug. "I know so. You just gotta have a little faith."

Sheri follows Jenni back to the quilting circle, which has dispersed to the food and drink table. She picks up her square and folds up her chair to lean it against the back wall before sneaking out the door. She's got some thinking to do.

2

Randall's phone buzzes. His cousin, Jan, who he's kind of reconnected with—if that's the right term for family—has been all sorts of interested in his life lately, though he doesn't know why. Maybe it's the fact that her parents passed recently. He figures since his parents have passed on too maybe Jan feels a kinship to him.

He picks up the FaceTime call. "Hey, Jan."

"Hey, cousin. What are you doing?"

Randall can't help but smile. Jan is so upbeat. "I'm, um, well, I'm reading over the strange contraband magazine my brother left me—a modern-day, mail-order bride catalog," he says, testing the waters.

"No way. Are you freaking kidding me? That's an actual thing? Isn't that like some sort of archaic form of female degradation?" Her blue eyes narrow. Her hand flies to her hip while she continuously moves around. Jan's phone is mounted to something in her kitchen, as baking is her favorite pastime.

Randall shakes his head. "I'm sure you're right. Calm

your little feminist heart rate down. I had no idea these things still existed. Don't yell at me. It feels wrong to read through these profiles that are attached to smiling faces of all these international women waiting to be chosen to come and live in America. I saw a few honest faces, but—"

"What do you mean, a few honest faces? What makes you think they aren't all honest? It's not a crime to want to improve your life; and if the only way to do it is to marry an American and make him very happy because he won't get that kind of package with his looks, then so be it."

"Whoa. Simmer down. Did you just go all superficial on me? Don't you think it's kind of cold to make such assumptions about men you've never met? I thought you weren't that kind of girl."

She slams something down on the counter and starts pounding away on it. "Whatever, cousin. You gonna tell me that there aren't a certain number of men who still exist and are interested in something frilly, feminine, and wrapped in a neat, simpering little package that lives to serve them? 'Cause there totally are."

He rolls his eyes. He's not about to take her man-hate sitting down. "Like you women aren't the same way. Why do you think the romance novel section is so popular with all the women? They love romance in any form they can get it, even if it's only in a book."

Jan shoves the dough around with her knuckles. "Women's romance novels are much less offensive than what men prefer to look at."

Randall gives a disagreeable snort. "Says you. I was never so relieved when they finally shelved that stupid *Shades of Gray* book." He shivers. "All I can say is good riddance. *Lonesome Dove* needs to make a comeback or something. I miss McMurtry." His voice drops off.

Another phone rings. Jan lifts a finger of warning at Randall. "Hold up," she says as she picks it up. "Hello. Yes, this she." There's a pause. "Oh, yeah, I know her." Another pause. "That's right, the Mothers Milk Bank just off 129th and Wilson. I'll meet you there tomorrow." A longer pause. "Yes, it's put on by the coalition. There will be drinks and snacks. It's all very informal. No, don't worry about that. You're in your last trimester. It's the perfect time. It's never too soon to choose the best nutrition for your baby." She leans back on the counter.

Randall makes yakking signals with his hand.

Jan gives him a glare. "Right. Sounds good. See you later, Addy. Bye." She hangs up the phone. "Now, where were we?" she barks. Her bright sweet-as-sugar tone is gone. If they weren't family, Randall might feel offended.

He clears his throat. "We were discussing the differences between women and men when it comes to what catches our eye."

Jan goes back to beating her dough into submission on the kitchen island. "Thank goodness I found Mark. He's the farthest thing from being a troglodyte. He manages art museums, and he loves history."

Randall feigns snoring. "Did you say something worth listening to, Jan? You're boring me to death over here with all your museum talk." He sighs dramatically. "Anyway, what I was going to say before you interrupted me is that the whole ordering a bride thing feels too cringey to me. I can't do it. The biggest issue I have with marrying a girl from another country is I would never know if she wanted to be married to me or if she was only after citizenship, and

I'm not okay with that." He lays the magazine down on the counter.

"Throw that magazine away, Randall. Right now. I can't look at it another second," Jan's mom voice demands through their FaceTime call.

Randall laughs out loud. "Jan, your mom voice might work on your children, but it certainly doesn't work on me. I'm mailing this back to Rodney. Don't you worry. He can be a real turd about his stuff. If I don't return this to him, he'll probably send me a bill for $26.99 in the mail."

Jan makes a face. "Seriously?"

He nods his head. "Yep. His idea of frugal and mine are clearly not the same."

Jan raises a doughy finger in the air. "Wait a minute. Isn't this the brother who has been married, like, four times?"

Randall rolls his eyes. "You know I only have one brother."

Jan giggles. "I can't believe you'd even consider taking marital advice from him."

Randall taps on the counter. "Well, he has been to the altar four times, so apparently he knows how to get a woman to fall in love with him. He just can't get them to stay."

"I guess that's fair to say. Has your brother ever married a mail-order bride?"

Randall shakes his head back and forth. "No. I think he just likes the idea. Besides, I don't think he can afford it. Divorces and alimony can be financially draining. It's probably a good thing Rodney's married to his job."

Jan shapes her dough. "So, does he have any kids?"

Randall can't help but snort at the thought of his

having children. "No. The women he married didn't stick around long enough to get pregnant—they maxed out his credit card and left."

Jan raises her eyebrows. "Is your brother rich?"

He chuckles. "Not particularly, and it gets a little worse with every divorce. His job is decent though, and I think he's had a few promotions over the years."

Jan stops her pounding on the counter long enough to stare right into the camera. "So you're not going all past president on me, then."

"Excuse me?" Randall is completely lost.

"You know, marrying a woman from another country with a serious language barrier because no woman in this country will speak to him, let alone marry him."

He barely holds in a smirk at the measure of contempt in her tone. "Wow. You really don't like him."

Jan does a giant eye roll. "Am. I. Female?" She sticks her front out as if to leave no doubt.

"Yes, you most certainly are."

She grins. "Well, then. There's your answer."

Randall slaps the magazine on the counter again. "I'm just glad Mom and Dad aren't around to know Rodney's stooped to considering ordering a bride. It's just creepy to me—on both sides. I watched a few episodes of women who came here, found themselves a sugar daddy, and the next thing you know, that man is either missing or dead. That can happen too."

Jan shakes her head. "I suppose so, but I'd be more inclined to believe most crimes in that kind of marriage are committed by the husband. He's got the woman away from her family. She has no money. She has no one to turn to if he treats her terribly. I'd say the woman is definitely risking more than the man."

He hears what she's saying, but he's still feeling a little burned from the one and only online relationship he'd ever had. "I hear you, but don't you remember what happened with that girl I met on an online dating site?"

Jan's face lights up. "What? You had an online dating profile? You never told me this."

He ducks his head. "It's rather embarrassing. That's probably why I didn't."

She abandons her dough on the counter and plops on a barstool in front of the phone. A curl or two of her blonde hair falls in her face. She swats it away. "Spill it, cousin. Spill the tea."

He can't decide. Her excitement makes him nervous.

"Don't leave me hangin'," she pleads.

"All right, fine. I was seeing a woman who looked a little too good to be true, especially for me. She was a real smooth talker, and she had a very sad story. She really had a way of making a guy feel special, and she knew it. Before I knew what was going on, she just about wiped out my bank account."

Jan's bright blue eyes bug out. "What?"

He nods his head. "Yeah. *Shannon* called my bank and impersonated a sister I don't have. Fortunately for me, Winifred, with her cold-cash heart and air-tight memory, gave Shannon some bs answer and got me on the phone ASAP. It hurt hearing Shannon was just after my money, but I was relieved to find out and promptly ended our four-month Internet relationship. I'm telling you, changing my email address, all my social media passwords, and my online banking information was a pain in the butt. After that fiasco, I stopped online dating, and I haven't been back since."

Jan gives a shiver. "It sounds like Shannon was one step away from being on that movie *Impostors*."

Randall blushes with the memory of how easily Shannon fooled him with her sad story. "Yep."

Jan looks a little less opinionated than usual. "I guess I could see why that would make you a little gun-shy from Internet dating, which is too bad because I can't imagine there are many women moving to Alaska." She raises a finger. "I understand you had a pretty bad experience, but do you want to be alone all your life? Mark and I have our moments and disagreements, but that's just part of being married. I'd rather fight with him than have silence all to myself."

"I don't know. I mean, I knew when I moved to Alaska I was seriously decreasing my chances at finding happiness and all that, but I also felt it was the right place for me to be. Mom always said that if I'm meant to find love, I will, and Mom was a very wise woman," Randall counters.

Jan nods her head in agreement. "Yes, your mother was. She had a lot of patience and faith too."

He pffts. "She had to. She was married to my dad." He looks down at the magazine once more. "Love might be overrated. I'm happy in my job, and that's something. I think I'll just let Rodney be the one to walk women down the aisle."

Jan shrugs. "Yeah, well, your brother is a bit of a puzzle. He seemed decent enough when we were growing up, but there has to be some reason women keep leaving. Maybe he just doesn't choose the right ones."

Randall shrugs his shoulders. "Yeah, maybe." There's a

pause in their conversation. He tries to think of something else to rile Jan. It's way too easy and so much fun. "You know breastfeeding is, like, outdated and the very definition of keeping women barefoot and pregnant," he needles.

Fire flashes in her eyes as they narrow in his anticipatory direction. "Excuse me?"

He chuckles. "I'm referring to your phone call, the one that interrupted our conversation."

Jan's fair complexion turns a shade of pink. "Not that it's any of your business, but I'm working part-time as a representative for the Breastfeeding Coalition. And breastfeeding is not outdated. It's a new health movement. It's the best way. I could give you statistics."

Randall shivers at the thought. "Um, no thanks."

"Did you say you want me to mail you free brochures? I'm all over it," Jan sings out with a bratty grin on her face.

Well, that little plan backfired, Randall thinks to himself.

"I'll even send you a poster to put up in the firehouse!" Jan's practically shouting with her enthusiasm.

His work pager goes off, saving him. "Oh, this is work, Jan. I've got to go."

"Yeah, yeah. If you ask me, your brother isn't the only one married to his work." She sticks out her tongue.

"Jan, some of us knead dough, and some of us make dough. I know which one I am," Randall retorts before moving his finger toward ending their FaceTime call. "And some of us do both so we can eat," he mutters under his breath. His finger hovers over the red bar on his phone screen. He's a cheeseball for a good pun, but he doesn't care.

"Were you saying something? I can't hear you over my

Christmas music," she hollers and cranks up "All I Want for Christmas."

Randall slaps a hand over his ear. "Geez, Jan. It's not even Thanksgiving. Turn that down."

"You're not squishing my Christmas spirit. Run along, fireman. Go fight some fire."

Their FaceTime call ends. Randall goes to the closet for his fireman's clothes and suits up. "Great, now I'm going to have Christmas tunes in my head all day. I hate Christmas," he mutters as he yanks up his coveralls and shoves a foot into a rubber boot.

3

Sheri can't believe it's been two long weeks since she made the decision to move to Alaska. Things fell into place fast, which can only mean this move is meant to be.

Jenni and her husband sold their house and bought Sheri's home. Sheri's pastor bought her dad's old truck. Sheri bit the bullet and found an adorable home in a quiet neighborhood for a great price in a small city in Alaska, which she intends to be completely settled into by Christmas, a mere five weeks away. Sheri giggles with anticipation, thinking to herself this is definitely what her fellow church choir member, Michelle, would call a "God thing."

Sheri ignores the fact that she paid a small fortune to ship her minimal amount of furniture north about a week ago, because there are some things she can't live without, like her favorite recliner, her sleigh bed, and her family keepsake trunk passed down from generation to generation. Sheri holds her breath and whispers a prayer as the puddle jumper plane descends.

She smiles and gives herself a mental congratulatory

pat on the back for learning some new lingo. "Puddle jumper," she whispers. "That's a fun phrase."

The old man next to her turns to her with a knowing grin on his face. "First time in Alaska?"

Sheri can't fight her growing smile. "First time. I'm moving here."

The old man chuckles as he looks her over. "Better get you some warmer clothes before you catch frostbite."

Sheri hears his words, but they barely register. She can hardly believe she's in Alaska. Her heart sings with joy in her chest. She just knows it's going to be so great. Sheri recalls the PDF file she downloaded the very day Jenni suggested she move to Alaska. Typically, Sheri doesn't put much stock in fate or destiny, especially when it comes to romance, but when she saw the words "New Year's Ball" in the email in her junk folder, she *had* to open it. Sheri clicked on the link, half scared she was going to open up a Russian virus of some sort, but her curiosity got the better of her. The invite floated down her screen in slow-mo. Confetti sparkles filled the screen. In the very middle sat a glass slipper on a pillow. The princess in her shrieked a little. Sheri sat on her hand to keep from reaching for the screen. She whipped out her phone and snapped a few pics, as it was so enchanting.

She brings up the picture in her phone once more and stares at the invite, focusing on not freaking out while the plane makes a bumpy landing. "Come one, come all, to the New Year's Ball! Stars in your eyes and two rings are the prize! Love is calling, so pick up the phone! No woman or man is meant to be alone!" she reads to herself once more while she dreams of her perfect prince.

Sheri tells herself she's not a sucker who is so desperate

to meet a guy she paid one thousand dollars to sign up for a New Year's Day weekend in a huge lodge where they guarantee she'll meet a potential soulmate. She shrugs off feelings of uneasiness and assures herself there's nothing wrong with being assertive in her quest for true love.

Her eyes stare into the Alaskan darkness—one more reminder that real life isn't like the fairy tales. There's no handsome prince on standby waiting to wake her with true love's kiss. Glass slippers and fairy godmothers aren't real, no matter how dreamy they may be.

She exhales slowly as she makes a silent resolution. "This is the twentieth century. Women can be as deliberate as men in their pursuit of happiness, joy, and happily ever after. There's nothing wrong with chasing a dream, so long as I don't lose my grip on reality," she whispers out the plane window into the darkness, thankful the old man next to her has headphones on.

She stares at the invite some more as she ponders. Finding the perfect dress and heels is a more realistic goal. She's never worn a tiara. These are definitely things to look forward to. This ball is the perfect excuse to let her inner princess out for one night.

The plane's wheels screech down the runway. She exhales slowly as they come to a stop. A quick glance at her watch shows it's two p.m., so why is it so dark outside? She wishes she could see some scenery. She was all prepared for mountains and shining blue waters in the distance. Sheri grabs her overhead bag and slings her messenger over her shoulder. She's so glad she opted for a backpack purse last minute. It's very accommodating as she stumbles down the plane aisle to the steps ahead.

Frigid arctic air slaps her in the face. There's darkness

all around. It steals her breath but not in a good way. She's never been so surprised in all her life.

"Think happy thoughts, think happy thoughts," she mutters her mantra as she slips and slides all the way to the building that seems so far away.

She whips open the doors to get inside, finds her footing, and scurries to find her luggage. Sheri spies Jerry, her friendly, former homeowner and new Facebook friend, standing by a door. He holds a sign with her name on it. She rushes over, dragging her suitcases behind.

"I'm ready to see my new home," she answers brightly.

He gives her a nod. "That's great. That's great." He seems a little jumpy, but it's pretty cold. He's probably just trying to keep warm. "Follow me," he orders.

She heads out into the cold once more. She's barely out the door when he opens the truck door and hops in, slamming it behind him. She hesitates a few minutes as she takes in his big truck attached to a snowplow. "Is this your vehicle?"

"Yeah, I drive for the city. Are you coming or what?"

Whoa. The happy-go-lucky personality she's gotten to know over the past few weeks is nowhere to be found.

She hurries around to the other side, tosses her luggage, and hauls herself up into the cab. He starts up his noisy truck, and they proceed to drive out of the parking lot.

"So Jerry, what do you do for fun?" she asks, trying to make conversation.

"I just told you. I drive a snowplow," he states in an irritated manner.

"Not for a job. Just for fun. What do you do for fun?" she insists.

He looks at her as if she can't hear. "I drive this snow-plow. It's fun for me."

"Oh. Okay," she answers, feeling embarrassed but also annoyed. She is only trying to be polite. She decides he's not very chatty, but she tries one more time. "How long have you lived in Alaska?"

"All my life."

Forty-eight long, silent minutes later, Jerry stops at the end of a quiet street. "Well, here we are," he says as he points to a little house.

She grabs her luggage and climbs down out of the truck. She barely gets around the front of it and onto the sidewalk when he pulls away with a wave.

"Good luck with your new home," Jerry calls out.

Sheri rubs her arms and stomps her feet. *There had better be central heat in there*, she thinks to herself. She drags her luggage inside and reaches for a light switch, but there's only empty wall beneath her fingers. She digs around for her phone and turns on her flashlight, which is a good thing, as she soon discovers all of her furniture is inside but just barely. Everything except for her bed sits in the middle of the front room.

"Did they forget my bed?" she groans aloud.

She runs up the stairs and peeks in every room. She sighs with relief when she finds her bed, at least. She hurries back down the stairs to search for the light switch, which she discovers at a level just above her knee.

"What in the world? Did dwarves live here?" she grumbles as she flips the switch. Nothing happens. "You've got to be kidding," she says aloud. "It's cold as an icebox," she mutters right before she starts shoving furniture across the floor.

After moving things around in her cold, dark house for at least an hour, Sheri's exhausted. She goes to turn on the TV, which is miraculously mounted to the wall, before she remembers she has no electricity. Sheri googles the city office on her cell and calls the number. No one answers about the time she remembers it's a Saturday.

"Crap, crap, crap," she mutters as she hangs up.

Sheri wills herself not to cry. After all, she's been here all of one day. These are just small inconveniences. *What's the worst thing that could happen?* she muses, but then she hears Jenni's voice in her head. *"You could freeze to death up there, Sheri. Don't forget to be careful."*

She rummages through her blanket trunk and drags out everything. She yanks the pile of blankets up the stairs. She then proceeds to put on every item of clothing she can find. Sheri spies a long, tall candle on the dresser. It whispers to her of longing and romance and gives her hope. Sheri sets it in the candleholder and puts it in the window before lighting the flame with the box of matches lying on the floor. She climbs into bed beneath all the blankets and gazes out the window into the dark night before she closes her eyes to dream of her future.

Tomorrow is a new day, she decides, *and it can only get better.*

4

Randall's pager goes off in the middle of the night. "This had better not be another call from widow James, who is weeks away from a nursing home," he mutters into the cold cabin air before giving Jake, his Saint Bernard, a hard nudge.

Randall stumbles around in the dark and shoves his bare feet into a pair of thick socks before he shuffles across the room to his ever-waiting pair of winter overalls hanging on the wall. He steps into them and clicks his plastic buckles in place before he leans over to shove his feet into a pair of work boots.

"If I have to answer one more come-hither house call from that lonely old widow, I'll drive her to the old folks' home myself. I am not Walt Longmire," Randall grumbles to Jake, who snuffles along behind him.

Jake and Randall walk out to his Outback. He opens the back door and Jake climbs inside. Randall plops into the driver's seat and starts it up. He's puzzled when he pulls up to the house just three blocks away. It sits on the corner, but it's been empty for so long that he almost forgot it was there. It's a strangely narrow, two-story house made of brick and stone. It reminds Randall of a gingerbread house in a fairy tale.

He turns to Jake. "Jerry must've done some fast talking to pull the wool over somebody's eyes. This place looks good on the outside, but I've heard the inside is a big ole mess." He glances around for a vehicle but sees nothing. "That's just great, Jake. We've probably got another temporary out-of-towner trying to fulfill their own version of *Wild*. When is everyone going to learn real life is not a TV show?"

Jake answers with a woof that comes out more like a sigh of resignation.

Randall gets out of the car and opens Jake's door. They stomp up the front stairs together and knock on the door. No one answers. Randall turns away to return to his Outback.

"I'm so glad I crawled out of my nice, warm bed," he grumbles. "This isn't my problem, Jake. When did everyone's curiosity become a 9-1-1 call? No one respects what constitutes an actual emergency anymore."

A feeling stops him. He glances upward, and that's when he sees the candle in the window, beckoning. It dawns on Randall that this is the first flame he's seen in all his years as a fireman that feels more welcoming than dangerous. Unease fills him from head to toe. He shakes it off and embraces his norm: irritation.

"Seriously. What kind of idiot leaves a candle burning unless they're trying to burn their house down?" He stomps back up the porch steps and jiggles the door handle. "At least they had the good sense to lock their front door," he says as he searches an empty front porch for any place to stow a spare key, coming up empty.

Randall cups the windowpane in an attempt to peer inside and is rewarded with visions of a black hole. His fingers find the lift and he tugs. It raises easily. His lips form a small smile. He squeezes his six-foot-three, 225-pound frame through, dropping his Maglite and cell phone somewhere behind him.

"Hold on, Jake. I'm coming," he mutters as he feels around for his light and phone, which he pockets.

Randall follows the beam of his Maglite to the front door. He opens it and Jake ambles in. They head upstairs. "For a big dog, you're pretty stealth," Randall whispers because the house is too quiet.

He heads down the hallway toward the candle's flame and the lightest snoring he's ever heard. He lowers his Maglite before turning it off. He steps through the doorway and peeks inside, feeling every inch the intruder. Randall sees a bumpy form beneath a pile of blankets.

For a second, he's at a loss for words. He doesn't know what to make of the feeling of calm that embraces him. He steps quickly to the window to extinguish the flame before he remembers he needs a source of light. He tiptoes across the floor, holding the candle, hesitating when he gets as close to the bed as he dares.

The light dances across the most perfect set of brows he's ever seen. He takes in her turned-up nose and those freckles, and he shivers a little. When his gaze falls on her lips, he just about goes to his knees. His head spins with the thought of laying the softest of kisses on her angelic smile. His eyes roam further to her wavy, brown hair.

He's so distracted that he doesn't notice Jake until he's

by her side, sniffing her hand that hangs off the side of the bed. Randall jumps about a foot when she flings a startled hand up to her chest. He turns away and heads straight for the door, tugging on Jake's collar. He can only imagine her shock if she woke to find the two of them standing over her like a couple of creepers. He tiptoes out of her room by candlelight and wanders back downstairs. He blows out the flame of the candle.

"Who is she and why haven't I heard anything about her?" he whispers into the darkness, which gives him no answer.

He thinks about Jerry, the previous owner of the house. Jerry has a big mouth, even when his information isn't firsthand, and this is definitely firsthand because this is his house—if you count inheriting a house from a distant aunt who had Alzheimer's so bad at the end she would have willed it to a rat. Jerry isn't too far from that detestable species.

He heads outside and grabs a few logs off the front porch, probably leftovers of Jerry's rustic staging act. Randall runs a hand over them to be sure they're dry before he tosses them in the fireplace and gets it going.

Jake sits on the couch and Randall follows suit. He gives Jake's big fluffy head a good rubbing. "Well, Jake. It looks like we're staying here tonight. Thank goodness I wore my thermals and winter overalls."

———

Randall wakes to someone poking him in the chest with a broomstick. Jake, his ever-loyal guard dog, snores beside him.

"Oh, thank God you're not dead," the woman answers in a soft voice.

"Are you suggesting I'm the incompetent fool who lit a candle in the window but left the fireplace unlit long enough to freeze your pipes?" Sharp words fly out of his mouth at her as his eyes follow suit. He waits for hurt to show up on her face. It doesn't.

The woman throws a hand on her hip. "For your information, sir, the candle in the window went out on its own just like the fireplace lit itself. I paid for a self-lighting home, and I got one."

He fights the urge to laugh out loud as he shakes his head. "Lady, this sounds like the words of Jerry, who shoots more bull than a Kansas farmer."

She blushes a little and lowers her broomstick. "Oh."

He swats the stick away just before it hits him below the belt.

"So it was you who blew out my candle and started my fire," she says with a slightly narrowed gaze.

"I'd like to," he responds in kind before immediately shutting his mouth and wondering where that thought come from. It's not like him to be so forward.

She turns away, but he sees the blush creeping into her cheeks. "I suppose introductions are in order," she announces as she turns slowly back to him and pastes a smile on her face. "My name is Sheri Mallo. I just moved up here from Wisconsin."

Her eyes hold more than just general curiosity in them as she looks him over. He thinks there's a little appreciation there.

"And you are?"

He studies his hands to sort his addled brain and clears

his throat before looking into her kind, hazel eyes. She's a little tall for his taste, and there's a little more to her than he usually prefers, but there's something about her that draws him in. "I'm the mysterious Alaskan magic you've been searching for."

She blinks a few times. "I wouldn't go that far, but I'd be happy to treat you to breakfast. Where would you like to eat? Maybe we can walk there. This looks like a pretty small town on the map."

He gives her a funny look. "Is that a joke?"

"No." She pulls out her phone and shows him pictures. "See there? That's a café. It looks good to me."

He clears his throat. "That's a city three hundred miles from here. This town has the same name as that city, but we're very rural. I'm afraid you've been tricked by Jerry."

Randall waits for tears or some lip quivering. White knuckles on a broomstick is what he gets instead, right before she chucks the broken broom pieces halfway across the room. "That lying piece of Kodiak bear poo." She paces back and forth in front of him in a pair of plaid pajama pants. Randall can't help but smile at her sweatshirt that has a big frowning moose on it along with the words "Mad Momma Moose." As fast as she started her furious rage, she stops and gives him a wave.

"Well, come on in the kitchen, then. I'll make us some coffee and breakfast. It's the least I can do to thank you for saving me from my gullible self." She strides into the kitchen, and he finds himself following her. "Do you know anything about how I can get my electricity going?" She stops in her tracks. "Oh, suck a sour gummy worm. I can't make breakfast with no electricity. How silly of me."

"How about you come over to my place and you can make me breakfast there?" he suggests.

He can't help but admire her determination to make the best of a crappy situation. He feels her studying him and can only imagine what she sees: a wooly face that hasn't been shaved in months and a shaggy head of hair in desperate need of a decent haircut.

He tries his friendliest smile as he extends his hand. "I'm Randall Graham, and that bump on a log, whose furry butt is glued to your couch, is my partner, Jake. Welcome to Alaska."

She reaches out and slowly lays her hand in his. "Nice to meet you."

She blushes clear to her cheeks, and it's positively enchanting. Randall fights the urge to shake his head and wonders why such strange words like enchanting and mesmerizing popped into his brain.

"I'm just gonna run upstairs and de-layer first if you don't mind. I don't really want to go out in public in my pj's. I kind of put on everything I own that I could squeeze into. I was trying not to freeze to death in my bed last night."

He gives her a wink. "That sweatshirt of yours would fit right in with the locals."

She giggles. "Are they really that bad?"

He shakes his head. "Nah. Some can be a bit reserved though. I think they're too used to people moving in and out. A lot of people give Alaska a try, but they don't last more than a few years, if that. Our winters can be hard on a person. Plus, all of the dark skies. It can test a person's spirit." Randall stops talking. He doesn't want to sound so negative.

Sheri gives him a small smile. Her eyes twinkle and shine. "So, how long have you been here?"

He can't help but smile back. "I've lived here most of my life."

"So you're tough to run off, huh?"

Randall laughs again. "I guess so. You're pretty funny."

She ducks her head. "Thanks."

5

Sheri doesn't know what to make of Randall yet, but she thinks he seems trustworthy at least. She can't believe he spent the night on her couch with no blanket. The fireplace must have kept him warm.

She rushes around and digs through her boxes for something to wear, but she's not sure what she's looking for. All she knows is it has to be warm. She settles on about three layers of shirts and two layers of pants before she traipses back downstairs. "I'm sorry to keep you waiting. I'm not sure I have the best idea of what to wear for the weather outside."

"You'll be all right for today. I just live three blocks from here. Do you not have a car?"

She shakes her head, feeling foolish. "I guess I was hoping to meet a few friendly locals who could give me some advice."

Randall gives her another big smile. She blushes all over again and hopes he can't read her mind. She could look at that smile all day long.

"Well, I hate to say it, but I'm kind of your guide. I, um, well, I know most everyone in town. At least, the people you want to do business with, and I can help you out with getting your electricity turned on as well as buying the right car. And I might even be able to find you a job."

"You'd do all that for me?" she asks, trying to decide if she's flattered or worried. *Who is this guy?* she wonders and thinks, *How bad off is this town if he wants her to stay so much?*

He throws a hand to his chest. "We don't get too many promising newcomers, so when we do, we try not to run them off. I'm just trying to be a friendly neighbor."

She walks past him to get to the front door. "Thanks for watching over me." She tries not to blush, but her statement feels so intimate.

Randall yanks a stocking hat on over his thick, dark hair. "No problem. It's part of my job as the local fireman. I like to keep everyone safe, you know." He lays a hand on her arm. "Do you have your house key? I imagine you'll want to lock up." His brown eyes search hers. For a second, she gets lost in them.

"Oh, yeah." She holds up her key ring. "It's right here." She walks outside. The sun is blinding as it glistens on all the snow. She turns back to look at her new house in better light from the outside. "I thought it looked different when I walked up the steps. This isn't the house I paid for online," she mutters.

"What? What are you talking about?" Randall is immediately concerned.

Sheri whips out a picture of a newer house with a white picket fence and pale-yellow siding.

Randall frowns. "I think Jerry took a picture of the house next door. Your house is right here." He points to a few bricks in the picture. "I'm going over to Jerry's right now. We'll get this straightened out. That guy needs to be taken to court."

Sheri takes a deep breath. "No. There's no need for any of that. This house might need a little more attention, but it's the house I was meant to have. You mentioned a little Alaskan magic inside. I might need some before this adventure is over. I kind of like this fairy-tale house."

Randall gives her a funny look. "If you say so." He pats his stomach. "I'm getting a little hungry. Let's go."

Sheri climbs inside his Outback. "So what do you do, Randall, when you aren't checking on people's unmonitored flames?"

A confused look settles on his face. "I just told you. I'm a fireman and an EMT. In small communities like this one, most of us wear many hats. We learn to be survivors."

Sheri takes in his shaggy hairstyle. "Do you have a local barber?"

He grins over at her. "Does it look that bad?"

She shrugs. "I suppose the *Grizzly Adams* look fits right in up here."

He laughs again. "It's nice to know someone in our generation still knows the classics. You've seen *Grizzly Adams*?"

"I thought it was a prerequisite for moving to Alaska," she pops off.

Randall laughs out loud again. "You're just full of opinions and one-liners. Were you a stand-up comedian back home?"

"No. I'm a librarian," she answers more quietly.

He does a double take. "No way."

She nods her head. "Yes, way. I've been one most of my adult life."

He grins and thinks she's not like any shy, mousy, librarian he's ever known. "It just so happens our town library has been looking for a librarian."

Sheri crosses her arms on her chest. "I didn't see any want ads for that. Trust me, I've looked."

"Yes, but I bet you were looking in the wrong place. I know my town. That position has not been filled," he persists.

"What's the pay?" she asks as she thinks about the income she's going to be needing soon enough.

He bites his lip. "Well, that's a tough question."

She shifts in her seat. "What did the last librarian make?"

He stares hard at the front windshield. "The last two librarians we had ended up working at the strip club down the road for supplemental pay."

Sheri fidgets as she stares out the window. "I'm not an exotic dancer. I don't work well with poles or bacteria." Her bubble bursts a little when she thinks of Randall frequenting the local strip club, but she's not about to ask him.

He busts out laughing. "Relax, woman. I wasn't suggesting you become a dancer. Trust me, you don't look the type, and that's a good thing."

He pulls into a garage and opens the back door. She follows Jake to the door leading to the house. She goes to turn the doorknob. Randall reaches around from behind. His chest bumps into her back, and she feels hot all over. She leans away from him to give him space.

"I'm sorry. It's just a little cold out here," she all but whispers.

He turns the knob, and the door opens. "Don't be. I'm just used to opening my house door. Go on inside." He clears his throat. "I'm just going to..." He points straight ahead. "You're welcome to my kitchen." He walks off in another direction.

Sheri heads for the kitchen coffeepot and spies some sort of weird bridal magazine on the counter. She picks it up and flips through it, feeling like an intruder but helpless to stop her snooping. She becomes more and more incensed as she reads article after article.

Thoughts race through her mind. *This man is a pig,* she thinks. First, he mentioned strip clubs, and now she finds some sort of whacked-out, mail-order bride magazine. She tosses the magazine in the trash and puts the lid down, feeling extremely disappointed. She thought he seemed so normal. Handsome even. She decides to keep her distance.

6

A charge of negativity radiates in the air as Randall sits down at the kitchen table. He side-eyes Sheri, not wanting to be caught staring, but it's hard as her movements are downright jerky. It's clear something happened between the time he went to the restroom and came back to the kitchen, but he has no idea what. She brews coffee and a few emotions he can't figure out. He sees she found his skillet. It smells like she's making some French toast, but she looks like she sucked on a lemon drop.

"So, do you want me to call my friend, Debbie, from the city office, about getting your electricity turned on?" he ventures.

She whips around to face him. "You'd like that, wouldn't you? Do you enjoy being the man around town, having everybody owe you something?" Her sharp tone affirms the vibe he thought he felt.

He blinks in confusion and wonders what happened to the easygoing woman who walked in the door with him. "Um, no. I was just trying to be nice."

She flips the toast. "Sure."

How can one word sound so accusatory? he wonders.

"So, I forgot to tell you. I'm an electrician and a house contractor. That's mostly what I do when I'm not on call half the time," he offers in spite of his urge to show her the door. He's not sure such a moody woman is worth all this trouble.

Her eyes narrow. "Do you get paid for being on call?"

He stares right back at her. "Of course I do, and I should. If that phone rings day or night, I answer it. This town's pretty small if you hadn't noticed, and I prefer to work close to home; so I don't always get too many contracting or electrician jobs, which is why I'm a fire-fighter and an EMT. I shouldn't have to apologize for working in a noble profession," he adds at the end with no small amount of smugness to his tone. He crosses his arms on his chest and thinks she's got a lot of nerve walking around his kitchen like she owns it and accusing him of getting paid for working.

"So, do you ever get a day off? I mean, aren't there other firefighters to give you a break or whatever?"

Randall mulls her question over in his head for a few seconds. He's not sure what she's fishing for. He shrugs in answer. "Our fire department can't afford to pay too many firefighters. And yes, I have substitutes or backups, but most of them are retired firefighters. There is another guy, but we have to share him with his town, so he's only here part-time." He clears his throat. "But I'm usually on call every weekend because there just isn't anyone else, and it's not about the pay. It's about civic duty and helping each other out. That's what small communities like ours do for each other. Is that so hard to understand?"

"No," she bites out as she scrapes his metal spatula across his nonstick pan.

"Watch it, lady. You're going to scrape the Teflon off my skillet," he growls.

Sheri stops mid-motion. She slaps the spatula on the counter. "What do you suggest I use? This was the only spatula I could find. You think I don't know that metal on Teflon isn't a good idea?"

He rises slowly from his kitchen chair and moseys over to a kitchen drawer. He tugs it open and pulls out a rubber-coated spatula. "Ask and you shall receive," he says in a flirty tone. His eyes sparkle and shine.

She snatches it from his waiting hand. "I'd know where it was if this was my kitchen, but I don't really make a habit of going through other people's drawers."

He bites his lip to keep from laughing. "It's nice to know you draw the line somewhere," he says with a smirk.

She gasps before whipping around to give him her back. "How many pieces of toast do you want?" she demands.

Randall returns to his place at the table. "Two or three oughta do it."

She fiddles with the flame beneath the skillet to find the right amount of heat.

"I don't think you need much more fire than that. You're putting out enough heat to burn my toast as it is," he scolds.

She side-eyes him as she flips his toast. She's hot all over. She tells herself it's from cooking at the stove, but she's not sure. His words about set her hair on fire. She turns to face him long enough to finish what she started before he interrupted her by telling her how to cook his breakfast.

"What's hard for me to understand is how you *seem* like a decent enough guy, but then you go and do something like *ordering* a bride through the mail." She points an incriminating finger at the offensive magazine. "How can any part of you think it's okay to pick a woman from a catalog, take her from her family and friends and any life she's ever known, and then expect her to fend for herself, let alone love you?" She shakes her head. "I can't imagine the level of desperation these women must feel to end up on this glorified auction block."

He supposes he should let her know how he came into possession of Rodney's magazine, but she's so fired up, and this is the most fun he's had in a long time. She's really reading him the riot act. He's not about to take it sitting down. He leans back in his chair and lays his hands on his chest. "I don't know. I mean, she is getting all of me plus a home to live in, food on her table, and my last name. That seems like a fair trade to me."

Sheri's eyes bug out just a little. She snatches the magazine up and waves it around, walking away from her skillet. "The only thing more appalling than these women lining up to be bought and purchased by total strangers is the consumer." She practically spits the words as she stares him down.

He's torn between bursting out with laughter or kissing the ever-loving crap out of this overly opinionated woman who showed up out of nowhere. He thinks she's as hot as a Fourth of July firecracker. "I don't understand what's got you so fired up. If you ask me, this isn't much different than a man meeting a woman down at the lodge or at a grocery store," he teases.

She sniffs as she returns to her cooking. "What on earth are you talking about?"

He knows he's probably completely in the wrong, but he's warming to his side of this highly enjoyable discussion that unfurls the longer he speaks. "Well, think about it. What draws two people together initially in most circumstances? Is it their winning personalities, or is it more about chemistry and mutual attraction?"

She squirms just enough to let him know he's hit a nerve, but her chin juts out. "For a relationship to work and to be something meaningful, there has to be more than just really good chemistry." Her face flushes.

He can't help but smirk. "That may be true, but as a fireman, I've got to say, you can't build a fire without a little spark."

She clears her throat. "I misspoke. All I'm saying is a relationship that lasts is built on more than just chemistry and something as superficial as what a person looks like. Most people can make a great first impression. You can't really know someone until you've been around them for a while."

He taps his fingers on the table. "I suppose you're right, but are you telling me you don't believe in love at first sight? Like ever?" As the words flow from his mouth he wonders why it feels like he's talking about something that has nothing to do with his brother's magazine, and he can't help but feel that he's in way over his head.

She rolls her eyes. "It's a little hard for a stranger to fall in love with a man if she doesn't have the chance to meet him before he flies over here and she's stuck."

He scratches the back of his neck. "You know there's plenty of these marriages that don't work because the woman leaves."

She grins at his comment. "If you ask me, those guys get what's coming to them." Her hand is on her hip again. "I would bet a high percentage of these men want a woman that will rely on him for everything. Therefore, she will do whatever he says, or so he thinks. If she happens to develop a mind of her own and leave him, well that's just too darn bad. Secondly, if the woman does leave him for someone else, that's what he gets if he marries an opportunist. And thirdly, any man who is stupid enough to think he can *buy* a woman's affection doesn't know what real love is and therefore will never find it."

He stares her down. "And you wonder why you've never married." He shakes his head back and forth. "Could it be because you're a little too opinionated for your own good?"

Her face turns red. She moves the pan off the burner. "Your breakfast is done. Never mind about helping me. I think I can survive another day without electricity, but what I can't survive is another second with you," she declares before she stomps toward his front door.

"Where are you going?" he demands.

"I'm going home."

"How are you going to get there?"

She sticks her nose in the air. "I'll walk."

He gets out of the chair and runs to the door right before Sheri can open it. He shuts it in her face while giving her as much space as possible. He doesn't want her to think she walked onto the set of *Misery*. "Sheri, just a second." He flashes her his smolder, or at least what he thinks is his most charming grin. "I didn't want to make you so mad you would leave. I thought we were having a spirited discussion."

She pauses.

"You do realize you were really on a rant. You can't expect me to just not say anything in return." He sighs. "That magazine isn't even mine. It belongs to my brother, Rodney, who lives in Tennessee, a fact you would have noticed by the address on the outside if you weren't so busy yelling at me."

She stares up at him. "How do I know you aren't lying?"

He crosses his arms on his chest. "For one thing, you can check the address on the magazine." He stares her down. "Do I really look like a guy who would need to order a mail-order bride?" He regrets his words as soon as he says them because he feels like he's asking for confirmation that he doesn't resemble a tree stump.

She blushes clean to her roots. "No."

He is encouraged more than he'd like to admit by her one-word answer, which must mean she finds him attractive. He can hardly speak as he nods. "Okay, then."

"Okay, what?" she demands.

"Okay. Now that you've decided I'm not a total jerk, would you like to come back to my kitchen and eat with me so we can decide what your next move is?"

She doesn't move a muscle.

"Please," he mutters under his breath as if it's a word he's not used to using.

She takes a deep breath. "I'm not so sure you're not a jerk, but if you can forgive me for chewing you out, then yes."

He shrugs. "There's nothing to forgive. I like an opinionated woman with some backbone. You'll need both if you're going to fit in around here."

His phone buzzes. He glances down at it. It's Jan. He hits End. Two seconds later, it buzzes again.

She looks suspiciously at his phone. "Are you going to get that or what?"

He holds it in front of her face. "It's my cousin, Jan, and if I get it, we might be on the phone a while. She's chatty." He wonders why he feels the need to explain himself so thoroughly to a woman he's just met. Randall is not in the habit of answering to anyone.

She shrugs. "Just tell her you're eating breakfast."

He opens up FaceTime. "Hey, Jan. I've got company."

"Oooh, a girl? Please tell me it's a girl. It's been so long since you've met anybody." Randall gives Jan a warning look through the phone screen. She ignores it. "Wasn't that what you just said the other day when we were talking?"

He regrets hitting the speaker immediately. "Jan, she can hear you, and she's right here with me."

Sheri snatches the phone from his hand. "She would be me, and I'm Sheri."

Jan claps her hands. "Hey, Sheri. I'm his cousin, Jan. I love to bake. Today I'm making a cranberry-orange scone to go with my chai tea."

Sheri grins. "Nice. I'm afraid I can't compete with that. I just brewed some coffee for Randall here and made him some French toast."

Jan wiggles her eyebrows. "Having breakfast with my cousin, are you? Do tell me more."

Sheri giggles. "It's not what you think. I just moved to town yesterday. My house has no electricity so your cousin sort of rescued me. I figured the least I can do is make him breakfast." Sheri whips around to face Randall. "That is if he'll stop creepin' on my phone call."

He reaches for the phone, but Sheri dodges.

"That's my phone call. You're talking to my cousin," he protests.

"Just sit down and eat your breakfast, mister."

Randall is torn. He's really hungry, and he wants his breakfast. Sheri seems the type to throw it in the trash if she gets mad enough, but her bossy librarian tone is a turn-on, and he kind of wants to hear it again.

She raises one eyebrow in warning while giving him the stink eye.

He sits down. "Okay."

Sheri lays the phone down on the counter face up, prepares his plate, and lays it on the table in front of him before she grabs him a cup of coffee. These two actions make him very itchy. He thinks he might have hives. He tugs at his shirt collar.

She smacks his hand. "You'll stretch out your shirt," she scolds.

He fights the urge to rip a hole in the collar just to prove a point that he won't be bossed around as a grown man before reaching his own conclusion that would be ridiculous. He picks up his fork and takes a bite of toast. She moves the pan off the burner, picks up the phone, and wanders into the other room, chatting away to Jan like they've known each other forever. He refuses to follow as he tries to shut them out. He doesn't want to be called a creeper again.

Ten minutes later, Sheri meanders back to the kitchen and lays the phone down beside him on the table. Jan's face is all smiles on the screen.

"Hey, cousin." She sounds like she's up to something. It makes his stomach hurt.

He frowns down at her. "Hey."

"Sheesh. What bug crawled up your butt?" Jan teases.

"What? Nothing. Why would you say that?"

"You're all Mr. Frowny Pants. That's all."

Sheri's at the stove. He wishes she'd go in the other room. He snatches up the phone and walks outside. Ice-cold snow seeps through his sock feet. "What did you two talk about?" Randall asks as his teeth begin to chatter.

Jan giggles. "Wouldn't you like to know?"

He has had enough of these two overly opinionated women sticking their noses where they don't belong. "You know what, cousin? Talk about whatever with whoever. I don't care."

She laughs at him. He can't believe how much it hurts. "Good. Because I'm not telling you. But I will tell you she passed my test," Jan answers.

"What test is that?" he answers in a tone that he hopes suggests indifference.

"The only one that matters. She's a decent human. That's all I've got to say," Jan says with a grin.

He frowns. "What about me? Am I a decent human?"

Jan rolls her eyes. "Barely, Randall. Just barely." A timer goes off in her kitchen. "Oap. I've gotta go. My baby ramekins are done."

He turns the doorknob and walks back inside with frozen toes.

"Take off your socks. You're going to get the floor wet," she instructs.

"I'll track water through this entire house if I want to,"

he growls as he stomps across the floor, leaving a dripping trail behind him.

Sheri fights the urge to throw a towel down to soak it up. "You are the most pigheaded, stubborn man I have ever met."

He steps into her space and stares her down. "Is that so?" His voice is deceptively quiet.

Her heart races in her chest as she looks up at him. "Yes. That's so."

He sighs. "I don't much care for being bossed around in my own home. No one likes a nag." She has the grace to look properly scolded. She opens her mouth and closes it again. She does this a few times before he chuckles, breaking the tension. "You about done? Or should I get out my fishing pole and land you?"

She's thoroughly confused. "Excuse me?"

He taps her bottom lip with his fingertip. "You look like a wide-mouthed bass."

In spite of his insult, she can't help but giggle. "Probably so," she agrees. She looks over at the table. "I'm just going to go eat before my breakfast gets any colder." She sits down and bows her head for a few minutes before she digs into her French toast with a fork and knife, cutting it into bite-sized pieces. "So, how do I become a volunteer firefighter?" she asks as she prepares her breakfast.

"I'm sorry, what?" he answers from the middle of his kitchen, where he still stands. He feels a bit stricken ever since he touched her lip.

"I want to be a part of this community, and I want to contribute, so what do I need to do to do these things?" she continues as if she didn't just set off a small earthquake inside him.

He can't begin to picture her lugging forty-plus pounds of pack around, much less dragging a body out of a burning building. "How about you be a volunteer search-and-rescue assistant?"

She wrinkles her nose. "That sounds incredibly boring, like I'd just be riding along on your coattails as a silent observer. No, thank you."

"We've never had a woman firefighter before," he tries to explain. Her whole demeanor changes. He does some serious backpedaling. "What I mean to say is that it's a very strenuous job and it involves some heavy lifting and running lots of stairs."

He thinks his explanation is more than reasonable, but she looks all indignant.

"So you're saying I'm out of shape and incapable of carrying more weight than a newborn baby?"

Between her words and her tone, he's not sure what sort of answer will appease her. "Yes. I mean, no. I mean, I don't know."

"Is there a physical test that I can take to settle this matter?" she challenges.

He relaxes a hair as she's finally asked a question he knows a clear answer to. "There certainly is, Sheri, but there's also a written test, and that can take a little bit longer and requires much preparation."

"And you think I can't do this?"

He wonders why her tone sounds so personal. He feels like he's talking to a brick wall, but he tries again. "I never said you couldn't do it, but are you saying you're a runner and that you lift weights on a regular basis?"

Sheri shrugs. "I lifted boxes of books at my old job. How hard can it be?"

"Lifting a body that is dead weight is totally different than moving a cardboard box. That's all I'm saying."

Sheri rolls her eyes. "Well, yeah. Duh."

Randall grows tired of the same conversation and the fact that he feels as though Sheri's trying to tell him how to do his job. What does a librarian know about being a fire-fighter? He decides it's time to change the subject. "So how is it you're still single? Have you been hanging out in a nunnery?"

She looks him dead in the eye. "Yep. It's a hard habit to break," she says with a straight face.

Randall laughs so hard his ribs are sore. She has the driest sense of humor he's ever heard. "You are hilarious."

Sheri throws out her hands. "I aim to please." She taps her fingers on her elbows. "I guess you could say I haven't found the right one yet. I don't know."

"Don't worry. You will. I just know it." Randall doesn't know why he said that so loud. It's not like him to speak of romance to anyone, let alone a kind of complete stranger, but there's something about Sheri that makes him want to pry.

7

She steals glances at him in between bites of French toast. She thinks he's a pretty funny guy. He's not easily offended, which is really nice. He's easy on the eyes too. She decides he must have a serious flaw somewhere, or maybe there aren't any single women within a hundred-mile radius.

"So, are there any women's groups around here?" she asks.

He gives her a funny look. "And why would I know that?"

She takes a sip of coffee. "You just said you know every-one's business because it's part of your job and you live in a small town, so I just thought..."

He nods his head. "Oh, yeah. Well, there's a group of women who scrapbook, and there's a group of women who have a book club, and then there's the church ladies." His voice drops on the last two words.

"What's wrong with the church ladies?"

He shifts in his chair. "I'm sure they mean well. They're just always in everyone's business."

She grins at him. "A bunch of gossiping old hens, huh?"

He shakes his head. "*They* call it a prayer circle." He looks a little uneasy.

"Hey, don't knock prayer circles until you've tried one. Sharing is caring," she says in a slightly teasing manner, but she means what she says.

He coughs. "If you say so. Anyway, if you want to hear the latest gossip, just go on down to the gas station first thing in the morning. The old men around here are worse than the women."

She nods her head in agreement. "That sounds like my hometown."

He takes a sip of coffee. "What did you put in this coffee? It's really good."

She reaches over to pour a tad bit more syrup on her breakfast plate. "I'd tell you, but then I'd have to kill you."

"A librarian and an assassin. I like it." He winks at her. "Silent but deadly." His eyes twinkle and shine.

She gets the giggles. "If you count the number of spiders I've executed, I guess that makes me a serial killer."

He shakes his head and grins. "Man, oh man. I'm shakin' in my boots."

She clinks her coffee cup against his. "That's woman to you, mister." She takes another bite of French toast. Her tastebuds sing. "Ho-ly map-le syrup. That's the real deal."

He grins back at her. "Yep. This is Alaska, honey. We don't mess around with our maple syrup. I don't allow synthetic materials at my breakfast table."

She has serious butterflies going on. She's never had a man call her honey before. She can't think of a word to say, so she takes another bite of deliciousness and tries to avoid his dark-eyed stare, his weathered face, and his bushy beard that ought to turn her off but doesn't. His lumberjack look is definitely growing on her.

His empty plate sits between them. He hops up. "I'll just go make myself another piece or two. You want any more?"

"Um, no thank you." She focuses on her plate so she doesn't stare at him standing in front of the stove in his thermal shirt and coveralls hanging halfway down over a pair of faded blue jeans.

"So what brings you to Alaska?"

She sits back in her chair. "I wanted a sense of adventure, but I was also on a bit of a budget."

He frowns. "I hope you got a good deal on that house of yours because it's going to need some major repair work."

Her stomach sinks at his statement. She doesn't have much left over from selling her house, and she needs that for a vehicle. "Is the house livable as it is though?"

He flips his toast in the skillet. "That depends on what you consider livable."

She sips her coffee and ponders his statement. "I'm hoping for not freezing to death in my bed or starting an electrical fire by trying to vacuum."

He shifts around at the stove as if he's uncomfortable. "My main concern is that your house is a health hazard. It's probably a few steps away from being a fire trap."

She bites her lip. "Really? You think it's that bad?" She fights tears. "It figures the first thing I try to do independently is a complete disaster," she mutters.

He pretends not to hear her.

"So you think I should sell it?" she asks again, speaking up.

"Um, I don't think that's a possibility. At least not to anyone around here." His seriousness causes pain in her chest. She thinks she's having an anxiety attack.

She ducks her head in embarrassment and focuses on breathing normally. "Only to someone gullible enough to buy a house over the Internet," she gets out.

He ambles back over to the table. "I tell you what. Why don't you live here for a few months? You might not even like living in Alaska."

She tries to remain passive as her heart rate skyrockets at the thought of sharing a living space with a man she barely knows—or any man at all. "You want me to live here with you?"

He throws up his hands in the air. "Hey, hey, hey. No one said anything about *want*. Relax. I'm offering, okay? You could stay here while you figure things out. This is a split-level house. The downstairs has its own kitchen and bathroom. It's practically another home down there. We wouldn't even have to cross paths."

She hears regret in his tone, but she can't tell if it's about her living there or avoiding him so easily. "I don't know. I mean, this seems kind of sudden. I don't know you all that well."

He crosses his arms on his chest. "You met my cousin, Jan. She seems normal enough, right? Don't you think she'd tell you if I was a freak?"

She studies him longer than she should. "She's your cousin, and you were here the whole time. How would she warn me?"

He sips his coffee. "You were in the other room for ten

minutes by yourself on the phone with her. She could have told you then."

Her head spins. "Why would you want to help me? What are you getting out of this?"

He tilts his head to the side. "Look, lady. I'm offering you a place to stay rent-free for a trial period. Take it or leave it. All I ask is you don't leave a bunch of hairballs in my drains. I don't do hairballs."

She leans back in her chair again and tries to focus, but it's hard with him staring at her so intently. "Just how many women have you lived with?"

He looks confused. "None. Why?"

She makes a face at him. "You're the one talking about hairballs."

He blinks. "Oh, well, I'm kind of a plumber for the elderly community." He winks. "It's another one of my many hats."

She tries to think of an alternative living option but realizes there aren't any. "I guess I could stay here."

He snorts. "You're welcome."

She stares off into space. "I never asked to live here. You offered."

"I'm wondering now if I should have," he grumps.

She stands up out of her chair. "If you want to take it back, fine. I could probably find a hotel to stay in."

"No, you can't," he says with a smirk. "There's nothing decent in the way of hotels for the next one hundred miles. The closest thing to a hotel for you would be taking up with a senior citizen at the assisted living center. Their apartments are decent, but they don't have much space. However, you'd probably make some elderly person quite happy as their new roommate." His eyes light up at the thought.

She thinks he has the same warped sense of humor as she does, and she also thinks she might be in trouble.

"While living with a grandma I've never known sounds somewhat attractive, I'll have to pass. Thank you for that kind offer though," she manages without laughing out loud.

"Well, then I guess you're stuck with me." He rolls up his sleeves to wash dishes, and her eyes fly to his forearms. "Besides, this town would not be happy with me if they knew I ran off the first relatively young librarian we've had for thirty years," he adds. "You do know what the young crowd reads, right?" He gives her a wink.

"I know all the best sites for what's trending in the literary world," she states. "And I wear more than one hat too. I'm also a barber," she answers in return, determined to feel useful.

His eyes light up. "Excuse me? How can you be a barber? You're a wom—" He notes the murderous glint in her eye and shuts up as he turns back to stare at the faucet.

"I was a candy striper once, okay? I learned a thing or two about shaving men in bed. I sort of have a natural way with hair," she says. She realizes her words came out all wrong, judging by the look on his face. She coughs. "Yeah, queen of awkward moments, right here. Thank you, thank you very much." She takes a deep bow before popping back up with a cheesy grin.

His face is red. "Nice recovery."

She giggles. "Well, I've had years of practice at sticking my foot in my mouth."

"It just so happens I could use a haircut and a good

beard trimming."

Her cheeks pinken. "Right...right now?"

He rubs his hands together. "Consider me your first customer."

She stares at his beard. "Really?" She chokes just a little at the thought of running her hands through his thick hair.

He clears his throat. "Yeah. I need to know if you're all talk or if you can put your money where your mouth is."

She gives him a miniature glare. "You want a straight edge, or are you more of a glider fan?"

He raises one eyebrow. "I don't know. How bad do you want to shank me right now, Piper?"

She runs a quick hand through his thick head of hair, something she's been wanting to do since she met him, and now she has an excuse.

He becomes still as stone in front of the sink.

"My name is Sheri," she insists in a hushed tone just above a whisper.

He turns toward her. She drops her hand from the back of his head and hides it behind her back. "I know your name," he answers in a tone with a look in his eye that suggests he knows so much more than that, even though they've known each other for all of two days. "That was a reference to a prison show."

She swallows hard. "Oh. Well, you'd better make it a glider." She takes his chin in her hand and gives it a little squeeze. She can only imagine the stubborn jaw that lies beneath that full beard. "I wouldn't want to go all *Color Purple* on you. We've only just met." Sheri shivers and fights the urge to check her arm for goose bumps while she wonders what it is about Randall that brings out the biblical Eve she'd rather not know she possesses.

8

Randall stands frozen at the sink and wonders why on earth he thought it was a good idea to ask Sheri to give him a haircut when he remembers what the touch of his finger to her lip did to him. The last thing he needs to know is the feel of her hands on him deliberately—for any reason.

It's such an intimate act having his hair washed, especially in his own kitchen. He relaxes a little as he watches her wrestle out of her layers of clothing until she's down to her V-neck cotton tee that's the same pale pink color as his grandma's roses. He blinks a few times and wonders why he's thinking about his grandmother with her standing so close.

"Do you have like a tank top or something?"

Her question interrupts his sentimental perusal. "Excuse me?"

She looks all flustered. "It'd probably be best if you wore something else when I wash your hair. Your shirt's going to get all wet, and you're going to need a few towels."

He hesitates. He doesn't know if he can take her leaning over him, all up in his space. "I can wash my own hair."

She fumbles with her earlobe, and it's adorable. "That's fine. Whichever way you want to do it. I just need a wet head if I'm going to give you a decent haircut."

He goes back and forth and feels quite silly. *What harm can there be in her washing his hair?* he reasons. "Where are you going to wash my hair, then?"

She eyes the oversized sink. "You have a great sink. It's definitely deep enough."

He shoves his hands in his pockets. "I was looking for practicality, so I chose a bigger basin so I could, um, wash my dogs in there."

She glances at Jake. "Are you telling me you haul big old Jake off the floor and put him in that sink? It's big, but it's not that big, and he's a lug to lift I would imagine."

He chuckles. "Um, no. Jake's bathing station is in the basement. I didn't intend to have a Saint Bernard, trust me. He's like feeding a small horse, but sometimes things just happen, and they work out." He's telling Jake's story, but it feels like he's only talking to Sheri, and all of a sudden, he has no more words.

She tilts her head to the side. "And?"

He looks at her again. "And what?"

"I think you were saying about how you and Jake met," she prompts.

"Oh, yeah. So, I was driving down the road. It was a blizzard that day. Snow was flying this way and that, and Jerry, your conniving realtor, was out plowing snow. He was going along, bopping his head around to his head-phones, and all of a sudden, I see this puppy in the middle of his path. I knew Jerry didn't see Jake, and I wasn't about to park my Outback in front of his plowing. So I stopped my car and ran over and snagged Jake from being run over by the plow."

She blinks. "So you threw yourself in front of a snow plow but not your car?"

What a joy killer, he thinks. She just turned his tale of heroism into pure stupidity.

"I love animals. What's so bad about that?" he argues.

She wrinkles her nose. "Nothing." She gives him a small smile. "I bet your mom was happy to hear you made it through that harrowing experience."

His heart pinches just a little, and his eyes water. "My mom's in heaven now," he says.

"Oh. I'm sorry. My parents are in heaven now too," she says with a sad smile.

He waits for her to say more, but she doesn't. "Do you have any siblings, then?"

She shrugs. "Nope. I was an only child. I just have my best friend, Jenni, and her family. She's like family to me anyway."

"And she's in Wisconsin?"

She nods. "Yes. She has a husband and three children, plus one more on the way."

He can't help but hear the longing in her voice when she talks about her friend. He wonders if she wants a family someday, and he can't believe how much he wants to help make that happen for her. The thought of having his own children makes him feel like he's just been tasered. "You were all alone and yet you left the one friend you have behind in Wisconsin." He smiles more to himself. "Alaska might be just the place for you."

She looks impatient. "I'm not all alone. I'm strong in my faith. I'll never be all alone."

Randall feels thoroughly admonished. He can't help but notice she sounds so sure of herself. He hasn't felt that sure about anything in a long time. He doesn't know how to answer. "Do you want me in front of the sink, then?"

She picks at invisible lint on her shirt sleeve. He finds it absolutely charming. "If you can lean down that far, it would be best if you're going to let me wash your hair."

Suddenly, he can't wait for more of her fingers in his hair. "I'll go get my shower kit and find that tank," he says before he marches off to his room.

9

Sheri does some serious scolding of herself while she stands alone in his kitchen. "Why did I have to be so direct with him? He was just making conversation," she mouths silently as she prepares her work area.

She can hear Jenni in her ear. "It's your age and the fact that you've been alone for far too long, Sheri. You're going to have to tone it down if you ever want to meet someone. People don't respond well to no filter."

"I know, I know," she answers to the voice only she can hear.

"What do you know?" His baritone voice interrupts her thoughts.

Her head pops up. "Nothing."

She takes in his white tank that he's wearing beneath an open button-up as he walks into the kitchen with his shower caddy. Sheri feels the heat crawl up her neck and into her face. She's severely perturbed at his ability to make her blush so easily, and he's not even trying. She takes a hold of his caddy and does a quick inventory of the contents. She's relieved for a distraction that isn't Randall.

She grabs a hold of his arm. "Come over here to the sink," she orders. She runs the water. He goes to stick his head in, but she stops him. "Hold up. Let me make sure it's the right temperature."

He grins down at her. "You think I haven't had a cold head of hair before? I live in Alaska."

She frowns at him. "That may be, but I won't be the reason you get pneumonia in the middle of winter."

He chuckles. "Fair enough." He sticks his hand in the running water. "It feels okay to me. I'm going in."

He grabs a hold of both sides before he ducks his head beneath the sink. She reaches over his back, doing her best to soak his head beneath the water. She gets her hands on some hair and tugs him toward her, crowding him as she lathers up his head with shampoo. She scrubs a little too hard but then stops.

"Is it okay if I do that?" she asks.

He groans. "Yes, please. Don't stop. I don't mind."

She digs both thumbs into the base of his neck and applies a little pressure as she moves slowly up the back of his head. She proceeds in the same manner with the rest of her fingers as she goes along for a few minutes before she steers him back beneath the water to rinse the soap out. She runs her hands through it a few more minutes, making sure all the shampoo is out. She grabs a towel and throws it over his shoulders. "Okay, you can stand up now."

He straightens up and turns toward her. He's so tall that he looks down at her, a feeling she's not used to. She's not exactly short. She glances down at his hand on her wrist. His eyes follow hers. He drops his hand as if he's been burned. "I'll just go sit down now," he growls.

She doesn't know what to make of what just happened between them. "Okay," she answers as if in a daze. She follows along behind him as if she's in a stupor. She absentmindedly picks up a brush and starts going through his hair.

He reaches up and grabs her hand. "Hold up. That's Jake's brush."

She snaps out of her Randall-induced stupor. "Oh, I'm sorry. I don't know what I was thinking." She lays it down on the table. "Do you want... Do you want me to wash your hair again?"

"I'm fine with my hair the way it is so long as you are," he answers.

She can't help but giggle as she scrubs his head dry with a towel and starts combing. "I don't suppose a little hair of the dog is going to hurt anything."

He throws his head back in laughter about the time she starts cutting his hair. She halts her movements in mortification and waits for him to settle down.

"And the hits just keep on coming." She swallows hard. "I'm at a bit of a loss, unless you count Murphy's Law as one."

He looks up at her. "What happened?"

She holds long pieces of his hair. "You moved while I was snipping."

His hand flies to his beautiful head of hair. He feels all around. "Okay. How bad is it? Do I have a bald spot?"

She coughs. "No. It's nothing like that. You just have shorter hair than you might have planned on. That's all."

By the look on his face, she can tell he's fighting annoyance. She braces herself for a good scolding. His knuckles tighten on the chair for half a second. "That's okay. I was due for a good haircut anyway. Go ahead and shave it."

She blinks. "You want me to shave your head bald?"

He tilts his head to the side. "Do whatever you have to, to even it out. Just don't tell me about it. I don't need to hear every gory detail of how you're chopping off my luscious locks."

She giggles. "Luscious locks? Who are you, Jason Momoa's cousin?"

He winks at her. "If you want me to be."

Her face flames. She's not sure when they officially crossed the line from teasing to flirty and fun. She's not sure she's prepared. "I'd rather you just be you. That'd be all right with me. I'm not much of an *Aquaman* fan."

He shrugs. "Your wish is my command."

She giggles again and wonders why it keeps happening and why she can't make it stop. She's hardly a teenage girl. "I wish for continual seventy degrees and an endless view of the ocean," she says dreamily.

His shoulders slump just a little. "You're on the wrong end of the map, lady. You sure you don't want to catch the first flight to Hawaii?"

She snips away at his hair. "I think if I try really hard, I can pull off a faux haircut. You could be like a GQ lumberjack," she teases.

He shivers. "What are you talking about? Please don't make me look like a Backstreet Boy or a Jonas Brother. I have to be able to hold my head up down at the lodge."

She flicks the back of his neck with a fingernail before she returns to snipping and trimming. "I happen to like the Jonas Brothers. Are you saying they aren't manly enough for the rugged Alaskan woodsman image you're striving for?"

He grins just a little. "Are you saying I'm rugged?"

Her stomach flips at his suggestive tone. "That's not what I said. I asked what kind of image you were going for." She nudges his head down with her hand as she continues working.

He ducks his head in response. "I'm not going for an image unless you're looking for a man who's not afraid of hard work."

She tries in vain to ignore how much his words spoken in earnest mean to her. "I didn't say I was looking for a man." She holds her breath for a few seconds before she continues working, forcing herself to focus on his hair. She doesn't want another mistake, especially when she feels as if she's applying for a job. She runs a hand over the top of his head before moving onto the back. "So, I thought I'd just shave this back here." The back of her knuckles grazes his skin, and he feels so bare.

He ducks his head once more. "Go ahead and do your worst."

She turns on the electric razor. "When's the last time you had your hair this short?"

"Never."

Panic fills her. She turns off the razor before coming around in front of him. "You've never had your hair buzzed, but you're okay with me doing this?"

He stares at her. "I trust you. It's just hair. If I don't like it, I'll wear a stocking hat until it grows back." His hand moves to the back of his neck. "You can't stop now. You have to finish what you started." Something in his tone makes her forget they're talking about hair.

She walks behind him and turns the razor on once more. "All right." It doesn't take long to finish up with that, but now comes the tricky part: shaping his beard. She's more than a little nervous. "It's been a while since I've worked with beards, so this might take a while."

He stands up. She thinks he's having second thoughts. "That's fine, but I'm moving to my recliner. It's more comfortable." She busies herself at the sink with readying her supplies before she carries them over to where he leans back with his eyes closed. She lays her hands on his face to get a feel for what she's doing. "I'm sorry this isn't a barbershop." Her voice is quiet.

His eyes pop open. "Are you kiddin' me? I can't think of a more relaxing thing to do in my living room than this right here. I'm just gonna lay back and enjoy my personal spa day in the comfort of my own living room."

"Just consider this part of my first rent check," she says as she glances around at the somewhat bare, but functional, living room. Something is missing. What is it? "Hey. Where's your Christmas tree?"

"I don't have one," he states as if it's the beginning and ending of the conversation.

"Do you not celebrate Christmas?" She feels sad at the thought.

He shrugs. "I do, but it's just me here so it feels a little silly to put one up."

She smacks his shoulder. "Well, we are *getting a Christmas tree*. That's all there is to it."

His eyes narrow a little in her direction. He crosses his arms on his chest. "And what if I don't want one?"

She shakes her head back and forth. "That doesn't matter. You're getting one."

He waves some sort of jazz hands in her face. "No, I'm not. This is my living space. You can put one in the basement."

She throws a hand on her hip. "So you're telling me if I have some women friends over I'm supposed to take them to the basement?"

He makes a face of mortification. "Why would you have women friends over? What are you planning on doing?" he accuses as if they're going to plan world domination over tea and cookies.

She rolls her eyes. "How am I supposed to get to know them better unless I have them over?" He starts to sit up. She surprises herself by laying a hand on his chest and shoving him back in his chair. "Hold it right there, mister. You about got it in the neck with the edge of this brand-new razor. You don't want blood all over your recliner."

He sighs all dramatically. "I never said you could have company over. Just get to know them at the library." A miniature battle of the wills goes on between them while each of them waits for the other to break the staring contest.

Someone knocks at the door. "You stay right there," she instructs as she hurries to the door with the razor still in her hand. She turns the knob. Two elderly women beam up at her from behind their bifocals, bright puffy coats, and matching lavender stocking hats with "Alaska" written on them with a magnificent Eagle head behind it. "Hello," Sheri answers as Randall buries his head in his hands behind her.

The first lady nudges the other. "Hello. I'm Bertie, and this is Mrs. Betts, and we were just dropping off a piece of correspondence for Randall."

The other one edges past her long enough to wave a gloved hand. "Hi, Randall," the woman calls out.

"Mrs. Betts," he growls from his chair where he sits in his tank top, blue jeans, and coveralls hanging halfway down.

Mrs. Betts inches past Sheri and drops the letter in her hand before going back outside as quickly as she stepped inside. "Bye, now." She slams the door shut. Sheri watches them walk down his sidewalk with their heads together.

"Well, that's just great," he mutters from his chair.

She looks over at him. "What's wrong?"

He waves at his front door. "You and I will be all over town before the day's over, that's what."

She can't help but grin. "They don't even know my name. How much can they really say?"

He snorts. "Trust me, a whole lot."

She crosses her arms on her chest while she clings to the letter. She doesn't know why he's so upset. "Shouldn't I be the one who's offended? They're talking about me and they don't even know me. At least they know you."

He holds out his hand. "Just let me see my letter, please."

She walks over and hands him the envelope. He tears it open and removes the piece of paper. His lips move silently for a few minutes. He flies out of his chair so fast he almost trips over his footrest. "Did you put them up to this?"

She is so confused. "That's not possible. I just met them." She tries to peek at the letter, but he's waving it around like a madman. "What is it?"

"It's a petition!"

She's so lost. "For what?"

"For me to put up a Christmas tree," he bellows.

She can't help but snicker at his outrage. "Calm down, Scrooge. No one can make you do anything."

"I am calm," he shouts before he shoves the letter under her nose. "Just look at what it says."

She snatches it from his hand and holds it under the light of a lamp. "It behooves me as Chairwoman of the Christmas Caroling Committee, whose sole interest is spreading cheer at every opportunity to everybody everywhere, to request that you join the rest of your friends and neighbors in our efforts in this cause by erecting a Christmas tree with lights and decorations that are easily visible to passersby as a demonstration of your support forthwith. We, the undersigned, agree with this reasonable request made by Mrs. Betts on November 13, 2021, as your friendly neighbors and urge you to respond ASAP." Sheri bites her lip to keep from laughing as she eyes the list of names that stretches out for the next three pages. "You have to admire her love for the holidays," she suggests.

"Bah humbug! They can't make me put up a Christmas tree, and neither can you," Randall hollers.

Sheri kind of understands why he's upset. Those badgering little old ladies are really throwing their weight around, but it's too funny. She can't help but be charmed by the use of Mrs. Betts's vast vocabulary.

"Maybe I'll invite them over and we can pray on it," she says as she gives him the most serious look she can muster, knowing she's sending him into orbit.

10

Randall sits in his recliner, fuming. "Great. That's just great."

She fights the urge to giggle more. "I don't know what you're going on about. They're two harmless old ladies."

He stares up at her like she's grown two heads. "You haven't even moved in here and you're plotting to turn my house into a house of prayer, and now I've got two old women threatening me if I don't put a dadgum Christmas tree. They can't tell me what I can or cannot put in my home. I hardly live in a HOA neighborhood. I live in Alaska because I need space to breathe." He points at the door. "They're infringing on my personal freedom as an American."

She is quiet throughout his ranting, but she's already decided he's not keeping her from meeting people and making new friends. "Back home we had a knitting group and a scrap-booking group. It was just nice to get together and visit," she says in a calm tone as if she's trying to soothe or distract him, but it's not happening. He's too riled up.

"I can't believe Mrs. Betts signed a petition. Do they really think they can make me put up a tree by guilting me into submission?"

She giggles. "That is what one does when they want something done. You can't say they didn't go about it properly."

Her rational words fall on deaf ears. "There's nothing proper about it. I'm not putting up a tree, and that's all there is to it." He catches the look of determination on her face, and he realizes she's just begun to fight but so has he. "How old are you? You do realize knitting is an old-lady activity."

Her answer is to pull a hair from his beard.

"Ouch, that hurt," he says as he rubs his offended chin.

"Just what sort of things should a woman my age be doing?" Her voice holds all sorts of warning.

He holds his tongue for all of half a second. "I don't know. You could start a book club, and then you could have it at the library." He thinks of his cousin, Jan. "Or you could bake."

She tugs on his ear. "I'm already pushing the limits with my cholesterol. I don't think my body needs any more carbs."

He groans as he flicks her hand away from his ear. "Okay?"

She gives his shoulder a shove. "Well, what do you think is in baking, except for carbs?"

He shrugs. "I don't know. I didn't think of that. Maybe you could sell what you bake."

She snorts. "I'm not looking to open a bakery anytime

soon. Four thirty in the morning doesn't sound like anything I want to do."

"How about the great outdoors? Do you enjoy that sort of thing?"

"I enjoy hiking, yes. But I thought there were bears in Alaska. It's not exactly my dream to become beef jerky on a nature trail." She gives him a nudge. "So, what do you do for fun?"

He leans back in his chair and wiggles his toes. "I love my job. I enjoy fishing. I enjoy peace and quiet."

She clears her throat. "What about spending time with friends? Do you do any of that?"

He flushes. "I usually spend the holidays down at the lodge with the guys. We have a few beers. It's kind of nice."

She snorts. "So basically you see your friends like four to five times a year *max*?"

He shrugs. "What's wrong with that?"

She smiles. "Nothing, I guess. It's just kind of hard to make a difference in anyone's life if you keep to yourself."

He frowns at being called out. "Wow. You're a little judgy."

She coughs. "No. I'm a lot judgy, and I'm working on it, okay? Just forget I said anything, and I'll just find myself a tiny tree that will fit in my space downstairs. You won't even have to see it." Her tone is filled with resignation.

"You think your pouting about a little tree is going to get me to change my mind?" He shrinks inside even as he taunts her.

"You can't blame a girl for trying," she says all flirty-like, and he kind of likes it. "But—" She raises a finger. "—you might reconsider putting up a tree. It's not wise to be at war with your neighbors."

He opens his mouth, and then he shuts it again. Mrs. Betts, his canning lady, is his main food supply. He studies Sheri. She's no dummy; she knows exactly what she's doing. If she intended to trick him into letting her have a Christmas tree, it's working.

"Fine. We can get a tree."

She shakes her head. He waits for her next response. "No. I don't want to make you do something that will only annoy you. You're going to look at that tree taking up your space and you're going to curse me every night."

He laughs out loud. "Boy, you're either really grudgy too, or you're laying it on thick for no reason."

She lets out a big sigh. "As you can see, there are many things I need to work on, and believe me, I'm trying."

He twiddles his thumbs on his chest. "So, where do you propose we get this Christmas tree that is eagerly waiting to invade my personal living space?"

Her hands run over his chin as she proceeds with her beard trimming or whatever she's doing. He fights the urge to stop them. He can't take much more of this. He's burning up. He decides it must be because he's not used to this much physical touch.

"I have no idea where to get a tree. You're the one who lives here," she pleads.

He clears his throat. "I guess we could start with Bob's Christmas Tree Farm. I don't know if he'll have any left this late in the season though."

She claps her hands and her eyes light up. "That sounds like a perfect plan." She whips out a round mirror and holds it up. "How do you like it?"

He touches his chin, something he hasn't done in months. "I feel bare."

She giggles. "Is that a bad thing?"

He looks up at her. "I don't know. Is it?"

She takes a step back and studies his face for what feels like forever. "I'd say you'll pass, but you might consider growing back that beard." Her eyes twinkle and shine.

She's kind of ornery. He goes to get up.

"Hold up. You've got something." Her brow is furrowed, and she looks all worried. She tilts his head toward the ceiling. Her finger traces the edge of his scar, making him feel all self-conscious. "What happened?" Her voice is full of concern.

"It was a long time ago. I was in a snowmobile accident."

"That's some scar you've got. I can't believe I didn't see it."

He coughs. He wishes she'd move her fingers away from his face, but at the same time he wants them there. "I keep it well hidden. I wouldn't want it to mar any of this," he says as he waves a hand in front of his face.

She giggles again. "I don't know. It might go along with that broken nose of yours."

He snorts. "So you noticed that too, huh? And here the doctor told me no one would know the difference."

She blushes. "Ah, well, everyone knows bumps and blemishes just add character. I wouldn't sweat it."

He stands up from his chair to look down at her once more. "I wasn't going to, but then you started in on me. You're kind of hard on a guy."

She looks contrite. "I don't mean to be. I'm not sure if it's my age or being alone too long, but I fear I've become too opinionated for my own good. I just have to stop myself and say, 'Lord, stop me from saying ugly things.'"

He studies her with more than a little curiosity. "So you're on really good terms with the man upstairs, huh?"

She raises an eyebrow. "Why do you say that?"

He feels weird. "I don't know. You sure talk about Him like he's pretty close is all."

She smiles again, and he feels all warm inside. "That's because He is to me, Randall. He's as close as you'll let Him be." She studies him with nothing but openness, but it's too much for him.

"Okay, then. Let's go find that tree, shall we?"

She takes a step back. "Sure. Just let me go layer up again first. I don't want to freeze."

11

She follows Randall through the empty parking lot. "Where are all the trees?"

He turns to her with his gloved hands in his coveralls. "I think they're gone. I think we came too late." He sounds so apologetic as if somehow this is his fault, and Sheri feels bad.

An elderly man wheels himself out of the mobile office with a friendly smile. "Hi, folks. How can I help you today?"

Randall clears his throat. "Hey, Bob. We just thought we'd come down to see if you have any trees left."

Bob blinks. "Randall? Is that you? I almost didn't recognize you without your bushy beard. Who's your lady friend?"

Sheri holds back a giggle when Randall looks all embarrassed.

"Bob, this is Sheri. She just moved here from Wisconsin. She's a librarian. Isn't that great timing?"

Bob frowns. "Well, I don't know. I mean, we kind of already have a town librarian."

Awkward. Sheri opens her mouth, then closes it again. She glances at Randall in annoyance and wonders why he said nothing about her moving in on someone else. "I don't have to be a librarian" is all she can think to say.

Randall stomps his foot. "Now, Bob. Don't you worry about it. I'm sure the township will agree with me that everyone loves Bertie, but she's getting up there in age. She's got to be like ninety-three. She can't hear. She can barely see. If you ask me, she's more of a liability."

Bob's jaw drops. "Randall, there's no need to be so hard on Bertie. She does her best."

Randall's jaw tightens. "I know that, Bob, but if you want our library to continue to stay open, you need someone in there who knows what's trending. Otherwise, no one will come in. Sheri, here, has a degree. She's worked in libraries for years. She knows the business."

"Well, now I don't know. I mean, I think this is definitely something the library board will have to discuss. You can't just bring somebody new in without getting the necessary approvals."

"Fine, Bob, but you should know you can't grow a town if you refuse to let newcomers in. Come on, Sheri. This parking lot has nothing to offer." Randall grabs Sheri's arm as if to go.

Sheri feels torn. She really needs a job, but she doesn't want to toss a ninety-three-year-old woman out in the street, and she certainly doesn't want to start a library board war. Sheri needs to make a good impression or at least a better one than grumpy butt Randall just did.

"Bob. I know it's late, but are you sure you don't have any Christmas trees for sale?" she implores.

Bob scratches his chin. "Well, as you can see, my lot is empty."

Her heart drops a little. "I see."

Bob flinches at the defeated resignation in Sheri's tone. "Well, I might have one left, but it's a bit on the thin side for a Christmas tree, and it's a whole lotta wonky."

She rewards Bob with a big grin at his description that he felt was lacking. "That sounds just right to me. Where is it?"

Bob looks all sheepish. "To tell you the truth, it's still attached to its roots. It looked so pathetic I was sure no one would want it. I didn't have the heart to cut it down."

Randall clears his throat. "I'm gettin' old here, Bob. Where is the dang tree? Sheri and I will just go and get it."

She glances over at Randall and tries to scold him with her eyes. *What is his problem?* she wonders. *Why is he being so rude?*

"It's in the back forty, Randall. It's the tallest one out there. The rest are just babies that won't be ready until next Christmas." Bob looks back at Sheri. "So, where are you staying? Did you buy a house here?"

Sheri's not about to tell him which house she bought, but she doesn't know what to say.

Randall steps closer. "Sheri will be staying with me for a few months. She bought a bit of a fixer-upper."

Bob chuckles. "Good luck with him. You don't need to meet a bear in the woods to get the Alaska experience. You've got Randall."

She laughs out loud. Bob and Randall both stare at her. "That was pretty good, Bob."

"I wasn't trying to be funny," he grumbles in response.

Randall hooks her elbow with his hand. "Come on, woman. I ain't got all day. Let's go get your tree."

Bob coughs. "I don't usually do this but go ahead and take the snowmobile and the wagon. You're gonna need help gettin' that tree back here, and I'm in no shape to be haulin' anything sizable. You know I've got a bad back."

Sheri beams at Bob. "Thanks, Bob. That's so kind of you."

Randall snorts. "Are the keys in the snowmobile?"

Bob frowns. "What do you think I am, some sort of idiot? The keys are with me." He pulls a lanyard out of the top of his jacket and holds a circle of keys to work through. "Just give me a minute to find it."

Randall walks over to the base of the steps in front of Bob. Sheri fights the urge to do the same as she grows colder by the second. She doesn't think twice as she steps up behind Randall and leans against his back.

"What're you doing?" he growls.

She digs her face into his shoulder. "You're blocking my wind. It's freezing out here," she mutters into his jacket.

"Here. I found it."

She peeks around Randall's shoulder at Bob's raised hand dangling a key. Randall reaches for it.

"Don't lose that key. I only have the one," Bob says in a tone that can only be interpreted as scolding.

"Don't worry. I'm not about to walk all the way back here with a wonky tree," Randall growls.

12

Randall hops on the snowmobile. Sheri climbs on behind him. She shivers through her coat. Her teeth rattle near his ear. She wraps her arms around his waist and leans up against him.

"Let's go. This is my first snowmobile ride!"

He can't believe the excitement in her voice despite the fact that she's obviously freezing.

He hits the gas, and they take off. He goes as fast as he dares with the wagon jumping around behind them. He follows the path between the tree lines. Sheri's about to think Bob has Alzheimer's when she spies the lone, tall tree at the end of the road. She can't help but be eternally grateful for the snowmobile. They pull up to it slowly. She hops off and grabs the chainsaw.

She looks at Randall with hope in her eyes. "Can I operate the chainsaw?"

Visions of blood and bone fill him, but he doesn't want to offend her. "I'd rather cut the tree down this time if you don't mind. We will have plenty of warm weather days for you to learn to chainsaw. Today's too cold."

She hands the chainsaw over and sits back down on the snowmobile, looking all kinds of dejected. "Okay."

"I'll let you drag the tree into the wagon," he says, feeling all sorts of ornery.

She nods her head. "Good! I'll take it."

He ducks his head before she catches him chuckling. He's never seen a woman so eager to do what he considers to be man's work. The tree falls quickly. He gets far too much enjoyment out of watching her wrangle the odd-shaped tree into the wagon. She grunts and groans but eventually manages to balance it enough that it doesn't fall out. She stands back to admire her work.

"I think I've got it in there far enough so it won't fall out if we go really slow," she says as she hugs herself.

He doesn't think it's his imagination that her lips are a little blue. He points to the plastic hooks hanging off the sides of the wagon. "Or...we could tie the tree down using the ropes and the hooks."

She looks all embarrassed and then a little mad. "I'm surprised you didn't wait 'til we got a little ways down the trail before you told me that, smart butt."

He rocks back on his heels and throws up his hands. "Hey, I wouldn't want to offend your independent nature. I'm just trying to help here."

She rolls her eyes. "Fine. Thank you for your assistance." She digs around in the wagon. "Where's the rope? I don't see any."

He unwinds the twine wrapped around the front of the snowmobile. "It's right here."

She jabs a hand on her hip. "How was I supposed to know that could come off there?"

He chuckles. "What do you think it's for? Holding this thing together?"

She holds out her gloved hand. "Just give me the rope."

He drops it in her outstretched hand. "Fine by me. But just so you know, it's twine." He gives her a smirk. "I'll just watch you hang yourself."

She shakes her head as she runs the twine here and there, looping it through the hooks, only to have it pop back out at her. She does laps around the wagon a few times before throwing her hands in the air. "Fine. I give up. Is there like some sort of secret Christmas-tree-tying knot trick that only you Alaskans know?"

He raises his eyebrows. "As a matter of fact, there is. It's top secret too. Right up there with the Witness Protection Program."

She stares at him like he's daft. "Are you going to show me, or do I have to turn around while you do it?"

He grabs the twine and works it through the hooks. "Well, since you asked so nicely." He bops his head sideways. "Get your butt over here and learn somethin'."

She walks slowly toward him. "All right, Father Christmas. Teach me your Christmas-tree-tying ways."

She watches his hands wrap the twine a few times before he knots it, then wraps it again, and then knots it again. He follows her around to the other side and waits patiently as she makes an attempt, but it doesn't work. She slows down and tries again only to have it unwrap itself. She holds the twine out.

"One more time, okay? But don't knot it. I want to get this down."

He can't help but admire her stubbornness. He does it once more and then takes it apart. She starts to go the wrong way again but stops, and this time she gets it right. Her face lights up. All his annoyance at freezing his butt off for a stupid, wonky Christmas tree disappears.

"Are you ready to go now, Christmas princess?"

She grins and claps her hands before making some strange gesture above her head.

"Now what are you doing?"

She sticks her nose in the air. "I'm adjusting my tiara. It slipped."

He hops on the snowmobile. "Let's go, milady; your chariot awaits you."

She sighs dramatically. "It's not a fancy carriage with snazzy wheels and you're no footman, but I suppose you'll do."

13

Sheri bounces around on the back of the snowmobile, smiling all the way. *Who knew cutting down a tree and tossing it in a wagon in ten-below freezing cold could be so much fun?* she thinks to herself as she clings tight to Randall's waist.

They fly over the snow-covered ground between the line of trees, and she sneaks more than a few backward looks to be sure they don't lose their Christmas tree. The wagon bumps along behind them. She feels silly as she realizes there's no way the tree would've stayed in the wagon without being tied down. She supposes she should be more than a little annoyed with him for letting her make such an independent fool of herself, but she knows she makes it way too easy.

As fast as they took off, they come to an abrupt halt. He hops off the snowmobile.

Bob throws open the door and holds out his hand from the doorway to his office. "I'll take the key, please, and put that twine back before you go."

Randall hands over the key. "What about the tree, Bob? How much?"

Bob shakes his head. "No charge. No one wanted that tree."

Sheri walks over. She reaches into her pocket and hands him two twenties. "This is my first Christmas in Alaska, and it's already been memorable."

They all look over at the pathetic tree that's a little bent in the middle and misshapen.

"That tree's a little odd-shaped, and its branches are sparse, but I'll fill in the gaps. We'll get along just fine."

Bob grins at her. He hands back a twenty. "I won't take both twenties, darlin'. Twenty is plenty." He gives her a wink. "I'd say by your words, you're the right person for that tree. You have a blessed Christmas."

Sheri lays her hand on his. "You do the same, Bob. I'm so glad we met."

A throat clears behind her. "You two hens done cluckin'? I ain't got all day," Randall growls.

Sheri releases Bob's hand. "Guess I'd better go. I've got work to do."

Bob smiles up at her from his chair. "He might be a bruised apple, but he's got a good core," he whispers.

Sheri doesn't know what to say, so she turns toward Randall, who is leaning on the truck bed with the tree already in it. "I was going to help you with that," she scolds.

He smirks at her. "Yeah, I know. But you women spent so much time talkin', I did it myself." He smirks again. "How you like them apples?"

She flushes with embarrassment and decides Bob's not a very good whisperer. "Just for that comment, you can wrap the twine around the snowmobile too. I'm gettin' in the truck." She stomps up to the passenger side of the truck and hops in. She jams her gloved hands in her coat and cringes as her breath leaves behind clouds of foggy air. "I've got to get a better coat. This is ridiculous," she mutters through chattering teeth.

The truck door slams. He puts his truck in drive. "Now where to?"

She looks over at him. "Don't you have a job to do?"

He grins at her and her toes curl. "I work on contract. Some days I make my own hours, and this is one of those days." He taps his fingers on the steering wheel. "So, where we headed?"

She grins as her next thought spills out. "We need to get some ornaments for our Christmas tree."

He closes his eyes. "You didn't bring any with you?"

Her eyes widen. She looks at him like he understands nothing, which is an accurate deduction. "I did, but I thought it would be fun to get some here."

He groans. She waits him out. "I'm sorry to be the bearer of bad news, honey," he says, not sounding the least bit sorry, "but the closest place to do that is about a hundred miles from here."

She can hardly believe it. She exhales slowly and decides this is another inconvenience she'll have to get used to. "Oh." She taps her fingers on the seat and tries once more. "Do you have any sort of craft stores around here? Like Hobby Lobby?"

"We have the basics here. If you can make Christmas ornaments out of toilet paper, office supplies, or school supplies, I think we have a chance," he says with a smirk.

She feels a little crushed and dismayed, but she's determined not to let on. Randall, aka Scrooge, is not getting the better of her. She'll show him she's not easily dissuaded. She grabs his arm. "School supplies it is. I can work with that."

He scowls. "I guess we're going to the general store."

She claps her hand and smiles. "I guess we are."

Four minutes later, they're parked in front of the store. He makes a shooing gesture. "Go on in. We're here."

She gives him a look. "You're not going to walk me in? You told me you would give me a tour of the town."

He crosses his arms over his chest. "I am. This is your friendly truck-guided tour." He waves his hand in the direction of the store again. "This is the general store. Have at it."

She grabs up her purse and opens the door. "Fine." She feels childish as she stomps toward the front door and flings it open. She walks slowly up and down every aisle, making sure she doesn't miss anything. Her frown quickly disappears when she sees there's plenty that can be made from ordinary items. Crafting is her specialty.

Minutes pass, and she's lost in thought. She notices a tall man standing near her. She glances his way a few times and is surprised to find he's checking her out, and he's being rather brazen. *Alaskan men must be really lonely*, she thinks, as well as reminding herself to keep that in mind as she meets a pair of chocolate-brown eyes accompanied by a bold wink.

"Can I help you?" she says as she realizes he's not going anywhere soon.

He grins at her. "I was going to ask you the same thing."

"I don't suppose you can help me, sir, unless your

specialty is making Christmas ornaments. Are you a crafty sort of person?"

He steps closer. "Some people would say so, yes." His eyes roam a little too much and a little too long. She doesn't think she's ever met anyone so bold.

She takes a cautious step backward. "Yes, well, I think I've got things under control. Thank you."

He lingers. "Would you like to go for a drink sometime?"

She blinks. "No, thank you."

His grin grows, shocking Sheri, as she thought she was rather clear. "May I ask why not?"

She sniffs. "I don't owe you any sort of explanation, *sir*. I don't even know your name."

He holds out his hand. "My name is Rick."

She shakes his hand because politeness demands it. He grabs a hold, giving her a gentle squeeze before grazing the top of her hand with his thumb.

"And your name?"

"It's Sheri, Rick, and she doesn't drink."

She blushes at the sound of Randall's warning growl. She moves backward just enough to peek around Rick at Randall, but she's still attached to his hand.

"Thanks, Randall, but I believe I can handle my own social interactions," she speaks in a clipped tone that borders on grouchy, but she can't help it but feel offended at Randall's overbearing ways. She's not some sort of helpless female who can't think for herself.

Randall raises his hands. "Suit yourself." He glares at their hands, which are still joined. "I was just trying to help. I'll just be in the truck." He pivots and marches back down the aisle away from Sheri, who drops Rick's hand like it burns her but not in a good way. She kind of wishes Randall would come back when she catches Rick's smarmy grin.

"As I was saying...about that drink."

She does her best to sound like the church lady, but she doesn't care. Rick is too aggressive for her taste. "Randall was right. I'm not much of a drinker. Or a barfly."

Rick glances at the floor before he looks back at her. "Who said anything about bars and alcohol? You sure make a lot of assumptions about a guy."

"Okay, fine." She forces a little lightness to her tone that she does not feel. "What kind of drink did you have in mind?"

He studies her a little longer than she'd like. "You seem like a coffee shop kind of girl. What about a cup of coffee?"

"Are you telling me there is a coffee shop in this town?" She can't help but get a little excited at the thought.

Rick looks caught. "Actually, no, there isn't." He raises a finger. "But there's no bar either, so... Although, there is the lodge." He stops and looks confused.

She taps an impatient toe. "So what do you propose?"

He scratches the back of his neck. "There's a coffee shop in the next town over."

"Which is forty miles from here, give or take," she offers.

He nods. "Yep."

She shakes her head. "That's a negative. I don't know you from Adam. I'm not riding forty miles down the highway with a complete stranger."

Rick snorts. "You moved in with Randall, and he was a complete stranger."

She's getting more upset by the second. "That was

different. He built me a fire and sat on my couch all night to keep me warm."

Rick's face changes, but not for the better. He opens his mouth, but she cuts him off.

"I don't owe you any sort of explanation. I said no, and that's the end of it."

He backs away with his hands in the air. "You can't blame a guy for trying. I think it's been nice to meet ya, but I'm not entirely sure. I guess I'll see ya around."

14

Sheri and her three bags of crap pile into Randall's truck. He glances her way as he backs out onto the street. "What'd Rick want?"

She snaps her seat belt in place. "Nothing much. Just a cup of coffee."

He tries to get a better read on her, but she's a closed book. "And?"

She glances at him. "And I said no. That's it."

His heart sings, but he tries not to show it. "Mind tellin' me why?"

She picks up her phone. "Do you want me to go out with him? 'Cause I can call him and tell him so. He gave me his number. I have it on speed dial."

He snorts. "Knock yourself out, sugar."

She giggles, and his anger rises. "I'm just teasing. I don't have his number."

He lightly shoves her into the passenger-side door. "You're a cruel woman."

She hugs the door handle. "Probably." She looks over at

him. "Can we go to my house again so I can get some boxes?"

He nods. "We could, or we could go unload this tree and then pile your boxes in the back of the truck and take them over to our place." He stops talking for a second or two. His last two words sound so permanent. Is it his imagination, or did her breath just catch a little?

"For now. It's our place for now."

Her words are quiet. They almost sound like a regret. He wonders what that means.

The two of them drag the Christmas tree through the front door while they listen to Jake about lose it. He stalks back and forth inside, giving the tree furtive glances as if it's going to come to life and attack him. After a few minutes, Jake gets the nerve to come and up smell the needles before one pokes him in the nose, making him jump. He backs up, plops down on his butt, and gives a little *woof*.

She giggles at his antics. "Oh, Jakey. You're ador-a-ble."

He frowns. "No one has ever called my St. Bernard ador-a-ble. He's more of a nuisance."

She rushes to Jake's side, scratches his ears, and kisses his head. "Don't you listen to grumpy old Randall. He's a stick-in-the-mud."

His frown grows deeper. "Hey, this stick-in-the-mud just spent the afternoon with you acting the part of Father Christmas. You might want to ease up a little."

She turns from Jake to smile at him. "Careful there, Randall. You almost sound like you're having fun."

He drops the Christmas tree on the floor. "Whatever. I'm going to find a bucket and some dirt to stick this wonky tree in. It'd better stand upright."

The pitter-patter of her footsteps behind him makes him smile, and he's surprised at how fast he's gotten used to having another person in the house.

They get the tree set up in the pot. The tall, gangly tree almost touches the ceiling but not quite. She claps her hands with delight, stirring up emotions in Randall's gut. "Yay. It's a perfect fit," she sings as her hazel eyes twinkle and shine.

It feels like someone punched him in the stomach and all the air has left the room. He can't ignore that Sheri feels like the perfect fit. He second-guesses his decision in inviting her to live with him and wonders how he'll handle it when she moves out.

"Sheri." He invades her moment of joy. "Let's go get your Christmas decorations."

They drive to her house and head inside using their phones as flashlights. She turns to him as they dig through the boxes. "Is it possible this place is even colder than before? It sure feels like it."

He stops moving for a second. "I suppose. I know what it sounds like, but I've gotten so used to the cold. I don't feel it as much."

She laughs. "Yes. There is some truth to 'everything is relative.' My cousin lives in Kansas, and she hates the north because of the six months of winter sometimes, but I'd take that over tornados and ice storms any day."

He chuckles. "Yeah, I tried living in the Lower 48 once in Oklahoma. I did not acclimate well."

She giggles. "There is a big difference between Alaska and Oklahoma. This is true."

He comes across a photo album. He pulls it out of the box. "May I?"

She smiles at him. "Of course." They flip through the pictures. She shares a few memories with him. "That was me when our team, Scholars Bowl, won third in state. That was me when I got second in state for copyediting in Yearbook."

"You were an accomplished student," he observes.

She shrugs. "Yeah. Well, when you're an only child, it's not hard to do. I mean, you're not vying for anyone's attention because you get it all. I had no siblings to share Mom and Dad with, so..."

He chuckles. "I was always glad that Rodney was there because he drew the heat off me."

She looks puzzled. "Were you into trouble when you were young?"

He feels a little sheepish. "Not the bad sort of trouble, like not the law-breaking kind. I was more of a prankster you might say, but Rodney was a little more than that; enough so that my parents didn't have time to notice my ornery side because they were too busy keeping him out of jail. Literally."

She gasps. "Oh."

He claps his hands. "Yes. Apparently, moving to what is possibly the most remote state on the continent was not enough to keep my law-breaking brother out of trouble." He sighs. "But...Rodney turned out mostly okay. He's avoided jail time as an adult, and he has a regular sixty-hour-a-week job. He loves his work."

She shakes her head. "I guess so. That's a long work week."

"Well, you know the old saying: 'Work doesn't feel like work if you enjoy it.'"

She nods her head. "True. I mean, working at a library

never felt like work to me either." She points to the four biggest boxes stacked against the wall. "Those are all my books that I couldn't bear to leave behind."

He nods. "And are they coming to my house?"

She giggles. "No." She stares at them with longing. "Well, maybe one box. I put all my very favorites in one box." She opens another box. "Hey, I think I found my Christmas ornaments."

They haul boxes back down her porch stairs and into the back of his truck. It takes a few trips. He settles in the front seat, and she climbs in beside him. She lays a hand on his arm. Her eyes get all serious. "Randall, I'm really glad I met you."

It's crazy. They've only just met, but he feels like he's known her a lot longer. "Me too."

15

After Sheri gets everything unloaded, she heads upstairs with her Christmas box, which she sets down by the tree before turning on Christmas music on her phone as she chooses her first ornament.

He plops down in his recliner. "Turn that music off. I'm watching the game."

She glances at his black TV screen. "What game? There's nothing on."

He grunts. "There will be in about two seconds. I'm serious. Turn it off."

She frowns at him. "I'll just turn it down. How about that?"

He shakes his head back and forth. "No. I'll still hear it. I don't want to hear it."

A tear forms in her eye, which is ridiculous. She turns away from him. "Fine. I'll just put headphones in." She jams her AirPods in her ears and wills her Christmas cheer to return. It does slowly but surely as she tunes into her music and resumes decorating the tree. She's in the happy zone, moving right along, when she hears a hand clapping. She turns back to face Randall, who looks like a grumpy old bear. If he wasn't so infuriating she would probably start giggling at the scowl on his face. "Now what?" she demands.

"You're humming."

She removes an AirPod. "What?" she asks even though she totally heard him. But so what? He's being awful.

He stares her down. "I said you're humming."

She shrugs. "Yeah, so?"

"Well, stop it. It's annoying."

She stomps her foot. "No more annoying than you growling at me for simply being cheerful and decorating our Christmas tree."

His face is a little red. She feels a little bad. "It's not our Christmas tree. It's your Christmas tree that I'm allowing in my living room, despite my better judgment, and now you are annoying me to no end with your off-key Christmas humming, so stop doing it," he yells.

Randall is really worked up, but so is she. She wonders what is wrong with her and why she's so turned on by a man towering over her looking like he wants to kill her for being overly cheerful.

She searches for neutral ground. "Would you like to make some microwave popcorn?"

He blinks a few times. She struggles to hide a smile despite his Scrooge-y ways and their most recent beginnings of yet another argument. He looks like he just saw a fork in the road that wasn't there a second ago. "What?"

"I said, would you like to make popcorn in the microwave?" she repeats herself.

He looks all sorts of confused. "Are you hungry?"

"No. I like to string popcorn on a string with a needle, and then I wrap it around the tree. My mother taught me. She and I used to do it together," she offers.

He smirks at her, which is a tad infuriating, but she'll take a smirk over an angry word. "Can I poke you with a needle?" he teases.

"Only if I get to poke you back," she answers before she sticks her tongue out at him.

He looks indecisive before he grabs the remote and flips off the TV. "Crank up your Christmas, Sheri, and let's make some popcorn." He waves a finger in her face. "But if you tell any of the guys at the lodge about this, I'll swear I never did any of it."

"Seriously? You don't want the men to know you like Christmas? O-kay," she answers in a tone full of doubt that suggests he's being ridiculous.

A few finger pokes and Band-Aids later, they have a pretty decent string of popcorn. They wrap it around the tree together. "Any other homemade Christmas decoration ideas?" Randall tries to sound grumpy, but she hears the hope in his voice.

"I brought a gingerbread house with me from Wisconsin. We could make that together."

He wrinkles his nose. "You make gingerbread houses? I thought those were for children."

She refuses to be shamed for her love of all things Christmas. "I do. I even have my own secret ingredient that makes the frosting twice as strong and stiff to hold everything in place."

He laughs. "Is it edible?"

"Um, no. But no one I ever knew ate the gingerbread house or the frosting anyway. They're just to look at." He's headed for his recliner, she can just tell. "I'll make us a couple of hot toddies, but only if you make the house with me," she bargains.

He drops the remote back in the chair. "You're on."

They sit at his kitchen table, sipping their toddies. She uses her phone to listen to Bing Crosby's "I'll Be Home for Christmas." Randall's face grimaces in protest, but she ignores him as she carefully removes all the pieces from the box. "Okay, now here's the floor plan." She lays it out on the table.

He gives her an incredulous look. "You need a blueprint to put together a gingerbread house? If I have to listen to your Christmas music all night, I'm not reading those darn instructions on how to build a make-believe house. Just let that magic frosting of yours do its job." He gives her a wink.

She eyes the instructions quickly as she slowly folds them up and sticks them back in the box. They manage to assemble the gingerbread house, but she has her doubts if it's structurally sound. She pushes that thought away and focuses on decorating. She uses her tweezers to place another gumdrop in a perfect line.

He smirks at her. "You use tweezers for your gumdrops?"

"I like a perfect line, and my hands are too awkward to get the job done. So what?"

His hand covers his circle of candy rocks in front of the house. "Don't look. It's messy."

She shoves his hand away and eyes his asymmetrical circle of candy. She tilts her head to the side. "I thought you said you knew something about landscaping."

He makes a face at her. "In real life, yes. No one judges my gingerbread house skills. This is just for fun."

She tries to move a red-hot rock with her tweezers. "Just let me scoot this one over."

He swats her hand away and grabs her wrist. "Don't touch my Red Hots." She tries to dodge and dive again. He slaps her hand. "I said no."

She leans back in her chair. "Fine. I'll just avert my eyes from your imperfect circle of red rocks."

He downs his toddy in a few gulps and stands up. "You do that. I'm going to go recline in my chair now in front of my game." He stops in the doorway. "It's art. It doesn't have to be perfect."

She feels bad, which she's sure wasn't his intention, but still. "Thanks for today. It was all very nice," she offers as her flag of surrender.

He doesn't answer except to turn the volume up on his TV.

"I'll just head downstairs and eat a ham sandwich, then," she mutters to herself.

"Make me one too, please," he hollers out.

She smiles in spite of her irritation. *There's no way the man can't make himself a dang sandwich.* "I'll leave it on the table for you," she answers.

16

Randall hides his grin behind his hand when he thinks about Sheri's particularness over a gingerbread house and its stupid circle of rocks. Now that he knows how to get under her skin and how much fun it is, he vows to do it more often.

He stops humming when he notices what he's doing. As much he hates to admit it, old Bing and his Christmas crooning are kind of growing on him, or maybe it's the bossy librarian who is one heck of a cook and has the most gentle touch for a barber he's ever known, despite her reckless clippers. He chuckles at the memory of her mortification over his first haircut. He quickly sobers at the thought of her not being around for the next one.

Minutes later, he walks into the kitchen to find a grilled ham-and-cheese sandwich with a side of cottage cheese and sliced apples. "Mamma mia. Now I know what smelled so good," he says to an empty room.

He picks up his plate and strolls back into his living room. He stops short when he spies the decorated

Christmas tree with its bright lights shining back at him from behind his recliner. He glances back at the gingerbread house on his kitchen table, and it hits him like a lightning bolt: his house almost looks like a home.

He looks around the kitchen once more. He is disheartened to see how empty it looks without Sheri in it. He shakes off the feeling and walks back to his recliner to sit down to eat in front of his game, but it's not as enjoyable. He can't help but wonder what she is up to in the basement. He walks quietly to the door at the top of the stairs and peeks in.

"It's going good. There have been a few hiccups. I bought a house. You know, the one I was so sure was the one since the sale went so smoothly and all, but then when I got here, it was a piece of junk! I was tricked," she exclaims.

He can't help but smile at her theatrics.

"That's so awful, Sheri. I'm so sorry," someone else's voice answers.

She must be on speaker. He knows he should walk away, but curiosity keeps him glued to the spot.

"That's all right. Things always turn out like they're supposed to."

"So are you in a hotel, then? It looks very primitive—and a little dark."

Rude.

Sheri giggles. "Not exactly. So I thought I was moving to a town with limited choices on restaurants and such, but there's, like, none—at all."

"What? What happened?"

"You wouldn't believe it, Jenni."

Jenni...Jenni... That's her best friend.

"So I arrive here at night, get off the plane, and the guy who sold me the house picks me up. He was a little jittery. I thought it was just the cold, but now I'm beginning to wonder if it was something else that gave him the jitters. So anyway, he picks me up and drives me to my house in a snowplow. He stops long enough to let me out and then just drives off. So I'm, like, stuck in the middle of the night in front of my new home, which has no lights on. I step into an icebox. There's no heat, no nothing. I go to turn on the light and the electricity is out. And the next day is a Saturday, which is the weekend, so I can't even call the city office."

"No way. So what'd you do?"

"I marched upstairs and found my bed. Then I put on as many layers as I could, dragged all my blankets out, lit a candle, put it in the window, and went to bed."

"You could have frozen to death," Jenni scolds.

"I suppose. But what else could I have done? There are no hotels here. It wasn't technically an emergency. I wasn't sick or anything, thank goodness."

Thank goodness for no hotel, he thinks to himself. He might not have met her.

"What happened next?"

"Well, it was kind of weird. I woke the next morning. My candle was out, but the house felt a tad bit warmer. I headed down the stairs and found a man sleeping on my couch in front of my fireplace, which was burning logs."

"A man. A man was in your house?"

Randall chuckles again at the thought.

"Yes. He was just sitting there. Sound asleep. And he had a Saint Bernard with him."

"Weird. Was he a squatter? I've seen shows about this."

Randall sniffs at Jenni's implications.

"What's she do? Watch *60 minutes* all day?" he mutters to himself.

"No. He wasn't. His name is Randall. He lives here. He's, like, a volunteer firefighter, among the other things. He blew out my candle so I wouldn't burn my house down. Then he lit a fire in the fireplace and slept on my couch all night."

"That's all very strange but also kind of sweet. Go on."

"Strange," Randall muses to himself. He'd like to give Jenni a talking-to. "I'm not strange. I basically saved her from freezing to death," he mutters under his breath.

"So in the morning, he tells me my house is essentially a firetrap. We argued about me leaving a lit candle in the window, which he was totally right about, but I wasn't about to tell him that."

"Ha. At least she admits I'm right to someone," he surmises.

"Hmm. So what are you going to do?"

Her best friend sure asks a lot of questions.

"For now, I'm living in Randall's basement."

There's an awkward pause.

"I know what it sounds like, but I've met his cousin. She's pretty normal, and he's been so nice to me since I got here."

"If you say so. I think it's a bit strange he'd invite you to live with him so soon unless he has ulterior motives."

What is it with these paranoid Wisconsin women? Randall wonders. He has no ulterior motive other than to lose his sanity by letting a crazy Christmas church girl take over his home.

"Well, so far we've gotten a Christmas tree together

and built a gingerbread house at his kitchen table. He seems pretty harmless."

"He did these things with you? I couldn't get Justin to do those things even when we were dating."

His heart swells with pride before his ego deflates just a little. There's no way Sheri's turning him into Martha Stewart. Not if he has anything to say about it.

"Oh, and guess what? This town needs a librarian. It has to be fate. I'm telling you, I think this is where I'm supposed to be."

Randall can't believe the amount of hope he feels at the thought of Sheri sticking around.

"So how is this guy? Are you interested? Is he handsome?"

Finally, Randall thinks, *they're getting to the important part.*

"I don't know. He's not so much handsome. He's more..." Sheri's voice lowers.

She's whispering as if she knows he's trying to hear. There's more throat clearing.

"Well, I'll let you go. It was so nice talking to you," Sheri says.

17

Sheri ends her FaceTime with Jenni, which was such a great surprise. Sheri didn't realize how homesick she had been to hear her best friend's voice. She'd tried to call her a few times, but Jenni wasn't able to visit. There's a knocking at her door from up above.

"Yes," Sheri answers.

"Can I come down?" Randall calls out.

"Yes."

His footsteps are on the stairs, and then he's standing in her bedroom. "I was wondering if you would like to see the library."

She glances at her watch, as she hasn't gotten used to Alaska's daytime darkness yet. "Is it open?"

He tilts his head to the side. "I think so, but even if it isn't, I have a key."

She watches him warily. "Do you have a key to every business in this town?"

He nods. "Pretty much. I'm the town fireman."

She considers this. "What if you go on vacation? Who is your backup?"

He looks all confused. "We kind of already had this conversation, but whatever. As I said before why would they need a backup? I don't go anywhere." He stops. "I mean, I could go places if I wanted, but I don't want to. Everything I need is right here."

"You've never had the urge to travel? To see new places?"

"Have you?"

There's challenge in his tone as he throws her words right back at her.

"I always thought I would, you know. Go new places. See interesting things. But I never did." Her voice is quiet and self-defeating. She hates that she hears Jenni's voice in her ears whispering, "I told you so."

He claps his hands and pulls her from her reverie. "Well, let's try and remedy that, shall we?"

She's not sure if she should be worried, but his enthusiasm is contagious, and she did just challenge him. "What do you think we should do?"

He leans against the wall. "NASA's predicting a great visualization of Aurora Borealis in the next few days. I say we improve our odds of seeing it."

She's confused. "What are you talking about?"

"The Northern Lights. Have you ever seen them?"

"Um, no."

"Well, they're something to see, especially in Alaska. I think you'd really like it." He sounds so excited about the idea that she finds herself wanting to follow him.

"Sure, I'm game, so long as Jake comes along."

His hands are moving a mile a minute. "I've got a tent I

never use and some heavy-duty sleeping bags in a closet. I've got some perfectly good snowshoes too. If we left within the next half hour, we could make pretty good time. I know a good hiking spot beside a clear mountain lake. It's about three to four hours from here."

She stares him down. "You can leave town? Just like that? I thought you said you were the only fireman."

He looks all sheepish. "I'm not the only fireman. There are a few others, which I told you. I'm just the youngest by far and the most reliable, which is why I have more than a few favors I can call in. You say the word and I'll call one in." There's a pause. "So, what do you say?"

She gives him a slow nod. "All right."

He sniffs. "Gee, you could sound a little more excited. The Northern Lights aren't that common. Who knows when they'll be this visible again?" He knocks on the wall. "I'll go make the call."

She stares after him as he goes to leave. "What do I bring?" she yells at his ankles that head up the stairs.

"Camping stuff," he responds. His vague answer frustrates her to no end.

"Will there be any outlets where we are going?" she hollers at him as he stands at the top of the stairs.

He laughs. "No, woman. This isn't glamping. That's for lightweights in the Lower 48. You're in Alaska now. We're roughing it." He sits at the top of the steps and looks down at her. "It will just be you, me, Jake, and the local wildlife for company."

A shiver of fear runs through her. "Bob had better be right about you being a bear."

He lets out a small roar before he shuts the door.

She rummages through her boxes for the warmest

clothes she can find and wonders what she got herself into. She closes her eyes for a second. "Please, dear Lord, watch over us on our little trip. Don't let me get mauled."

True to his word, thirty minutes later, they are headed down a bare stretch of highway, listening to the radio. Sheri is squished up against Randall, as Jake insists on sitting by the window. It's a good thing Randall has a big bench seat. Jake takes up quite a bit of space.

They're about an hour into the drive when Randall turns the music down. "Do you know any games?"

"What kind of games?"

"Like games you can play in the car on a road trip."

She searches her mind. "Well, back home we played the license plate game, like count how many different states we saw, but that's probably not going to be very productive in Alaska."

He laughs. "No. Probably not."

She thinks some more. "How about the word-association game?"

He nods. "Okay."

"So I just say a word and you say the first thing that comes to mind, and then we go from there."

He waits.

"Shall I start?"

"Yeah, go ahead," he answers.

"Okay. Fire."

"Water."

"Balloon."

"Hot air." He smacks his forehead. "That's two words. Sorry."

Sheri laughs. "That's all right. Fiction."

"Story."

"Bedtime."

"Insomnia."

"Robert DeNiro."

"Raging Bull."

"Boxing."

"Rocky."

"Mountains."

"Valleys."

"Death."

"Heaven."

"God."

"Holy."

"Water."

Sheri giggles. "We're kind of back where we started."

He nods. "It would seem so." He taps his steering wheel. "I thought about what you said. It would be wiser to go to the library when it is open. I don't want anyone thinking I'm giving you an advantage or anything like that."

Sheri looks over at him. "How long has Bertie been the librarian, then?"

"About ten years, I think. Yeah, ten years."

"Hmm. And how long has it been since somebody new moved to your town?"

His jaw tightens. He looks embarrassed. "A while."

"Are most of the town residents from Alaska?"

He sighs. "Yeah, probably."

She fidgets in her seat. "How are they with outsiders?"

He laughs out loud. "Are you asking if all of them are as friendly as me?"

She glances out the window. "Yeah, I guess that's what I'm asking."

He clears his throat. "Some of them might make you prove your salt, but I'm sure you expected a little of that."

She giggles. "True. I mean, the same could be said about small towns everywhere." She can't help but razz Randall a little. "So, are you this friendly to every newcomer?"

"The last few residents who moved in were an old couple and their forty-year-old son, Jerry. So no, I did not take them camping."

A light bulb goes off in her head. "Jerry...as in Jerry who sold me the house?"

He nods again. "Yep. One and the same. Jerry, the snowplow guy who can't drive a straight line, but he has the job because his uncle is our mayor and has been for the past twenty years."

"Speaking of years, how long have you had all those jars of food in the basement?"

He looks over at her. "They're all kosher. Trust me, I keep a close eye on my inventory." He gives her the once-over. "I keep an eye on things that are important to me."

She shivers beneath his searching gaze. Just when she thinks things are comfortable between them, he throws her a curveball.

She looks away and tries to focus on something safe. She thinks of his food supply. It didn't look that complicated. "Did you, like, do all your canning yourself?"

He's a little too smirky, like he knows exactly what he just did. She thinks she should be annoyed, but she's not.

"Heck, no. I don't do the canning," he answers.

"Then where does it come from? Is there like a farmer's market or something?"

"Nah. I have a neighbor, Mrs. Betts. We have a thing going."

She coughs. "A thing?"

He laughs again. "Give me a break, Sheri. You met her. She's married, not to mention seventy-five years old."

She feels ridiculous. "You're talking about the elderly lady who dropped off your Christmas tree letter?"

He nods his head. "Yeah. So anyway, she's my canned goods person. I do odd jobs for her around her house whenever she needs them done, and I shovel her walk, that sort of thing. In exchange, she pays me with canned goods."

"That's a lot of food. Are you telling me you'll go through all of it before it goes bad?"

He nods again. "I don't like to grocery shop much because it's so far away and kind of an inconvenience. Besides, Mrs. Betts's canned food tastes so much better than anything I'd get from a store. Her cousin has a garden and a chicken house. They come to town about every two weeks to check on their great-aunt and swap food. Most of her groceries come from them. *And* she makes her own bread. It is delicious."

She pokes him in the shoulder. "Who needs a wife when you have Mrs. Betts?"

His face turns red. He coughs. "I guess I don't. I've done fine so far without one."

She feels bad about his reaction. "I was just teasing you. I didn't mean anything by it."

18

Randall kicks himself mentally, telling himself he should have known church-going Sheri wouldn't be much for small talk. He can't believe how fast she went from talking about food and his neighbor to marriage. He feels like he's suffocating inside his truck. The doors are closing in on him, and he's not sure he likes it. It's true that he's not getting any younger at thirty-eight, but he thinks he still has a few good years left before he settles down.

"Now look here. I'm not looking for a wife," he states.

Her whole body tenses. She looks at him like he's crazy. He starts to wonder if he is. His statement kind of came out of nowhere.

"Who said you were?" She leans away from him and snuggles up to Jake. "Did you think I was fishing for an invitation?"

He tries to focus, but she makes him so mad he can hardly see straight. "You're the one who brought up the subject of a wife. Not me."

She snorts. "I was just joking. Calm down."

He knows he should stop, but he can't. "Well, how am I supposed to know? You move to Alaska for a change of scenery. You're obviously a serious church-going girl who doesn't want to mess around for fun."

She crosses her arms on her chest. "So what if I don't do casual relationships? Is that a crime? I don't have to explain my sexual habits to you."

Her jaw drops like she can't believe what she just said, and frankly, neither can he.

She turns to stare straight out Jake's window. "I'd like to go home now."

He sighs in irritation. "We're three hours down the road. We're almost there."

Her hand moves to her face. He feels inadequate. He has no idea what to do with a crying woman except to wish she'd stop.

"I said I'd like to go home now." Her voice is more insistent.

He lays a careful hand on hers.

She jerks it away and whips around. "Don't you touch me," she yells at him.

Jake startles at her tone, and so does Randall. He raises his hand slowly from hers. "Okay, okay? If you really want to go home, we will, but it'd be a shame to miss a once-in-a-lifetime light show because you can't take what you dish out."

She lifts her chin a little and sniffs. "What's that supposed to mean?"

He slaps the little bit of truck seat between them. "You know *exactly* what it means. You started the conversation about marriage and a wife. When I responded in kind, you didn't like what I had to say."

She side-eyes him. "I don't care if you're looking for a wife or not. I never said I was applying for the job." Her jaw loosens just a hair, but his remains clenched.

"What's that supposed to mean? Are you saying I wouldn't be a good husband? Do I not meet your standards?" he protests.

She slowly turns toward him and raises her index finger. "For one, I don't know why we're having this conversation at all. You just said you don't want a wife, so it should not matter what I think of you being someone's husband." She raises another finger. "For two—"

He stares hard at her.

She shuts her mouth for about half a second. "You know what? I'm just going to sit over here and pray for a while before I open my mouth again."

He's so annoyed he almost misses his turn to the state park. "You do that."

She glares like fire, burning Randall clean through. "I just said I would."

He knows he should keep his mouth shut, but the urge to get the last word won't go away. "I know."

"So I am."

"I know!"

She sniffs. "You don't need to tell me to do what I already said I would. I don't need reminders."

"You just need the last word," he mutters under his breath.

Her eyes flash. "What did you just say?"

He exhales slowly. "Don't let me interrupt your prayin'."

She closes her eyes and lifts her face toward the truck ceiling. Her lips start to move.

He supposes he's seen stranger things happen inside his truck, but he can't think of any of them right now. He looks at Jake who sits on the other side of Sheri. Jake stares back at him as if to assure him he's not the crazy one. He smiles at Jake, thinking he's definitely the kind of friend he needs.

Randall searches the area as they come around the bend and is happy to see it's empty, which suits him fine. He doesn't like other company around when he's camping, as the whole purpose is to have peace and quiet. Her eyes are still closed. *That must be one long prayer,* he thinks, or she's somehow managed to take a power nap.

He clears his throat. "Sheri, we're here."

Her eyes fly open. "There are no buildings. Where will we shower?"

He grins at her. "I brought a bowl."

"To pee in?" her voice squeaks.

He laughs out loud. "No. I brought a bowl and a washcloth for you to wash with in the morning if you want."

"That's it? That's all I get to wash my entire body?" She sounds like she's on the verge of hysteria.

He nods. "Yep."

She shoves his arm a little too hard. "Well, come on, then. Let's get this tent up while we still have daylight." She follows him out his side of the truck. "You mentioned a lake. Maybe I can rinse off in there tomorrow."

His eyes widen at the thought. "No can do. Trust me, that'd be more Alaskan experience than you want or need. That lake this time of year would feel like a polar plunge."

She claps her hands. "Oh, fun. I've never tried one. I've always wanted to do that."

He shakes his head. "I was kidding, Sheri. You shouldn't

do that unless you have a heat source nearby for immediately after. Otherwise, you run the risk of catching pneumonia."

"Oh." She sounds so disappointed, and he almost feels bad.

They unload the truck together. It doesn't take long to set up the tent. She stomps her feet and bounces up and down. "Where's that sleeping bag? I'm freezing."

He gets it out and hands it to her. "Did you bring your thermal wear? It's going to get pretty cold tonight."

"I brought the warmest clothes I have. You didn't give me much time. I don't think I own any thermal wear." There's an edge to her tone, but her face remains passive. They climb in the tent. She snuggles into her sleeping bag. "This feels so much better already." She looks over at him. "What's for supper? Did you bring hot dogs or things to make s'mores with?"

"Um, not exactly. We're going to catch our supper."

She looks a little worried. "Do you expect me to chase down a rabbit or a deer? 'Cause that's not happening."

He can't help but chuckle at her comment. "No. I left my bow and arrow at home. If I shoot a rabbit, it'll have so much lead in it, there will be nothing left to eat. We're going to catch some fish."

"Oh. With fishing poles or nets?"

He keeps his eyes on her to see her reaction. "With our hands."

She stares right back at him. "You're kidding, right? I can't do that. The fish are too fast." She closes her eyes. "Besides, I didn't bring any rubber boots, and I'm not stepping in that ice-cold water and freezing my toes off, which I already can't feel."

"Do you want to come watch me catch a few, then?"

She snuggles deeper in her sleeping bag. "Do I have to? I'm almost warm."

He chuckles. "Fine, but you're going to help me gather sticks and twigs for our fire. You're camping too."

She buries her nose in the sleeping bag as if to chase away the chills. "Fine."

19

Sheri sits on a log as close to the fire as she dares. She fights the urge to pinch herself to be sure she isn't dreaming. Despite everything, she can't help but smile in wonder at the thought that if someone had told her just four months ago that she'd be sitting in the middle of the Alaskan wilderness in front of a fire eating smoked fish right from the river with a freshly shaven lumberjack, she would have called them straight-up crazy, but that's what she's doing, and she's loving every minute of it.

Well, almost every minute of it. It would be nicer if Randall wasn't glaring at her like he'd like to throw her in the fire. She smiles at the thought of being an Alaskan Joan of Arc. She's always admired martyrs. She's not sure she could ever be that brave.

"Why are you smiling into the fire with that strange look on your face? I'm not sure I want to know what you're thinking about over there," he says, interrupting her morbid musings.

She strokes Jake's head. "Actually, I was thinking about

Joan of Arc being burned at the stake."

He harrumphs. "Told you I didn't want to know."

"And yet you asked the question. Don't ask if you don't want to know," she grumps.

"Do you always have an answer for everything?" he demands.

She thinks he doesn't need to be so irritated, but he did catch her supper for her in the freezing cold water while she sat in front of the fire.

She fidgets on the stump that digs into her butt while she tries to find a neutral subject that doesn't lead to another argument between them. The stump is hardly a cushioned chair. "You know how we talked about me fitting in earlier as part of the town?"

"Yeah, I guess." He sounds confused.

"Well, is there anything I can do to, like, fit in faster?"

He shifts in his seat. "What do you mean?"

She takes another careful bite of fish. She's a little paranoid about fish bones after hearing a terrible story of a girl who swallowed a tiny bone that perforated her esophagus and started a massive infection that they thought was tonsillitis. "I don't know. Like, is there some sort of charity I could make a donation to or some sort of half marathon I could participate in?"

He gives her a slow grin, and she knows she's in trouble.

She raises her pointer finger. "I am not eating mountain oysters," she declares.

He laughs out loud. His laughter warms her clear to her toes. "Good to know." He leans back and stares at her through the fire for a second too long as if he can tell how fast it gets to her. "How well can you swing an ax?"

Where did that come from? she wonders. "Excuse me?"

He nods his head and rubs his hands together. "Yes, I think this will work. It'd be a great opportunity for you to make a good first impression."

"By swinging an ax," she answers in the driest tone possible so there's mistaking her doubts. She wonders if he's trying to pull one over on her, and she's not falling for it. The next thing he'll be doing is showing her how to swing it.

He raises a hand halfway up with his palm facing downward. "Hear me out. I'm totally serious. Every year, the town has a festival, and they have a log-splitting contest. Whoever splits the most logs in so many minutes wins a trophy."

She chews on her lip. "What makes you think I could do this? It's like you said. I don't have the upper-body strength to carry a full-grown man anywhere."

By the look on his face, it's like he's not hearing her. "Trust me. It's the best way to win them over in such a short time. If you want to win their respect and their trust in you as someone who's going to stick around, this is the way to do it."

She stares back at him. "Two questions: is this a co-ed contest, and are you going to be in it?"

His helpless smile hits her in the middle of her chest. "I've been the champion five years running. It's my thing. I can't not do it."

She nibbles on her fish. "You didn't answer my question. Is this contest co-ed?"

"What if it is? Are you going to give up before you even try?" he goads.

She rolls her eyes. "I didn't say that, but what makes

you think I have a fighting chance? I'm sure everyone else in it is experienced ax swingers or whatever." She feels ridiculous just saying the words. She has no idea what she's talking about.

"Maybe, but they don't have what you have." He sounds so confident.

She lifts her chin. "Oh, and what's that? No experience whatsoever? I wouldn't know the difference between an ax and a hatchet."

"Stop being such a negative Nancy. You'll have me for a coach. That'll make the difference. What you lack in experience, we'll make up for with training and practice. It's not so much your strength. It's the total movement and the angle at which the ax hits the log. You'll see. You never know. You might be a natural."

She giggles. "What are you going to do, turn me into a professional log-splitter?"

He tosses his fish bones in a nearby trash can. "Something tells me swinging an ax might be a natural calling for you."

"Whatever. You're just butt hurt because I was winning the argument," she answers.

He stands up and stretches. His shirt raises just a little, and she sees the stark whiteness of his skin just above his belt. She averts her eyes to Jake and holds the remaining fish bone in her hand, contemplating.

"Don't even think about giving him that fish bone. He'll choke on it."

"How did you know?"

He chuckles. "Your face is as readable as Jake's. You can't stand eating in front of him, which is just silly. I do it all the time."

She looks down at Jake's big, sorrowful eyes as he waits patiently by her side, watching every bite she takes. "I can't take him watching me eat without him," she says as she tears the biggest piece of fish she can find with no bones in it and tosses it in his direction. She glances at the thin-looking sleeping bags in the tent, and she *knows* no matter how many blankets she has, they won't warm her. "I've got dibs on sleeping with Jake," she announces before getting up to go and change into her jammies. She steps through the zip-up tent door, and Jake tries to follow. "I'm changing into my pajamas, Jake, so please make sure no one comes in," she calls out to him as if he can speak English.

Apparently, he can't because Jake walks right in. She reaches out and pats his head. "Gee, Jake. You're not exactly the best guard dog, but I'll take what I can get. You're sleeping with me tonight, and you better not snore," she says as she yanks on her long underwear before laying down in her sleeping bag. She throws the top halfway open before patting the sleeping bag.

Jake startles and backs away.

"Here, Jakey. Come here and lie down," she says.

Jake stares at her with incomprehension.

"Jake." His voice floats in on the breeze.

Jake, ever obedient to his master, nudges his way out of the tent.

"Stop calling him. Let me have him. Please, just for tonight," she begs.

He ducks his head inside the tent and rolls his eyes. "Fine. Jake," he barks out. "Go lie down," he orders.

Jake ambles back in, bumping into her in the process. He looks up at her unapologetically as if to ask what she's doing laying in his path.

"I'm sorry, Jake," she says, even though she feels ridiculous as she pats the space beside her.

Jake sits his big butt down right before going to all fours and laying his head on his paws while looking at her with nothing short of longing. She reaches over and scratches his ears for a while.

Before too long, he steps inside the tent and zips it down in the front from the inside. "Gotta love double-sided zippers," he says.

"What?" is all she can manage at the thought of being stuck in this tiny space with Randall overnight. The realization hits her a little too late. Why did she think camping was such a hot idea? She has nothing to prove to anyone, especially not freezing to death with only her pride to keep her warm. She snuggles into Jake, and lucky for her, he doesn't resist.

He gives her a look. "The tent has a double-sided zipper. That way, you can close it from either side." He glances at Jake. "It figures the only guy you'll snuggle up to has four legs and a tail."

"Why you ripping on Jake? He didn't do anything wrong." It's the coward's way out, but she's not having another discussion with him about sleeping arrangements, no matter how cold it gets.

He crawls into his sleeping bag and turns on his side to face her. "I'm not ripping on Jake. The way I see it, he's the only one getting a little lucky tonight."

"Oh? And why's that?" she answers with no small amount of warning in her tone.

"He gets to lie in the arms of a beautiful woman. It's as simple as that."

Is it her imagination, or does he sound a little wistful?

That can't be.

"Goodnight, Sheri."

If she didn't know better, Randall is smiling.

"Goodnight, Randall," she says to the darkness between them. The day catches up to her, and she's on the verge of falling asleep.

"Look up."

She opens her eyes, even though she doesn't want to. She's just so tired. Between the long drive and arguing with Randall, she's plum worn out. The tiny window in the tent roof seems endless as she stares out at the stars that shine so bright. She can hardly believe the vibrant greens and blues that fill the night sky. The colorful hues are fantastic —as sure as someone dipped a paintbrush in some paint before dragging it halfway across the night sky. It's marvelous. How long she watches, she couldn't say, but she's never seen colors in the night sky like these.

"How can you look up at all that and not believe?" she whispers.

"You know, the lights are a result of the particles from the sun hitting the earth's atmosphere as they pass through space, which causes atoms in the atmosphere to react, and this releases energy in the form of light, so that's what it is," he answers in a matter-of-fact tone.

She can't help but grin just a little. "That's just man's explanation for the world's greatest artist, our Creator."

"It's science, Sheri," he argues.

"Think what you want. I know what I believe. He could light up the night sky with every color imaginable if He wanted to. I don't need science to explain everything. It takes away from the beauty of creation."

20

Randall lays there, staring up at the night sky filled with waves of bright greens and blues, and he can't help but think about what Sheri just said. He doesn't know everything, but he knows the sky looks amazing. And the woman who lies beside him is pretty amazing too.

Sleeping in this tent beside her has him so confused. In ways he can't explain and doesn't want to acknowledge or examine, she reminds him of home, even though he's known her for such a short time. And those sorts of feelings are new and more than a little frightening. He's never felt them before, and he's not sure what to think about that.

Maybe it's the way she talks about nature, and the sky, and God. That's gotta be what's throwing him for a loop. Or maybe it's her sense of calm. He doesn't know. All he knows is he doesn't want to want to be around her, but it's like he needs to be around her, just like he doesn't want to know more about her. Because the more he knows, the more he'll like her, and he already likes her too much, and she's not really his type. He's better with quiet women who keep him guessing just enough to be mysterious, or at least he used to be.

He looks over at Jake lying next to her. He never thought he'd be jealous of a two-hundred-pound St. Bernard. He can't help but laugh just a little at the thought.

"Randall." Her voice is almost a sigh, or maybe it's just wishful thinking on his part.

"Yeah," he answers, hoping for some sort of invitation. If she gives him anything, he'll be across this tent in half a second.

"Tell me something about you."

His mind races. Is this some sort of test? Because if it is, he doesn't want to fail. "What do you want to know?"

She giggles, and he feels the heat in his neck just before it creeps to his face.

"What was your father like?" she asks.

He closes his eyes. "He had broad shoulders and blue eyes." He smiles. "That's what my mom always said caught her eye."

She giggles again. "I didn't ask you what your mother liked about him. I'm asking you who he was to you."

He stares up into the sky and imagines his father looking down on him. "He was kind of quiet. He didn't really make small talk. He was a provider and a hard worker. He was the happiest with his family. He was really smart, but he didn't go on about it or whatever." His throat feels a little tight.

"You must miss him." Her words cut into his memories.

"Some times more than others." He turns to face her, but all he sees is Jake's big, fluffy head. "He would have liked you."

"You said he was a smart man," she answers.

He laughs out loud. "You don't quit, do you?"

"Not when I'm right," she counters.

They lay in silence for a little bit. "Tell me about your father."

Sheri sighs. "He loved me in his way, but he was kind of closed off. I think some of it might have been the fact that I'm female. I'm not sure."

"That sounds sort of lonely," he answers.

"I never thought of it that way. He probably was."

"Or he was a bit of a turd who missed out on his daughter's life," he answers again.

"I'm going to go with lonely," she says, and he feels bad about what he said.

"I'm sorry. Sometimes I can really stick my foot in my mouth."

An awkward pause follows, and he thinks she's trying to sleep. "What is that yoga pose called?" she says with a smirk.

He laughs. He can't hold it in. Her sense of humor is funny and so dry.

An hour passes, and Randall can't sleep. His mind won't shut down. It's been so quiet that he's sure she's sleeping. Jake contentedly snores. His eyelids finally start drooping, which means sleep is within half an hour, or at least it had better be. Insomnia is getting old, and tomorrow's going to be a long drive home, especially if he can't get to sleep. A chattering noise fills the tent and interrupts his thoughts. It has to be her.

He doesn't think twice as he climbs out of his sleeping bag, shoves Jake to the side, and crawls in next to her. "No, Randall. I'm fine," she protests in between her teeth chattering.

"Be still so I can warm you up," he suggests, but it sounds more like an order in her ear as he smooshes all along her back. "There's no reason for neither of us to sleep tonight, and you won't get any sleep if you freeze to death." He waits anxiously for her to turn toward him to look him in the eye—any excuse to feel her lips against his—but she's calmly indifferent. It stings more than he'd like to admit.

He sticks out an arm. "Lay your head there," he says as he wraps his other arm around her and lays a light hand on her hip. "Relax and go to sleep."

Sheri slowly relaxes and settles in. He catches a hint of lavender and spice. *Home never smelled this good, so why does he want to run for the hills?* Randall wonders what he's really afraid of.

21

Sheri wakes up sandwiched between Jake and Randall. She's warm as toast. She considers snuggling up to Jake, but he smells a little too much like something dead. She snuggles up to Randall as quietly as possible before she digs her nose into his shirt-covered shoulder. She can't help but notice that he smells just like a man should: a little dirt with sweat mixed with day-old deodorant. She closes her eyes and prays for more sleep, but after about five minutes, she decides there's no hope for another REM cycle.

"Can I have my armpit back? I need to step outside," Randall growls near her ear.

She moves away slowly. She doesn't want to startle Jake, who's happily dead to the world.

"Sure," she answers as she scoots forward just a hair, making space for Randall to crawl out, but he gets all tangled up in her sleeping bag, and it makes her giggle.

"What's so funny?" he demands.

She shrugs. "Nothing. You're just having a little trouble crawling out of my bed is all."

He's almost to his feet when he falls backward onto his butt. "Yeah, well, I've probably got the fastest record for crawling into it, so I guess there's that."

Her face flushes as her anger goes through the ceiling. "How dare you? Are you seriously trying to shame me for being discriminating about who's in my bed? 'Cause that's not happening."

"Wouldn't dream of it, sugar," Randall mutters at her once more.

"Don't you go calling me sugar or anything else sweet," she yells. She's shocked at the sudden urge to chuck an alarm clock at the back of his head.

He snorts. "Don't worry. I won't make that mistake again."

Her mouth flies open, but she can't find any words as she watches him struggle with the tent flap zipper in the dark. She wonders what time it is. She turns over her watch that glows in the dark. It's eight o'clock in the morning.

"Just go outside and pee," she yells at his retreating back and feels bad when Jake is close behind. She takes a deep, calming breath. She can't believe she ran them both out of the tent.

Seconds later, Randall returns and plops down on the one makeshift cot-like seat parked in the corner. "So I was thinking..."

She's not too sure how she feels about the tone of his voice or his words. "About what?"

"About your training to be a volunteer firewoman."

Her heart lifts but her morning body droops. "Oh, yeah?"

He gives a decisive nod. "Yeah, and what I'm thinking is

you could use all the practice you can get. So to start your training you can carry the big pack today."

That doesn't sound so bad, and maybe it'll keep her warm. "All right."

He clears his throat. "So that means you carry my stuff and your stuff."

Sheri swallows hard. "Wait. What? Um, why?"

"Well, when you go into a building that's on fire, you're not just carrying forty pounds of heavy hose and other equipment. You might end up hauling out a human being. So you'd better start practicing carrying other people's loads."

She sniffs. "Listen, mister. I'm a prayer warrior. We think of others each and every day."

Randall looks a little uncomfortable at her statement. "Fine, but do you physically lift them off the ground? Because that's what I'm talking about." He stares her down.

"Just give me a minute to get around, all right. I'm not even out of bed yet." She bites her lip. All that water she drank last night just caught up with her. "So, where do I... you know..." She forces herself to look at him. She's so embarrassed.

"Any tree will do," he says, followed by a smirk.

She cringes at the thought of brushing her booty up against tree bark and catching poison oak on her backside or something crazy like that. "Um, that's a negative."

He digs around in his pack and hands her a bowl. "Here, use this."

"But that's our bathing bowl. That's what you said." She waits for him to crack a smile.

He doesn't. He digs around and pulls out another bowl.

"You're in luck. I have a blue bowl for bathing and a yellow bowl for peeing. That's how we'll remember." He gives her a huge grin.

She swallows hard. "Are you serious right now?"

He rolls his eyes and digs around once more before holding out a roll of toilet paper in one hand and hand sanitizer in the other. "How about this too?"

She pouts while she crosses her legs and does some Kegels. "I really hate you."

He looks excited at her words. "Good. You're going to need that anger for fuel. We've got a long day ahead of us."

She clears her throat. "So, where do I go?"

"Wherever you think is a good place, but you better get going before you can't hold it anymore. You look like you're in pain."

She shoves her sleeping bag down and whips on a pair of boots before she snatches up the toilet paper and sanitizer. "Come on, Jake," she pleads, thinking she'll take a St. Bernard for an audience over peeing in the great outdoors alone.

She manages to hide behind a line of trees, but she's still within ten feet of the tent. Her business done, she hurries back. She's surprised to see everything where it was, except for the tent. Sheri thinks Randall must be some sort of tent magician, but she'll be darned if she's going to give him any sort of compliment. She's still angry with him for trying to make her feel like a prude and being such a know-it-all.

She tosses off her boots and starts layering. She notices him staring at her, but she keeps going. Her modesty went out the window after she peed in the forest. She gives him little glares here and there as she wiggles into the next layer, thinking if he doesn't like watching her jump around while she tugs everything on over her long underwear, he can look somewhere else.

"Are you really going to wear your long underwear all day?" he questions.

His advice is the last thing she wants right now. She's still feeling sour over him offering her a bowl to pee in and a few other things. "Is there some reason I shouldn't?" she pops off.

"You're going to sweat twice as much if you do," he responds.

"Good. A little sweat never hurt anyone."

"All right, but keep in mind you're going to be carrying extra weight today. My pack isn't exactly light."

"Just give me a protein bar and some water mister, and let's get going already." She looks down at the tent packed neatly away and feels a tad bit bad about not helping. "You made short work of the tent," she offers.

"Is that admiration I hear?" he asks before giving her a wink.

"I don't know. Is it?" she answers as she gets situated in all three to four layers of clothes, which she's already regretting, but she's not about to tell him.

He approaches. "Are you ready?"

"For what?"

"To feel like a pack mule."

His eyes are all lit up. She's a little frightened. "Sure," she replies.

He claps his hands. "Okay! Here we go."

Sheri shifts a little under the ever-growing weight of the pack on her back that he keeps adding weight to. "Isn't there like some sort of hauling equipment I can put this on? Like a sled or something."

He laughs at her, and this gets her back up all over again. "You going to sit down in the middle of a fire and build yourself some sort of Eagle Scout rescue contraption that'll potentially turn into a burning bed when you only have seconds to search and rescue?"

His question makes her feel stupid, and this angers her further. She sees his point, but he didn't need to be so rude about it. "Gee, Mr. Merry Sunshine, I can't *imagine* why you haven't gotten more locals to join the volunteer fire department."

His eyes fly to the ground. "There's not that many guys locally who have the time or the interest. It takes more dedication than you'd think just to be sure everything is done proper in the safest manner possible."

"So, how do your men practice? Is there some sort of simulation lab?"

He shakes his head back and forth. "That's a negative. Too expensive."

"So you literally learn on the job," she says in a voice more skeptical than she intended.

"Yes."

"And that's not considered a liability?" she says with too much satisfaction.

"I don't expect you to understand, but sometimes we have to work with what we've got. I do my best to train every man—" He glances her way. "—or woman to prepare them for every scenario and to know all the protocols, but there's only so much you can learn from a book. With that being said, I spend a lot of time on the clock because I won't let an inexperienced fireman work on a fire alone.

Being a fireman is not just about saving lives, and it's not just about how much I can carry. It's about how much my team and I can carry and what we do together. We've got each other's backs, and that's true from day one because it has to be. We depend on each other because that's the only way we'll survive, which helps others survive."

She opens her mouth and then closes it. She feels more than a little foolish. "I'd sit down for your lecture, but I may not get back up," she quips.

Surprise registers on his face. He throws his head back and laughs. "I'm done, so let's get going. It sounds like you're ready for a long hike."

The packs dig into her shoulders, which surprises her because she didn't think she'd feel anything under all her layers of clothing. "How long?"

He gives the bare space on her shoulder a hearty pat. "We'll walk until you're tired of talking. How 'bout that?" His voice is muffled beneath the ski mask that covers his mouth.

As warm as she feels, she can't believe it's only two degrees outside. Thank goodness he came prepared with heavy-duty gloves and extra-warm socks. She's grateful she's wearing the men's socks and gloves without difficulty.

"What if I'm there now?" she answers.

His face fills with exasperation. "You can't be tired. We've only just begun." His face turns beet red. There's an awkward pause. His last four words grab a hold of her heart. As much as she'd like to shove them away she can't. Something is happening between them. She knows he feels it too because he's staring at her as much as she stares at him.

Jake bumps into Randall, and the spell is broken. He snaps out of it. His hands fly to his head. "Hats. How could I forget those?"

"We're wearing ski masks," she answers.

"True, but these are special hiking hats. You can't ever keep your head too warm," he says as he unzips a bag on her back and rummages around for what feels like forever.

She hears a merry jingling, and she giggles. "Jingle bells? How did you know they're my favorite? That'll be fun. Thanks!"

"Good grief. If I'd known how excited you get over jingle bells, I'd give them to you every morning with your coffee," he answers dryly.

If he's trying to embarrass her it won't work. She loves jingle bells, and she doesn't care if it's silly. "Whatever. Just give me my merry hat."

He steps back around to face her before he arranges it atop her ski mask with a smile. He puts his on next. "We wear bells to warn the bears we're coming so they don't startle and attack us out of fear."

Well, there went her Christmas cheer. She swallows hard. "Oh. That's good to know."

He raises a finger. "One more thing."

"What's that? Skunk spray so I'll smell repulsive to anyone or anything within a twenty-mile radius," she cracks a joke to calm her jangling nerves.

He laughs out loud. "Um, no. That's not the worst idea, though. I'll have to google it when I get home." He taps her shoulder. "You never know. You might be onto something. Maybe you could create some sort of foul-smelling perfume that repels predators to market for people who love the great outdoors."

He digs around in another pack, and she's beginning to think they'll be here all day. "Now what are you after?"

He clears his throat. "Ordinarily I wouldn't suggest hiking in the dark because it's not safe. In fact, it's a big no-no; and so is hiking with dogs or small animals that are potential prey for larger animals. *But* Jake here is well-trained, and if your dog is well-trained, it can be an asset when you are a hiker especially if you are hiking alone. The best time to hike is during the day when it is light out with a friend or a well-trained animal as your companion."

"So we're idiot hikers today, testing the laws of nature," she asks. "We're hiking in the dark, which is an invitation to be stalked."

"If we were hiking with no blinding lights and no bells, yes. But we're going to be noisy lit-up hikers, and that should improve our odds."

"What else did you bring? Do you have like a disco strobe light that sets off pacemakers or a giant beam to guide a small plane?" She knows she should stop, but she's on a roll. "How about a great, sweeping light that can be seen from Mars?" She giggles at her own joke.

"Sheri." His voice is mixed with humor and annoyance.

"Yes."

"Sometimes you should keep your humor to yourself," he says as he wraps something around her head.

She hears the Velcro snag together. He fiddles with it long enough that his warm breath falls on her lips, which is about the only part of her exposed beneath the ski mask with additional customized layering inside. His hands are at the base of her throat. She feels a little nervous. He peels her ski mask up.

Ice-cold hair hits her throat and face, and she gasps. "What are you doing?"

He peels his mask up too. "I wish I knew," he all but whispers before his lips meet hers.

Her knees go weak. She fears she'll fall backward with the weight of the packs on her back. She almost gets the giggles, as she never thought stocking hats with bells and a light strapped to her forehead could feel so sexy. His hands rest on her hips. It feels so strange to feel weightless and grounded at the same time. She grasps his upper arms and leans into their kiss. She's hot from head to toe.

He pulls away first. She wants to say something, anything, but she can't find the words. She has no idea what he's thinking. He slowly pulls his mask down, and she does the same. He turns sideways before reaching up to turn on his light. It's blinding, even from the side. She reaches for hers but can't figure it out.

"I could use a little help here, please," she manages.

He turns toward her as her hand flies in front of her eyes. "I'm sorry. I wasn't thinking." He flips off his light.

She can't tell if he's talking about his light or about their kiss. All she knows is she's blinded either way. "Obviously," she retorts, feeling annoyed.

He clears his throat. "You gotta watch out for that Alaskan mistletoe. It'll get ya. It grows wild around these parts."

His attempt at a joke almost breaks the ice, but her emotions are all over the place. What kind of guy apologizes for kissing a woman?

"Just turn on my light," she snaps.

His footsteps move. She feels his hand on her head. "There. You can open your eyes now."

She moves her hand slowly from the front of her face and peeks one eye open. His back is to her.

"Are you ready to go?" he asks.

Sheri feels injured, sore, and emotionally exhausted. She could go home right now. "Sure."

22

Randall's mind buzzes as they hike along. Thoughts of Sheri have him all over the place. One thing is for certain: being around her isn't boring. She may be a church girl, but she's not exactly meek and mild. And neither is her kiss. He doesn't know what he was thinking, coming on to her like that, especially when he knows she's looking for a husband. There's just something about her that draws him in.

He's not used to a woman who is so honest and opinionated. He rolls his eyes. The woman's got enough opinions to fill up a book or two. She doesn't play guessing games. She's not exactly flirty, which is usually the type of girl he goes for. She's no lightweight either, not her personality or her build. He glances backward to check her pace. If he's not mistaken, he receives a challenging glare.

"Keep your light out of my eyes," she barks.

"My apologies. I was just checking on you."

"Use your ears," she gets out between pants.

Jake, the intuitive traitor, trots by her side. Randall is

proud of him for keeping her safe, but it stings a little that Jake seems to prefer her.

They walk the mostly-flat ground and keep up a decent pace. He can't help but admire she's walked all this time without a single complaint. In fact, she hasn't uttered a single word since they started walking until he blinded her.

He smiles to himself, feeling clever. He thinks she took his comment about being silent seriously, or she wants to stop hiking, which he's not about to do. He pauses for a few seconds to give her a rest before they start up a trail that steepens gradually. But it will be worth the effort once they reach the top.

"Why did you stop?" she asks the side of his face between breaths.

He looks away from the light attached to her head. "Just taking a breather before we start the incline." He side-eyes her, noting her hands are on her hips.

"Incline?"

He points to the top of the hill that's more like a small mountain. "Yeah. I thought we'd hike to the top there."

She studies it with a resigned look on her face. "All right." Her hands rummage through her little pack before they pull out her AirPods case. She sticks one in her ear.

"What're you doing? If you have those in, you can't hear anything sneaking up on you," he informs her.

She stares him down. "If you expect me to climb that mountain, I've gotta have my Daigle."

He's so lost. "Excuse me? What on earth is a Daigle?"

"She's my favorite singer, and she's very inspirational." She shoves him to the side. "Excuse me." She takes a few steps.

"I wasn't joking. It isn't wise to not be aware of what's around you in the wilderness," he insists.

She turns sideways and pokes him in the arm. "I've got you to warn me. You're not exactly subtle. I'm sure I'll be fine. Just throw a rock at me if you need something." She puts the other AirPod in, adjusts her ski mask, and turns back around to start hiking up the trail.

He follows along behind her. Jake walks by his side. She's humming or grunting. He's not sure which. All he knows is it's going to be a long morning. They go on for a bit more when suddenly, she stops and removes a headphone.

"Why'd you stop this time?" he asks.

She holds it out. "Would you like one?"

After their kiss that turned him inside out and sideways, she's been acting a little chilly or hurt. He can't decide which. All he knows is it's one-hundred-percent his fault. This is kind of like a peace offering, and he ought to take it, but she's annoying him because she's not taking his advice, which, in fact, puts her in more potential danger. Although, her off-key humming could probably scare off more than a few animals.

He shrugs. "I don't know." The side of her smile looks a little ornery.

"It's either that or continue to listen to my humming, Randall, which I know you hate, so pick your poison."

He takes the AirPod. "Fine."

They resume their march up the hill. There are a few breaks here and there, but she keeps going, and he pretends not to hear her grunts and moans. They are finally three-fourths the way up the trail when she stumbles and catches herself on a big rock. Her one hand is on her knee, and the other is on a big rock. She stares at the ground. He takes a few steps closer, but she holds up a hand. He stops moving.

"Give me a minute. I need to do this myself," she gets out in between breaths.

He looks ahead. All he can see are the packs on her back. He wonders if he gave her too much at one time, but then he sees her lips moving, and he waits a little more. She's praying. Slowly, she stands straight up, lifts her chin just a little, and takes a step forward.

The rest of the hike is slow and strenuous. They take more breaks than before, but he hangs back. Finally they reach the top, and there are two boulders sitting near the edge as if they were staged. He sits down on one, and she plops down on the other, slowly leaning back until her packs rest on the boulder, and she falls into a slump. Her lantern points toward the sky. She removes her AirPod and he removes his.

"Can we set the tent up again? I need a nap," she says.

He chuckles. "If you really want to, but you might miss out on what's coming."

She sighs. "And what is that?"

He studies the dark horizon. "Any minute now the sun's going to come up."

Not long after, light peeks out from between the silhouette of the mountains in the distance. It slowly grows, and the darkness fades to light. There's a lake down below. The waters light up in the reflection of the sun. A fog appears over the waters, and a few large birds fly overhead.

"Majestic," she whispers in awe.

He couldn't agree more. If he hadn't fallen for her a little already, he has now. His hands tremble at his sides, and he feels slightly nauseous. Whatever this is, he's not ready for it.

"I could carry all this again, but what if I fall?" Her voice quivers.

"I already have," he answers before he knows what he's saying.

"Excuse me?"

He clears his throat. "I mean, that's probably enough for today. I'll carry it on the way down. You don't want to overdo it." He stands up with the need to be anywhere but where he is.

"We don't have to go yet," she answers in a dreamy voice. Her gaze remains on the scene in front of her.

He kicks at the dirt, feeling a little lost. "Oh, right. Well, I'm just going to walk around a bit. I need to stretch a little."

"Go ahead," she answers as an afterthought.

23

Randall walks ahead of Sheri on the trail, carrying his pack and the tent. She feels like a weight has been lifted from her shoulders. He walks like he carries the weight of the world. She knows his pack is heavy, but she thinks it's more than that. Something happened at the top, but she doesn't know what. All she knows is he's in a hurry to get down the mountain.

"Is weather coming in?" she asks as they near the base of the trail.

"Not that I know of," he answers.

"Then what's your hurry?" she can't help but ask.

"I never said I was in a hurry," he answers with an edge to his tone.

"You didn't need to," she mutters under her breath.

"What does that mean?"

Great. Now he's all defensive.

"Nothing. Just forget it. What are we doing now?"

He looks around, and she follows his gaze when it stops on a pile of bigger logs. "We could practice log splitting."

"But there's no stump," she says.

"You don't need one."

"Yes, you do. That's what they do at all those tough-man contests at the fairs or whatever." She regrets the words as soon as she says them. She feels like she may as well be citing Wikipedia as a source, and she's relieved he can't see her ignorance beneath her ski mask.

"Anyway, as I was say-ing, we don't need a tree stump. We just need a decent log to lean the other log on."

She's still doubtful. "How's that going to work? Won't the log just roll away?"

He taps his toe. "Not if you do it right. Do you want to learn or not?"

She exhales. "Yes, I do."

"All right, then."

He shifts out of his pack and pulls the ax from behind his back, which should be creepy, not hot. She shakes off her appreciation for all things lumberjack as she tries to focus. He lays the log vertical to the log laying horizontal on the ground.

"So, you want to aim for the middle of the log, and you want to hit the side of it. If you hit the top of it, your ax will get stuck in the log. And you don't want too big of a log because it won't split if it's too wide."

He takes a swing. She instinctively backs up just as the ax cracks the log. It splits right down the middle. He flashes her a killer grin.

"Just like that." He holds out the ax, handle first. "You want to give it a try?"

She drops her pack on the ground. "Okay."

He grabs the handle at the end. "Grab it closer to the blade, or it's going to swing down and hit you in the leg."

"Oh." She does as he says, and he lets go. The ax is heavier than she thought, but she keeps a hold as she lowers it slowly to the ground.

"First, you want to select a log," he instructs.

She looks at him. "Which one?"

He laughs a little. "This is your thing. Pick out your log, but I'd start small."

She wanders through the logs strewn here and there, looking them over carefully before she picks one up with both hands and sets it up just like he did. She stares down at it as she raises the ax.

"Stop," he says. "Your feet are too close together. You need to spread them farther apart. Now find your center on that log so you know what you're aiming for. Where is it?"

She points to the middle of the log with her toe. "Right there."

"Okay. So that log should be centered between your feet. Keep that ax close. Start with one hand on the lower part of the handle and the other hand near the ax head. You just want to raise the ax in front of you, push off with that lower hand, and then bring your hands together as you bring the ax down to hit the log."

She starts to raise the ax head behind her head.

"No. Don't do that. You don't need to do that. That's just a waste of energy," he stops her.

She starts over and twists a little as the ax head goes over one of her shoulders.

"No. Don't do that either. You're going to pull muscles that you don't need to be using."

She stops moving. Her muscles are all tense and sore, but she doesn't know if it's from the ax or his constant nagging. She sighs loudly.

"Gimme that ax," he demands. She hands it over. "Now, watch what I'm doing. I'll go in slow motion."

She knows she should be grateful, but she feels more than a little insulted. "You know what? I'll just watch some YouTube videos when I get back to the house and I'll practice by myself," she says between gritted teeth.

He purses his lips. "If that's what you want to do."

"Did I not just say so?" she answers.

He stops what he is about to do and holds out the ax. "Take it. I'm gonna go sit in the truck."

She feels bad but not bad enough. She waits until he's out of sight before she picks up the ax again and thinks about what he said. She focuses on the movements of keeping the ax in front of her and letting it drop straight down a few times. She stares down at the little log that feels so big. She lets the ax fall, and it hits it right down the middle with a satisfying crack. She drops the ax and leans over to pry the log apart.

"That's right. I can do this," she says to herself.

She stares down at it, feeling victorious, but then she hears a noise of something shuffling and moving around behind her. *"Bear"* is the first thought she has. She knows she should turn around, but she doesn't want to. She leans down slowly and grips the ax handle before peeking around. It's a fuzzy creature. It kind of looks like a calf and a deer. She thinks it's a caribou. She tries to hold still as he stares back at her, but she can't fight her grin behind her ski mask that feels like it's going to split her face wide open.

She moves slowly as she digs through her pack for her phone blindly, never dropping her gaze from the caribou's. Her fumbling fingers bump into it. She inches it out of her pack. She glances down as she touches the camera and slides over to video mode. She starts recording and raises it as quickly as she dares. Just as she frames him front and center, she hears a strange noise and hoofbeats. In the corner of her eye, she sees a much bigger caribou. It's running right at her.

Her phone falls from her fingers. She grabs up her ax and raises it, screaming as loud as she can, hoping to startle the crazy caribou that's making all sorts of guttural sounds, but it keeps coming. She drops the ax and runs for the nearest tree, tripping over rocks.

"Stay away from the baby!"

Randall's words register in her ears as she throws her pack at the charging caribou. She stops mid-step, changes direction, and does as he says. She bails behind a rock half the size of her, feeling ridiculous as she curls up in a fetal position and hopes somehow it doesn't see her. She doesn't know how well caribous can see. Jake tears by her, barking with all his might.

The caribou grunts. She opens her eyes enough to see around the rock. Jake and the crazed caribou face off for a few seconds, but it feels like hours. "Dear Lord, please save Jake," she mouths through quivering lips as she tries not to hyperventilate. She can't believe she ran toward the baby. *No wonder big momma caribou is so mad,* she realizes now that she's not running for her life. Jake backs off, and the momma manages to corral her baby out of sight.

She fights the urge to run to Randall, who stands on the edge of the line of trees. "Can I come out now?" she squeaks.

He gives her a nod.

She stands on unsteady feet and feels all her pockets for her phone. "I think I dropped my phone," she says as she heads back to where she just was. She shuffles her feet through the leaves, hunting. She's about to give up when she bumps something that slides from beneath the debris on the forest floor. It's her phone. She picks it up. "Found it," she calls out.

"You would have found it a lot faster if you would just ask for my help," he grumbles.

"Or you could just help me," she answers back.

"I don't have your number in my phone," he says.

"Well, there's only one way to get my number."

"What's that? With google or Facebook, which I don't do," he replies.

She exhales. "No. You could get it the old-fashioned way. You could ask."

"Where's the fun in that?" he says before he spins on his heel. "I think we should go before you have any more encounters with strange wildlife."

She grabs his ax up off the ground. She slings the pack over her shoulder. "I didn't ask momma caribou to chase me, you know." She thinks some more about the caribou now that it's gone and she can halfway think straight. "Wasn't that a boy caribou?"

He laughs as they walk out of the woods. "Um, no. He didn't have a...you know..."

She blushes inside her mask. "I wasn't checking out his package. I was too busy staring at his antlers."

He turns off his light and pulls up his mask. His face is all smirky as he turns toward her. His eyes sparkle. "Interesting fact, Sher-i. With caribous, both females and males have racks." He grins. "That's another name for antlers."

She fights the urge to slug him. "I know that," she answers.

He snorts. "Well, I *thought* you knew getting near any baby wildlife is an invitation to be attacked, because that's just common knowledge."

He's so smug. It's infuriating. "I know that too, but I was in panic mode, okay? That caribou was huge, and it was making all sorts of noises as it charged. I was terrified for the baby. I was just trying to help." Her voice is all trembly, and she's shaking all over again. She ducks her head. "I think I have caribou PTSD."

He throws an arm over her shoulders and gives her a side hug. "That's nothin' a long ride home won't cure."

24

Randall swears his heart stopped in his chest when he saw that caribou charging at Sheri. He can't believe she raised an ax and yelled. Most women would have crumpled on the ground or fainted dead away. She may not be what he's ready for, but she's ready for Alaska. She was definitely shaken, but she didn't fall apart, and then she even made a joke about it. Caribou PTSD. He grins at her smart mouth and shakes his head.

She sits beside him in the truck. Her ski mask is bunched up around the top of her head and her forehead light is turned off, but it's still in place. She's sprawled all over Jake, sawing logs. He should probably wake her from her snoring, but she's out like a light. And after that harrowing encounter with the caribou, he'd say she more than deserves some rest. It's a long ride home, so he turns up the music to keep him alert.

Many country songs later, they're pulling into town. She stirs a little. "What are you doing for Thanksgiving?"

He's confused and more than a little wary. *What's she planning now?* "Like in four days?"

She nods. "Yes."

"I don't know. I usually go down to the lodge and buy their meal to bring home and watch a game or two on TV."

She frowns, slaps the seat, and startles Jake. "That's just sad. This year, you're getting a home-cooked, seven-course meal. I'm pulling out all the stops."

His stomach grumbles and his mouth waters at the thought. "That sounds real nice. Thank you."

Her motherly smile relaxes him a little. He feels more than a little bad that he thought she was plotting.

"I'll just borrow your truck, please. I'll pay for the gas," she continues.

He interjects. "No need to pay for gas. Not when you're doing all the cooking."

Her face changes just a little, and he knows he's in trouble.

"Oh, it's not just for me and you. That would be a waste of time, energy, and food. I'm inviting a group of ladies over too."

His jaw instantly tightens. "Excuse me." All he can envision is a bunch of women traipsing through his home making so much noise he won't hear the game.

She waves a hand. "Don't you worry. You won't have to lift a finger. I'll do all the house cleaning, the cooking, and the preparations. As soon as we get home, I'm doing an inventory of your kitchen." She snaps her fingers. "You know what? I'll just do paper plates and plastic utensils. That'll make it easy to throw away. That will be even less hassle."

He doesn't know how, but he's got to shut this down. "How are you going to invite women you haven't met yet?"

She smiles at him like I'm a simpleton. It's kind of creepy. "You're talking to a woman who's run church circles for years. I know how to draw people in." She gives him a slug. "Besides, do you really think there aren't women who are just itching to see the inside of your home? You're the most eligible bachelor in a hundred miles."

He cringes at the thought. "I don't really think myself that way, but now that you say it, I'm not sure I like any part of this idea."

She rubs her hands together, not even trying to hide her scheming ways. "Now that I think of it, this is the perfect plan. Given the fact that you gave that creepy mail-order bride magazine a second glance, I'd say you need to start looking for a wife."

He chokes on air. "But we shared a kiss," he blurts out before he shuts his mouth. He can't believe he sounds like a lovesick schoolboy.

She pats his hand. "Yes, Randall, we did. And it was very nice, but don't you worry about that. I won't hold you to any sort of commitment. It was just a kiss under the mistletoe, just like you said."

Her tone is light and airy, like she's talking about watching a sunrise or something. He's more than offended. His kisses mean more than that. He's never been blown off so easily. It's a very unpleasant feeling.

She levels him with a look as if she knows he's about to protest. "Those were your words."

He wants to say something, anything, but he doesn't want to sound more stupid than he already feels. He stares at the road. "We already had this conversation. I very clearly stated I don't want a wife."

"I'm sure you only say that because you haven't really given the women in your town a chance. There's got to be at least one woman who might be a good match for a grumpy lumberjack who'd rather stay home 360 days of the year when he's not out fighting fires. Even if we can't get you married, you really need to get out more. There's got to be someone you'd like to spend more time with."

Her words are kind of hurtful, but her tone is so bright. He glances over at her. "How much joy did you get out of saying I only go out four days a year? You're practically singing."

She gives him a wink. "I just call 'em like I see 'em."

He snorts and looks at her again. *Two can play this game.* "What about you?"

"What about me?"

"Are you going to invite any men to this little dinner of yours?"

"No. That would be rather forward. Despite my independence, I'm an old-fashioned girl. I will not be doing the chasing on Thanksgiving." Her mouth shuts tight like she let too much slip, and it clicks in his head.

"When will you be doing the chasing, then? 'Cause I gotta see this," he answers with a smirk that doesn't quite meet his eyes.

She lifts her nose in the air. "On New Year's Eve."

She sounds so sure of herself that he almost hates to burst her bubble. He laughs out loud. "If you think our little town's going to have some sort of New Year's Eve celebration when a bunch of singles come out of the woodwork, think again."

She looks way too satisfied with herself in his opinion. "There's more than one place to find singles. Alaska is a big state. I signed up for a singles retreat. It *guarantees* the first step toward finding true love."

For reasons he doesn't care too much to examine, he gets a terrible stomachache. He lays a hand on his gut. "Is that right?"

They pull up the driveway.

"Yes, that's right. There's a ball and everything."

He raises his eyebrows. "I thought you said you were an old-fashioned girl."

She leans back on the truck seat. "I am. That was my one hiccup in this decision, but I'm not getting any younger, and everyone at this retreat is supposed to be marriage-minded." She side-eyes him. "Unlike some people I know. So I decided to give it a try. I've got to step out of my comfort zone sometime. Besides, I've always wanted to go to a ball." She sounds all dreamy.

"A ball, huh? You'd better start hunting for that glass slipper now, *princess*," he mutters in a tone that suggests she's anything but a princess. He glances in her direction to see her reaction. She's still wearing that silly grin that tells him she's somewhere else. Between her longing for marriage and her obvious scolding of him not being ready, he figures now is a good time as any to get out of the truck. "I'm going inside. I've got stuff to unpack."

"Sounds good. I've got Thanksgiving Day guests to round up."

25

Sheri rushes inside to climb out of all her clothes. It takes her ten minutes just to get to the toilet. She's about to finish de-layering and hop in the shower when she changes her mind as she's washing her hands at the sink. She runs back upstairs, snags Randall's keys, and rushes outside to his truck.

The fastest and best way to meet people is to do it in person, she decides.

She heads downtown to the lodge. She opens the big red door, just to find another set of doors. Determination pushes her through the French doors. They slam against the wall. Her face turns beet red. She didn't mean to push them that hard, but she's so nervous.

The first person she sees is Rick, the pushy creep from the store. She quickly moves on to other faces and stops when she spies the woman behind the bar. Emboldened, Sheri heads in her direction.

"Hello. I'm a friend of Randall's, and I—" She stops short when the woman bursts out laughing.

"You're a friend of Randall's?"

"Yes."

"Randall the firefighter?"

Sheri rolls her eyes. *Honestly, how many Randalls can there be in this one-horse town?* "Yes."

The woman looks her up and down. "What can I do ya for?"

She leans in with both elbows on the bar, and it's like a wave of leans happens behind her. The room grows quiet. "I was wanting to plan a Thanksgiving dinner at his home, and I'd like to meet some of the local women around here, particularly singles. What is the best way to do that?"

The bartender taps her chin. "Well, it is Thanksgiving this week. That's awfully short notice."

Her heart sinks.

"Buutt, given that it's at Randall's home, and this is the very thing that's going to shove him over the edge I'd say you've got pretty good chances these women'll show up for ya."

"And how do I invite them?" she asks again.

"Oh, just post a sign on the lodge's window outside. People will see it, and maybe post a few on the church doors too."

Something about what she's saying doesn't feel right. "Are you sure that's okay?"

"Oh, yeah. This is a small town and all. We're very informal around here," the bartender assures her.

"So do you know how many people might show up? I'm just thinking about my grocery list," she explains.

"Just make it a potluck. That way, everybody brings at least one dish, and no one will go hungry."

She smiles with relief. "Thank you. I wanted to, you

know, but then I thought that's not very hospitable to invite people over and ask them to bring their own food." She taps her fingers on the bar. "Plus, I'm kind of excited about making a stuffed turkey, old-fashioned gravy, twice-baked potatoes, mashed potatoes, about three pies, and a few casseroles."

The bartender's eyes are wide open. "You're making all that for Thanksgiving?"

She nods her head and looks her dead in the eye. "I sure am. I love cooking, and I love to share."

The bartender slaps the bar. "Well, I'd hate for all that good food to go to waste. You want to bring me a few plates? My son's visiting. I haven't seen him in forever. I want it to be special, but I'm not the best cook."

She gives her a friendly wink. "I've got you. If you don't cook, you'll have that much more time to visit."

The bartender looks as if she might cry. "You're exactly right. I'm gonna close early that day just for him."

She gives her a smile. "I bet he'll really like that."

The lady leans toward Sheri. "You could always post your meal on the flyer and then a tiny note about if they want to bring something they can. This way, if you get any quirky guests who only eat their own cooking, they'll have something they like."

She never thought of it that way. "This is true." She gives the lady a parting smile. "Thank you for all the great advice. I'm glad we met. What did you say your name was?"

The lady gives her a sassy wink. "I didn't." She points a finger at her. "You'd better get going before these men start cornering you."

She doesn't cherish that thought. She turns to go and

nearly bumps into a man sitting right beside her. He doesn't look a day younger than sixty. He's as quiet as a mouse.

"Hey, there," he says as if he's talking to a skittish horse.

"Pardon me, sir. I was just leaving." She rushes in between the tables. She's almost out the door when a man sticks out his foot and almost trips her.

He hides beneath his black cowboy hat, which he tips back. Strong jaw. Bright blue eyes. A smile that should be outlawed. He looks a little weathered, but that's not necessarily a bad thing.

"Whoa, there," he drawls.

What's with all the men in this bar talking to me like I'm a horse?

"You'd better slow down there, darlin'" is all he has to say.

How'd his hand find the backside of my thigh? It's a good thing I'm not holding an ax. She smacks his hand.

He chuckles.

She resists the urge to slap his cheek and not just his hand. "You might want to move your feet before I step on your toes." She waits for him to move. He doesn't.

"What's your name, darlin'?" he drawls.

She throws a hand on her hip. "It sure isn't 'darlin'.' I can tell you that."

"Her name is Sheri," Rick calls from across the room.

"Sherry, like the drink? I like that," he continues in the same slow manner.

Words flow from the man's mouth like bourbon in a glass, but it doesn't matter. Sheri doesn't care much for bourbon. She imagines it's smooth just like this man.

His eyes take their sweet time getting to her face as they

roam. "Don't you want to know my name?" he says with a wink.

She's so annoyed. She backs up to find a different escape route. She hates showing signs of retreat, but she's desperate. She marches clear out of the way to make a point of avoiding him. "Did I ask your name?" she bites out in his direction right before she hits the swinging doors with her hand. Darkness is already setting in. She has no idea what time it is.

"Oh, ho, Bill. You've met your match. I've never seen you get rejected so fast," she hears as she exits.

Laughter follows her out into the parking lot. She walks faster. She's not so sure the lodge was the best idea.

Her phone vibrates nonstop. She looks down. "Dang it. I've missed like fifteen texts from Jenni," she mutters to herself.

SHERI:

> Hey, girl. I'm sorry. I went on a camping trip. Saw a baby caribou. Mama caribou chased me. I threw a pack at her. Split a log with an ax! Planning a Thanksgiving dinner for the women in town. I'll find a woman for Randall yet!

JENNI:

> Oh, thank God. I imagined the worst when you didn't answer me for two days. You've got to give me more details than that! I'm so excited for you! It sounds like your life in Alaska is off to a great start!

Sheri climbs into Randall's truck, still talking to herself.

"I don't know why I didn't text her sooner. She always has encouraging words for me, and right now I need them."

She starts it up and heads for home. Her foot taps the brakes just a little when the word *home* registers in her head, and that's when she realizes she never thought of her parent's house as her home. At least not as an adult. It was always their home, but it wasn't hers. She wonders if she really considers Randall's house home, or if she can, when she's not sure he even wants her there.

He definitely won't want her there after Thanksgiving Day.

Sheri shoves that thought aside. She's got flyers to make.

26

Randall gets more annoyed every time the second hand makes another lap on his bass clock hanging on the wall. He can't believe Sheri took off in his truck without asking. She didn't even have the courtesy to tell him how long she'd be gone. About the time he tosses on his coat and hat to walk downtown, she barrels through his front door, tosses the keys in his lap, and heads for the kitchen stairs.

"Where did you go?" he demands. He instantly wishes he hadn't asked because it makes him feel like they're an old married couple.

Her footsteps stop and then start again, but they're getting louder. She stops beside his chair and stares down at him. "I didn't know I needed to check in with you every second that I'm gone," she goads.

Her tone is mixed with injury and warning, but it's her words that set him off. "If you don't want to tell me, I guess I don't need to know," he hollers. "But I do need to know when you're going to return since you took my truck and all."

She taps her toe. "Who do you think you are, my father? I wasn't even gone that long," she replies.

He is more than a little curious about where she went, but he'll be danged if he's going to drag it out of her. "You know what, Sheri? You're right. I don't need to know. Next time you borrow my truck, tell me before you leave, all right? If there's an emergency, I need to know where it is in case I need to find a ride to the fire station." She looks so sorry he has to look away, but he can't help but feel satisfied. "Even if *you* don't need my help, some people around here do." He side-eyes her.

She looks properly chastised, which was exactly what he intended. "Oh, I'm so sorry. I didn't think of that."

"I know you didn't. I just want to be sure you know now. I'm going to need your phone number, please."

She rolls her eyes. "I told you all you had to do was ask."

He grits his teeth. "This is me asking."

"Well, fine. Give me your phone and I'll put it in there."

"Or you could just tell me, and I'll put it in there. I'm not a child," he says, feeling every inch a kindergartener.

"All right, fine. It's 755-242-1056," she rattles off.

"Hold up. I don't even have my phone out yet. You're going to have to say it again."

"Are you ready?"

"Almost." He fumbles around with his touch screen. He's so flustered he enters the code wrong. Twice. "Okay, I'm ready."

"It's 735-262-1079."

He starts to type it in. "Hold up. That's not what you said before."

She gives him a look. "So you *are* capable of listening."

"Yessss." He is so annoyed he almost doesn't want her number anymore. She's the most irritating woman he's ever met.

"I told you before I left the house earlier today that I was taking your truck. Did you not hear me then?"

"*Sheri*, I was unpacking our camping stuff. Give me a break. Are you going to give me your real phone number, or am I going to have to creep down your stairs and steal it in the middle of the night?" He smirks at the thought.

"All right, fine. 755-242-1056."

He types it in and puts her name in as "Scary Sheri." He looks up to see her frowning, and he almost feels bad but he can't. "Creep much," he demands.

"'Scary Sheri.' Really?"

He shrugs. "It's my phone," he says as he watches her. "Do you want my number?"

"No. I'll just wait for you to text me, and then I'll have your number." She taps her fingers on her phone. "Can I go now? Because I need to get my flyer made so I can put it up downtown."

"What's that now?" He hopes he heard her wrong when he thinks of his address plastered all over downtown.

"I told you I was going to invite women to dinner here on Thanksgiving Day."

"Yes, you did, but I didn't think you were going to post my personal information all over downtown."

"Technically, it's my address and my name I'm posting, so don't you worry about your name being anywhere on the flyer," she protests.

"Sher-i. I've lived here most of my life. They're going to know it's my house."

"Rand-all, I'm having a Thanksgiving dinner in the basement completely outside of your living space. The only time you'll see them is when they'll walk through your living room to get to the kitchen. You need to chill out," she insists, though she prays he'll change his mind because she's not sure how she's going to fit them all in her somewhat small space that somehow constitutes being a bedroom.

She walks out of the room. He feels anxiety in every nerve of his body. His skin starts to itch. He thinks he might be breaking out in hives. He glares at the empty space where she was and decides she can have her pack of women on Thanksgiving Day. He's going to the lodge. No homemade meal is worth half the trouble she's sure to stir up.

27

Sheri smiles at the colorful flyers she created as they come off the printer. "Not too shabby," she says with a smile as her eyes scan them.

Inviting all neighbors, female and single.
I'm new in town and looking to mingle.
It may be too soon, but I've got a hunch.
Let's all bond over Thanksgiving Day lunch.

Come as you are with an optional side dish.
The rest is on me, and it'll be dee-lish.
This lunch is not without a few door prizes.
But that's not the only secret surprise.

I'm a newcomer, but I'm a matchmaker too.
My landlord's a real catch. It's just a matter of who.
He's a confirmed bachelor, but it only takes one.
In the meantime, eat, spill a little tea, and just have fun!

4–6 p.m. Thanksgiving Day – Have a meal or a pre-game snack!

   RSVP at 755-242-1056 – Sheri Mallo
   327 Spring Street

She gathers up a handful and marches back upstairs. He's still in his chair. "Hey, Randall. I need your truck, please, for like ten minutes."

"Why?"

"I'm taking the flyers downtown to put them in windows and tape them to business doors."

He eyes her papers like they're declaring war. "You're really going to do this."

"Um, yeah. I pretty much announced it down at the lodge. I was talking to the lady behind the bar, but they're a shameless bunch of eavesdroppers down there."

He chuckles. "They have nothing better to do. What did you expect?"

She shrugs. "I don't know but I didn't expect that." She recalls the lady behind the bar. "What's the bartender's name?"

"Why do you need to know?" he asks all confrontational-like.

"I guess I don't. It's just she wouldn't tell me her name."

He gives her a look. "What did you say to her?"

Indignation fills her. "All I said was I was your friend and I was planning a Thanksgiving dinner for the single ladies in town at your house."

He closes his eyes. "You said all that down at the lodge?"

"You *know* I did. I don't know what the big deal is. It's

not like you ever go down there. By the time you go there again, they will have forgotten anything I said that has to do with you."

He shakes his head. "This is so embarrassing. I'll never live this down."

She kicks the footrest on his recliner. "You're acting like an old woman. There's nothing scandalous about me meeting women in town so I can make some new friends. If you're so terrified about a few women coming into your home, then find a reason to stay in your room. I'm making Thanksgiving dinner, and there's going to be company, and I don't want to hear another word about it."

He's out of his chair and in front of her in a heartbeat. His hot breath hits her lips. "Listen, lady. I don't know who you think you are coming into my home, stirring up my routine, and getting me all kinds of bothered."

His hand falls gently on her cheek, and it feels as foreign to him as the look in her eyes before he bumps into her, tilts her head a little, and dives in. Their kiss is pure magic just like the first time. There's no other word for it. She is walking down that church aisle in her head by the time he pulls away.

"I do," she whispers with her eyes closed.

"I'm sorry. That was a mistake. I forgot myself," he all but groans.

Her eyes fly open. She's more than injured. She can't believe how fast she lost her head over a man who yells at her, kisses her, and then apologizes. For the second time. And she fell for it. All over again.

"Go to your room, Randall," she mutters in a voice filled with disgust.

"Yes, ma'am," he answers before he walks past her and quietly closes the door.

Her fingertips fly to her lips as a tear rolls down her cheek. She picks up his keys in a daze as she clutches the bag of flyers and scotch tape in her other hand. "I'm going downtown to post invites. I can't wait to fill his house with women. Randall and his hot lips can jump off a cliff," she whispers to the empty room. "And there's no Alaskan mistletoe growing in your house," she hollers at his closed door for good measure right before she makes a beeline for the nearest exit. "What's your excuse this time, buster?" she mutters as she shuts the front door.

28

Thanksgiving Day arrives. Randall finds himself praying for a forest fire, anything to get him paged and out of the house for the day, but it seems he's run out of luck.

He hardly recognizes his kitchen as he enters in search of coffee. Every counter is covered with some sort of food. Steam rises from a pie sitting on a hot pad, and it smells heavenly. He grabs a spoon to dig in. A hand pops out of nowhere and smacks the spoon from his grasp.

"Don't you dare touch my crust," she orders.

He groans. "No one will care if a slice of pie is missing. This is my house. If you're going to cover every inch of counter space and prevent me from packing my lunch, the least you can do is feed me breakfast." His whining hurts his own ears, but he's not about to admit it.

She swipes a cereal box from a cupboard and a bowl from another. She whips open the drawer and motions. "Grab a spoon and have yourself some cereal. This is Thanksgiving Day. I don't have time to cook you breakfast."

He leans over and takes a big whiff of the pie that taunts him. "I'm not asking you to make me breakfast. All I want is a piece of that pie."

She gives him a shove. "You can have one later. Now stop breathing on my pie."

He sniffs. "Isn't it a little early to be making potatoes?"

She throws a hand on her hip. "If you must know, I'm making twice-baked potatoes. They're my specialty."

His eyes light up when he spies the turkey roasting in the oven. "You're cooking a turkey," he says stupidly.

She rolls her eyes. "It is Thanksgiving."

"When did you bring all this food into the house?"

She smirks. "When you were at work the other day. Remember? I came in and borrowed your keys to go out of town."

"Oh, yeah," he answers, even though he doesn't remember that at all.

Her hazel eyes narrow in his direction. "I totally just lied to you, and you lied right back. I didn't borrow your vehicle, and I didn't drive forty-five miles away."

"Then how'd you get all this food?" he says, feeling belligerent and tricked.

She stares him down. "It's called having friends. You ought to try it sometime. They're kind of nice."

"I've got friends. They're down at the lodge."

"They're more like acquaintances. Do those guys know your dreams?"

How could they when I don't even know my dreams? he thinks.

"Dreams? Seriously. What are we, five?"

She looks all wounded. "There's no age limit on dreams. At least not for me."

Foolishness fills him. "You may be comfortable talking about all this with an audience, but I am not."

She looks at him with pity written all over her face. "I don't know how you live without dreams. I certainly couldn't."

He feels bare, exposed, and a bit ridiculous. He's no one to feel sorry for. "It sounds like you did for forty-two years, so don't go feeling too sorry for me."

Her face tightens a little. He feels terrible as he stares her down. There's just something about her that has his back against the wall the majority of the time, and he's getting tired of it. All she's done since she moved in is make his house more of a home, and that's what makes him so itchy; that and the fact that every time they speak it turns into an argument. He was fine before she came along, but he's not sure how he'll be when she leaves.

He can't help but feel like a wolf with one foot stuck in the trap. And the only question that keeps popping up in his mind is if he can chew his paw off to escape when this is all over and she leaves, or will he even want to? He shakes his head to clear his crazy thoughts and decides her overactive imagination is rubbing off on him. It has to be her fairy-tale wishes that have him thinking about wolves and traps.

"Randall."

"What?"

"Did you hear anything I just said?"

Her librarian voice is back. He likes it way too much.

"I'm sorry. What?" he answers.

"Do you want mashed potatoes and twice-baked potatoes? And do you want gravy?"

He slaps the counter. "What kind of question is that? Are you not an American?"

Her eyes widen. "Of course I'm an American, but what does that have to do with anything?"

"Yes, I eat gravy on Thanksgiving Day," he says with a smirk because he plans on eating gravy, but not in the middle of her single-women party. He'll be down at the lodge throwing back a few beers and relaxing in front of the big game on the TV that takes up half the wall. Sure, the guys down there are a bit much, but if he holes up in a corner he thinks he can escape their gossiping.

"Well, we'll be having gravy here, but you won't get any down at the lodge," she mutters into the floor that she's scrubbing away at like she's going to break her Swiffer in half.

Admonished and annoyed, he keeps his mouth shut. He's not about to ask her how she knows he's going to the lodge today. He hasn't told anyone.

"If you don't want me to know you're going to the lodge for the day, maybe don't wear your blue fireman's jacket and khaki cargo pants." Her voice is filled with sleuthing satisfaction.

He supposes he should be angry, but how can he be? She just revealed herself to him.

He moseys over and lays a hand on the Swiffer handle right next to hers. "Your statement is spot on for a person who doesn't pay much attention to me or what I'm doing," he growls near her ear.

Her whole face turns red. "It's pretty hard not to notice when you come home smelling like whiskey and cigarettes, always in those clothes." She sniffs the air near his shoulder. "No amount of washing can get that smell out."

She sounds all snooty, but he doesn't hear her words. All he can think about is how much she noticed.

"Hmm mmm. Right." He skims the top of her hand with his pointer finger. "You've been checking me out. Just admit it."

She swallows hard and jerks the Swiffer from his grasp. "I'm busy. I need to finish cleaning before the ladies come, so unless there's something you need." Her eyes widen as they meet his. He can only guess what's there.

He steps into her space and snags a belt loop on her jeans before he tugs her to him and lays the softest kisses on her lips. "If you want me home for dinner, dear, just ask," he suggests before he kisses her again.

Sheri was torn between dropping the Swiffer to the floor and grabbing him by the collar to pull him even closer. Randall has the hottest lips she's ever kissed, and he says the nicest things in the nicest way when he wants to, except for when he's telling her he doesn't want marriage or a wife. Argh. She has no business kissing a man who doesn't want to put a ring on her finger. She fights her own feelings as she shoves him away. Her hazel eyes blink a few times. Confusion fills her face, but then determination sets in. "There are women coming here today to see you."

He gives her an ornery grin. "I'm not askin' if they want to see me. I'm askin' if you do."

She looks all confused. "What is going on here?"

He tugs her close again. "We're just having a little fun. There's no harm in that." His hands cover the small of her back. "Let's just see where it takes us."

She lays a firm hand on his chest and straightens her spine before looking him straight in the eye. "I'm not here for fun or for your amusement." She swallows hard. "If you're done toying with me, I'd like to get back to work."

Her words might as well have been cold water to his face. He admires her sincerity, but honesty never punched him in the face so hard.

29

Sheri continues with her sweeping. She's thankful to have something to wrap her hands around besides Randall's neck. She takes in the clean kitchen and all her cooking that's not quite done and welcomes the distraction from the one man who drives her crazy. One minute he's kissing her, being all sweet and cozy and asking her to beg him to stay home, and the next he's practically running for the front door.

"I'll be dipped in caribou poo before I ask him to stick around. He's a grown man. He doesn't need a woman telling him what to do," she mutters as she sweeps the dirt out the back door, but then reverse psychology smacks her right between the eyes.

She walks into the living room and is surprised to see him sitting in his recliner, which must have slowed his retreat. She sneaks up behind him as quiet as a mouse before she leans down behind his right ear. "Go ahead and go to the lodge, darlin', since you're already dressed to go down there," she says as sweet as sugar. *There, let him think about that*, she thinks.

Satisfaction—and a giggle or two—fills her as he flies out of his chair and runs a hand over his ear like he's batting at a gnat. His face is beet red. "I'm goin' already. Geez. Way to run me out of my own home on Thanksgiving Day. A man can't get any peace and quiet around here," he grumps before he stomps out the front door.

She waltzes back to the kitchen, feeling slightly victorious but a little blue. Her plan backfired on her. She thought he would stay because she told him to go.

Her phone buzzes from the other room. She races to answer it. She grins ear-to-ear when she sees it's Jenni. She opens FaceTime and props it up. "Hey, Jenni." She ducks to see her best friend face-to-face on the screen for a few seconds. "I'm doing Thanksgiving dinner here at the house for a bunch of women, so I'm doing last-minute cleaning," she explains.

Jenni giggles. "That's so sweet. You're on your way to making loads of friends. I just know it!"

"What're you doing?" Sheri asks.

Jenni sticks her belly out. "Check out my preggers that just keeps growing. I think it's a boy this time. He can really kick," Jenni declares. "We're going to Justin's mom's house. Thank goodness. It's been a few years since we've seen my parents, but I didn't want to be far from home in case I go into early labor or something."

"But you're just six months along. Is everything okay?" Sheri's brow furrows with worry.

"Of course. Don't you worry. It's just with my parents living four hours away and the baby pushing on my bladder all the time, it becomes more of a six-hour drive, and that's not easy for a two-year-old either."

"Yeah, I get it," Sheri answers.

"Soo, how's your lumberjack? I haven't heard much from you since you had a face-off with the caribou."

She fidgets in front of the stove while she starts the gravy. "Things are going okay. I chased him out of the house again. He brings out the worst in me, and I bring out the worst in him. I don't know."

Jenni giggles again. "Give him a chance. You know what they say about how opposites attract."

She takes a deep breath. "Well, I've mentioned marriage. He's definitely not ready for that."

"What?" Jenni yells at her friend. "Why would you do that?"

"It's like you said. I'm not getting any younger. I'm not just looking for a good time. I've never been that kind of girl. I'm ready to settle down. I've been ready for the past ten years." Her voice cracks. She hates herself for sounding so desperate or pitiful. That wasn't her intention.

"You're right. I'm sorry. What good is being an independent career woman if you can't speak your mind?"

There's an awkward pause, but Sheri doesn't say anything because she thinks Jenni has more to say.

"It's just...you might be a little more subtle. Most guys don't like an opinionated woman who says what she thinks despite popular opinions, and you've got a lot of your own opinions."

She hears what Jenni says, and she doesn't disagree, but she's still feeling defensive. She's never taken constructive criticism well. "Men are allowed to have all the opinions they want and no one faults them for it. I don't see why I can't have my own."

"This is true, but there's also the saying of 'you catch more flies with honey.'"

She rolls her eyes. "Just think of where people would be if Harriet Tubman had not been who she was. Or Mother Theresa. If those women had listened to society in their day, nothing would have gotten done that needed to be done."

"All right, already. Fine. All I'm trying to say is if you really want a husband you may have to change that foghorn of yours into a megaphone. There is a difference between blaring and being heard."

Sheri rolls her eyes again. "Fine, Jenni. Thank you for your advice." She barely gets out the words between her gritted teeth.

Jenni laughs at her friend. "You are most welcome. I think." There's another awkward pause. "So, tell me what you're making for your ladies."

She clears her throat. She can always talk about food. "Turkey with stuffing inside, cranberry sauce on the side, homemade gravy, twice-baked potatoes and mashed potatoes, creamed corn in the Crock-Pot, Dutch apple pie, pumpkin pie, cherry pie, green bean casserole, sweet potatoes in a casserole dish, and Grandma Connie's almond sugar cookies with homemade frosting."

"Oh my goodness. I so wish I was coming to your house for Thanksgiving." Jenni groans.

"Stop salivating over food, Jen-ni," Justin scolds his wife from somewhere out of sight.

"I can't. It all sounds so good. And I'm supposed to eat. I'm pregnant."

Sheri can't help but giggle at their bickering. "Hi, Justin," she hollers.

He peeks out from behind Jenni's right shoulder. "What's up? How's Alaska?"

She's surprised at her immediate smile. "It's perfect. I love it."

He gives her a thumbs-up. "Cool, cool."

"So you going to ask your guy to stick around for Thanksgiving dinner?" Jenni asks.

Sheri thinks Jenni's always been too good at reading between the lines, and she doesn't want to answer her. "No. If he wants to, he will," she says with a pout on her face.

"Justin, would you want to have Thanksgiving dinner with a bunch of single women vying for your attention if we weren't married?" Jenni asks.

For the first time, Sheri feels a little bad that she's trying to set Randall up.

"Do I get to watch my football and eat as much turkey as I want?" Justin answers off-screen.

"Yes," Sheri answers with absolute certainty.

"I guess I could get on board with that, but it might be a little uncomfortable. I mean, I might feel better if a few of the guys came too so I wouldn't be the only guy in the room." Justin pops back into the picture briefly.

She thinks of Randall's question about finding a guy for her, but there aren't any decent men around. She shivers at the thought of Bill or Rick chasing her around the kitchen island.

"Oh, shoot. Babe, we gotta go. It's later than I thought." There's a smacking sound. Jenni blows a kiss through the phone. "Byeee. Have a great day. Be sure to tell me how it went. I can't wait to hear."

Sheri ends the call and goes to the fridge to take out the bowl of cookie dough before glancing at the clock. She's going to be cutting it close, but that's nothing new. She enjoys the rush.

She rearranges a few things on the counter to make some space before she starts rolling out the dough. Face-Time goes off again. It's Randall's cousin, Jan. That's weird. She hasn't heard from her since the day they met. She hits the speaker with her pinkie, the only finger not covered with dough.

"Hey, Jan. What's up?"

"What did you say to my cousin?" Jan's tone is kind of sharp.

Sheri wishes she could see her face, but Jan's too busy rushing around, giving Sheri her back. Sheri's mind races. She's not sure which conversation Jan is referring to. There have been so many. "I'm not sure what you mean. What happened?"

"He called me just now. He sounded so confused. I don't have time for this. I'm trying to serve five-plus families Thanksgiving Day lunch, all right? So I can't have him messing with my holiday spirit." Jan speaks so quickly that if she didn't enunciate so well, Sheri would have no idea what she said.

Sheri bites her tongue and holds in her argument. Jan doesn't have much holiday spirit unless you count being really grouchy, but that's neither here nor there.

"What did he say?" she manages.

"That he got kicked out of his own home on Thanksgiving Day, and all he wanted was peace and quiet to watch his football, and not some crazy woman running around his kitchen stirring things up and sticking her nose in his business where it doesn't belong." Jan's words are like a firing squad.

Sheri takes a deep breath. "Did Randall tell you I'm having a bunch of women over to play matchmaker?"

Jan giggles. Sheri relaxes just a little. "No, he did not. Keep talking."

"If I tell you, you can't act like you know," Sheri warns, though she doesn't know why, as she's pretty sure Jan will do whatever she wants. Sheri exhales. "So, we went camping. I saw the Northern Lights. They were crazy amazing. We talked about marriage."

Jan tips her head sideways and squeals in the phone. "I knew it. I told my husband, Karl, that you two were going to get together."

"Jan," Sheri says a little too loud and a little too harsh.

"What? When's the wedding date? I've always wanted to see Alaska. Karl can't tell me no this time."

Sheri groans. Jan is so not hearing her. "Jan."

"Yes, I'll be your bridesmaid."

"Hey," Sheri hollers.

"What?" Jan answers in a distracted tone.

"We aren't getting married. Not even close." Sheri feels like she's on the verge of tears.

"But you just said..." Jan protests.

"I said we talked about marriage. I didn't say he proposed," Sheri whispers.

"Oh." Jan's tone is a little less harsh.

"Yeah." *We hardly know each other,* Sheri thinks to herself. Then why does it hurt so much to acknowledge he has no interest in marriage? "So, anyway, the subject came up. He shut down, said he wasn't ready, not for a few years, and I, um, I told him I wasn't a casual-relationship type of girl."

"You go, girl," Jan interjects.

"I guess," Sheri agrees. "So then he kind of gave me a hard time, so I told him I was having a bunch of single women over to the house for him to mingle with, and that's what's going on."

Jan giggles again. "But what about you?"

"What about me?" Sheri isn't sure what Jan is getting at.

"How are you going to meet that special someone if you don't invite any men over?" Jan suggests.

Sheri chuckles. "Trust me, Jan. I've met the men down at the lodge. I won't be finding any keepers down there."

30

Randall sits at the bar down at the lodge, pouting into his beer. He can't believe he let one woman run him out of his house. On Thanksgiving Day, no less. It's the biggest football game day of the year apart from the Super-bowl. "This is just stupid."

Chelsea pops up from behind the bar. "Woman trouble?" she asks with a knowing smile.

He frowns. "No. Why do you say that?"

She raises one eyebrow. "All I know is women are the only thing that can make you men talk to yourself and wear a sorry look on your face like your dog just died."

He gives her a frown. "Why you gotta talk about dogs dying? That's just cruel."

She giggles. "Ain't it just like a man to change the subject when what he really needs to do is man up."

His irritation level raises a few notches. "Who made you the relationship expert?"

She laughs out loud. "No one." She uncaps another beer

and sets it down in front of him. "This one's on me. Let's just say the lonely recognizes the lonely."

He takes a sip of the cold beer. "Thanks, Chels." He stares her down. "So you're closing early?"

She gives a little nod. "Yep. My boy's coming to see me."

He nods his head. "Well, that's real nice."

He stands up. He looks more uncertain by the second. "Sit back down, Randall. I ain't leavin' yet," Chelsea says in a teasing tone.

He gives her another nod and glances around the room at Rick, Bill, and the new guy he hasn't met yet. The guy sits at the other end of the bar. *He looks a little younger than the usual crowd*, Randall thinks. He gives him a nod and raises his beer in his direction. "Hey."

The guy gives him a nod back but doesn't answer. Randall hears footsteps behind him. It sounds like two sets. He turns on his barstool to face Rick and Bill, who are closing in on him with knowing grins on their faces. It's too much. He almost gets up and walks out. "Rick. Bill."

Rick shakes his head. "So the rumor's true, then? She's havin' a bunch of women over."

Randall nods his head. "Yep."

Bill snorts. "And you're just gonna hide out at the bar all afternoon." He sounds so disgusted.

Randall shrugs. "I was, but Chelsea's closing early, so I guess not."

They look a little sheepish. "Sounds like you're having quite the meal," Rick answers.

Bill nods. "Yeah, it sounds pretty good."

Someone slaps the bar hard behind them. "Last call for alcohol," Chelsea announces.

Randall turns back to look at Chelsea. "Why do I think

Sheri has something to do with you going home early today?"

"Now don't you go blamin' your houseguest, Randall," Chelsea warns. Between her flaming red hair and her flashing brown eyes, he feels properly chastised.

"What do you know about my houseguest?" he demands, and Chelsea looks caught.

"Who said I knew anything?" she says before she turns and marches back in the kitchen to hide.

"Why are you closing' early, then?" Rick calls out after her.

"You think you all are the only ones I live to serve?" Chelsea sounds injured as she hollers back at them through the tiny window in the wall. "It so happens I have a son, and he's flyin' in today to see me. I'm pickin' him up at the airport."

Bill looks skeptical. "How come I've never heard about 'im 'til now?"

Chelsea marches back to the bar and drills Bill with a stare. "I don't have to tell you all my business. There are some things you don't need to know."

Randall throws up his hands. "All right, fine." He knocks on the bar. "That's real nice, Chelsea. I hope you have a nice visit with your son."

She gives him a wry grin. "Thank you."

"That's just great. Now what are we going to do for supper tonight? I don't really want to eat beans from a can on Thanksgiving Day," Rick whines. Randall can hardly stand it.

He knows he'll regret this, but he figures seeing the look of surprise on Sheri's face will be worth the headache of dealing with Rick and Bill for one night. "You guys want to come over to my place for dinner?" he says in a haphazard manner.

"Yeah, sure. What time?" Bill practically pounces.

He gets out his phone and texts Sheri.

RANDALL:

What time is dinner? In case I come home.

He hits send and stops thinking about the words "home" and "Sheri" and how well they fit together in his head.

Rick nudges Bill. "He's checking in with his old lady," Rick says as he chuckles.

He looks up from his phone to glare at Rick. "I can uninvite just as fast, you know."

Rick doesn't look the least bit worried. "No, you can't. You said it, and you can't take it back."

He sighs loudly. "What are we, in kindergarten?"

"I like recess," Rick answers in the same childish tone.

He bites his tongue. He's not arguing with a grown man who acts like a child. He can't help but notice Sheri must be rubbing off on him. He hears her inside his head with every step he takes toward the stranger at the end of the bar. "I don't know if you heard, but the bar's closing early today. A bunch of people in town are having Thanksgiving dinner at my house tonight. You're welcome to come over too."

The man's face is full of surprise. He looks a little wary, but he hands Randall a business card. "My name's Matt. I just moved to town. I'm a traveling nurse, and I'm looking for a more permanent place to stay."

Randall thinks of Sheri's broken-down, fairy-tale

house. "I don't suppose you know anything about fixing up houses."

The man scratches the back of his neck with a grin. "As a matter of fact, I do. It kind of runs in my family, you might say. We've got an electrician, carpenter, plumber, and a contractor; and I know a little bit myself."

"Do they enjoy a challenge?" he asks.

The man's smile grows. "Have you met a house flipper who doesn't?"

He sits down with his beer. "I've got a houseguest who got taken on a house she bought from a local. The place she bought needs a lot of work. I'd like to keep this between us if I could."

Matt gives him a knowing smile. "She sounds like a special woman."

He frowns and holds in a groan. "She's something." He takes a swig of his beer and thinks of Sheri. All he feels is chased. "The sooner I get her out of my home, the better."

Matt's smile disappears. "She's that bad, huh?"

He leans in. "She's husband-hunting, and she's not the least bit subtle."

Matt laughs out loud. "And you don't want to be caught?"

He leans away from him and wonders why it is that everyone takes Sheri's side. Matt hasn't even met her yet. "There's nothing wrong with being alone," he mutters.

Matt reaches out and knocks his beer bottle against his. "No, there isn't. You can survive alone, this is true, but life's much better when you share it with someone else." Matt holds his up hand, and Randall spies the ring. "Marriage isn't all bad. I wouldn't knock it 'til you've tried it."

He feels so scolded. "How's your wife like Alaska?" he manages.

Matt's eyes look a little sad. "She would have loved it." He tips his head back and finishes his beer. He's so quiet. He slides off the stool and walks past. The beer hits the trash can with a *thunk*. He stops at the French doors. "I'll see you later...maybe."

31

Sheri's thankful her afternoon flies by. The longer the day goes on, the more her nerves jump around. She's beginning to regret her decision. Randall came home at 3:15 looking a tad bit glassy-eyed. She fought the urge to throw a bucket of water on his head. How dare he come home on Thanksgiving Day with a buzz? And then as if to add insult to injury, he plopped down in that chair of his and went right to sleep. She snaps a pic of him and sends it to Jenni.

SHERI:

Look who fell asleep in his chair on Thanksgiving Day. So much for him helping me out in the kitchen.

JENNI:

Oh my goodness. He really is an Alaskan lumberjack!

SHERI:

You only say that because you haven't
tried to talk to him.

JENNI:

Whatever. Are you really telling me you
don't like his full head of dark hair and
that three-day old beard? You always
were a bit of a Wolverine fan.

Jenni sends a Wolverine GIF. Sheri turns to take
another peek at Randall with his head tilted back as he
snores like a logger. She fights the urge to plug his nose
with her fingers.

SHERI:

That's stretching it, Jenni.

Better go. I've got a few more things to
do. The ladies will be here before I
know it.

JENNI:

Happy Thanksgiving, friend.

SHERI:

Happy Thanksgiving back. ☺

She vacuums around Randall three times. He doesn't
move a muscle. It's 4:30 when the doorbell rings. This sets
Jake off. Sheri comes through the kitchen door as his
recliner hits the floor. He shuffles toward the front door and
opens it. A dark-haired man in a sweater and jeans steps
inside. He removes his shoes. He's carrying a bottle of wine

and a bouquet of flowers. She resists the urge to clap her hands.

"You're early," Randall grumps.

Sheri is embarrassed by his poor manners. She rushes across the room. "Please, come in! I'm Sheri. I'm so glad you're here."

He smiles at her. She can't help but notice he has a nice smile. "Hi. I'm Matt," he says.

She shakes his hand. "If you don't mind heading to the kitchen, I'll be there in a second."

"Sure."

As soon as Matt is through the kitchen door, she grabs a hold of Randall and jerks him into his bedroom which she's never been in until now. She shuts the door and catches a whiff of beer and cigarette smoke.

"Good night. You smell like a brewery. Go take a shower before anyone else shows up."

He whips off his shirt and steps closer to her.

"What are you doing?" she squeaks.

"Just what you told me to." He reaches for his jeans.

She turns away. "You're being a real jerk," she mutters.

His hands rest on her upper arms. "I know. You just bring out the worst in me," he whispers over the back of her ear.

"Enough of this nonsense. I've got Thanksgiving dinner to serve," she scolds.

His breath falls on the back of her neck. His lips follow. Sheri thinks she's going to melt at his feet. She wonders what she's doing in his room when she has a guest in the kitchen. "I need to go. Matt's in the kitchen."

His soft, warm sigh falls on her skin. "You'd better go, then."

She lifts her head. "I just said I was."

He chuckles. "Then do it already."

"Fine. I will." She feels ridiculous as she forces herself to walk at a normal speed from his room without turning back. Something else hits the floor. It has to be his pants. She gasps and stares straight ahead. He chuckles behind her. She lays a hand on the doorknob and fights the urge to fling his door open while she opens it a crack and sneaks out. She heads straight for the kitchen and finds Matt arranging his flowers in a glass mason jar.

"Thank you for the flowers, Matt. They're beautiful. I'm sorry. We—I mean, Randall doesn't have any vases."

He holds up the jar. "That's fine. This will do." He clears his throat. "Jerri always told me never to show up to an invite without flowers and a bottle of wine."

She notices the ring on his finger. "Jerri must be your wife."

He smiles. "Yes, she was." He shakes his head. "I thought I was doing just fine until I met her." His eyes water a little. "Let's just say she had her work cut out for her." There's so much love in his voice that it pains Sheri.

"Jerri was a very fortunate woman," she answers.

He turns away. "And I was a very fortunate man."

"How long has she been gone?" she asks quietly.

"About two and a half years, but sometimes it feels like it was just yesterday." His tone is so melancholy.

She walks over and lays a hand on his shoulder. "I'm sorry. She sounds like a lovely lady."

He turns back to face Sheri. "She was." He takes a deep breath. "So, what can I do to help?"

She searches her mind. "Um..."

"You'd better let me do something because I'm seconds

from running out on you. I haven't been to a dinner party since before Jerri," Matt's voice breaks, and his words stop.

She holds his gaze. "Matt, one step at a time, right?" She reaches down to pet Jake. "Jake, here, is a friendly guy. He enjoys walking around in the backyard. With company. Any time you need to step out, he'd love to go with you."

Matt blinks. "Thanks."

She takes a deep breath. It just now occurs to her. "How many guys did Randall invite to dinner tonight?"

"There were two other guys at the lodge besides me," he offers.

She does the numbers inside her head while picturing the layout of Randall's home. "We'll be scattered here and there for supper, but we'll just have to make do."

There's a throat clearing. She looks across the room. Randall fills the doorway. His head is wet. He's wearing a light green sweater and blue jeans. He stands there in his socks. Her mouth goes dry. This is absurd.

"Yes," she answers. Her answer means so many things.

"I have a table and a bunch of folding chairs in the garage. If we rearrange furniture in the living room, we can make it fit," he says in a somewhat robotic voice, but he almost sounds needy.

He sounds so unsure of himself, and it's so strange. Sheri can't help but think it's like he can read her mind. "But what about your recliner and your game on the TV?"

He looks at her like she's silly, like they've never had a disagreement about that very thing. "It's just one night. I'll be fine," he assures her.

Matt claps his hands and rubs them together. "Take me to your table. We don't have much time. Let's get going."

Matt walks between them. Sheri mouths a big "thank

you" to Randall. She can't fight the smile that spreads across her face. Randall swallows hard, looks confused, and turns to head out of the kitchen.

She hums as she continues with her food preparations. This is going to be a Thanksgiving to remember.

32

Randall could hardly stand to listen to Sheri and Matt's conversation right before he walked through the door. He's never been one for eavesdropping, but when he couldn't make out the words, it drove him crazy. The even flow of conversation between them is something he's never had with Sheri, and she just met Matt. The pattern between them was like they'd known each other for years.

He doesn't know what comes over him whenever he's around her, but he just wants to make her happy. He stops in his tracks when that thought slaps him upside the head.

"Is something wrong?" Matt asks.

Yes, I need my head examined.

"No, I just had a thought," Randall says before he opens the garage door.

"Want to tell me?" Matt asks in a voice that suggests he already knows.

"No," Randall answers too quickly, and Matt laughs. They pick up the table, which is a little bigger than Randall remembers. They angle it to get it through the door. "You're going to have to wipe that down," Matt says.

Just like a typical married man who's been bossed around, Randall thinks.

"It's just a little dirt," Randall protests, even though he has to admit he wouldn't want to set any food on it.

"Suit yourself," Matt pops off just as Sheri walks into the room.

She gives the tabletop one look and shakes her head. "Where's the bleach?"

Matt laughs out loud.

"It's not that bad," Randall argues.

Seconds later, Sheri's back with a bucket. "Don't worry. I've got it," she mutters.

Matt takes the bucket from her. "Go ahead. We've got this. You're doing all the cooking."

She beams at him. "Thanks, Matt." She gives Randall a look before heading back to the kitchen.

"See how easy it is to be agreeable," Matt says to him.

"Kowtowed is more like it," Randall grumbles back.

Matt dips the rag in the water and starts wiping the table down. "I've been in the doghouse a time or two. Believe me. No one likes fleas."

Randall focuses on moving his few pieces of furniture closer to the TV. It doesn't take long. "I'm just going to go get those folding chairs."

Matt nods. "Sounds good. I'll wipe them down too."

"Of course you will," Randall mutters under his breath as he walks back out the garage door. Sheri had better be one heck of a cook to make him go to all this trouble. He still can't believe she was in cahoots with Chelsea, and

Chelsea went along with it. Chelsea doesn't get along with anybody.

His bad mood keeps him going between the garage and the house. He's down to the last chair to move when he turns around and almost runs into Sheri, who stands before him with a cardboard box. "I hate to ask you for another favor." Her voice is as sweet as sugar.

"I'd say you've met your quota for the day and then some," he growls.

She blinks once. "I need you to take this to Chelsea."

Aha. Sheri must have bribed her. "You do know her name," he accuses.

"Matt told me. I just learned it today."

"Why were you and Matt talking about Chelsea?" Randall accuses.

Sheri rolls her eyes. "Why does it matter?"

"Chelsea closed down early because you cooked her a Thanksgiving dinner."

"If you must know, Chelsea asked me if I would make two plates for her and her son who was coming home. She hasn't seen him in four years, and she wanted to be sure they had a special meal. Is that so terrible?" She sounds like she might cry.

"No, but you better put it in a cooler. If I have to leave it outside, the animals might get it. She was going to pick him up at the airport today."

"Thank you. It means a lot to me. I would take it to her myself, but I'm kind of busy in the kitchen. I'd hate to not be here when everyone shows up." She nods as he hits the button to open the garage door.

He spies Shannon getting out of her SUV. His stomach knots. He turns back to Sheri. "You invited Shannon."

She doesn't understand his strange reaction. It's like he's trying to crawl into the shadows on the garage wall. "I guess. You know I put up invites downtown. She seemed really nice on the phone."

"She's been chasing me hard since the day we met," he whispers.

She fights to keep a straight face. "We're in a group, Randall. What can she really do?"

He fidgets. "Lots of things. Trust me. And none of them are good."

"You'd better get going over to Chelsea's, Randall, or you'll miss the whole dinner," she urges. She doesn't want to be caught talking about a dinner guest.

"Fine." He turns to go, but Shannon's almost to the garage door. He turns back to Sheri. "I'm sorry," he says before he takes her face in his hands and kisses her long and deep.

That'll give Shannon something to think about, he thinks. *Maybe she'll back off.*

But somewhere in their kiss, he forgets all about Shannon. Until Sheri steps on his toe—hard. He backs away slowly, holding her gaze.

"Right. I'll just put that food in a cooler and head out," he says.

She hands him the box but doesn't say a word.

"That kiss looked yummy. Am I next?" Shannon announces.

His face flushes. He hurries over to the cooler, but not before he sees the shocked look on Sheri's face. He can't help but feel a little triumphant. If Sheri didn't believe him before about Shannon, she does now.

"You must be Shannon. I recognize your voice from the phone," Sheri says in a not-so-friendly tone.

"The one and only," Shannon responds before she giggles.

"Let's get you inside and out of the cold."

Sheri's librarian voice is back, and Randall loves it.

33

The nerve of Randall, kissing me like that, Sheri thinks to herself. It was all for show, but some of it felt real. She can't believe Shannon, who is going to kiss a man right after he laid claim to another woman. Even if none of it was real, Shannon doesn't know that. Sheri gets the shivers as she watches Shannon saunter around the garage as if she owns it. Alaska really is for hunters.

Sheri fights her inner cavewoman as she half drags Shannon into the house before Shannon tries to crawl into Randall's truck. Jake growls low in his throat as Shannon walks by him. *Bless him for his loyalty,* Sheri thinks as she gives him a pat on the head.

Shannon struts into the kitchen in her body-hugging outfit that outlines every curve. She stops mid-step when she spies Matt. "Hell-o there. I don't think we've met. I'm Shannon, and I'm single."

"I'm Matt, and I'm a widower," he answers.

"I'm so sorry, Matt. That's so tragic. You're so young," Shannon goes on.

"Thank you, Shannon." He stares past her to meet Sheri's wide eyes. "Did you mention Jake needs walking?"

Sheri smiles back at him. "Thanks, Matt. That would be wonderful."

"I'll go with you. I love walking. I love any type of exercise," Shannon says.

"I'm sorry. Jake prefers one person walking him," Sheri interjects.

The doorbell rings, saving them from further awkwardness. "Shannon, would you like to answer the door?" Sheri asks in as pleasant a voice as possible.

"You have guests answer your door?" Shannon pouts.

"If you'd rather check the inside of the turkey to see if it's done, I'll get the door," Sheri suggests.

"No, I'll see who's here," Shannon says as she glides past Sheri.

Matt whistles. "Come on, Jake. Let's go outside."

Jake's ears perk up. He lumbers around the island to the back door. A brief blast of cold air sweeps through the kitchen. Sheri shivers before busying herself with transferring some foods to other dishes and digging up as many hot pads as she can find.

The kitchen door flies open. Shannon steps in with Bill and Rick on her arms.

Oh, boy, Sheri thinks. "Hey, guys," she says in a perkier voice than she feels.

Bill steps up to the island. "Whooeee, Sheri. You made all this? It sure smells good."

She can't help but give him a wink at his praises. "I did. My mom was a wonderful cook, and she taught me all she knows."

Bill walks toward her. She heads around the other side

of the island. "If you guys want to hang out and watch the game in the other room, we'll wait just a little longer for everyone to get here, and then we'll have dinner."

The back door opens. Jake and Matt step back inside. Matt walks up beside Sheri. "Hey, guys. Would anyone like a glass of wine?"

Bill frowns. "I'll take a beer."

Matt goes to the fridge. He stands back up. "You're in luck. It looks like Sheri bought some for today." He holds one out to Bill and Rick. "Here you go." Matt looks at Shannon. "What about you, Shannon? Would you like a beer?"

She shrugs. "Sure. Why not?"

He hands her one too.

"You going to come out in the TV room with us?" she coos.

"I'd love to, but I promised Sheri, here, I'd give her a hand in the kitchen."

A look of disgust rolls across Shannon's face. "If that's what you want to do."

He gives her a small smile. "I don't mind."

Cheryl and Dani show up together. They're chatty and easygoing. Sheri takes an immediate liking to them. It isn't long before they strike up a conversation with Matt in the kitchen.

"How long have you two been here?" he asks.

"About three years," the two women answer in synch.

Sheri laughs. "You've got to be roommates. You answer each other's sentences."

Cheryl nods her head. "Yeah. We met in college. We have a lot in common. We just sort of hit it off. We have a lot of the same interests." Cheryl stands with one hand in her jeans pocket and the other in her hoodie. She turns her head just enough to reveal a long braid.

"I love your hair," Sheri comments.

"Thanks," Cheryl says. "Dani does it. She's a hair magician."

Dani giggles and covers her mouth with her colorful nails. Her magnetic eyelashes blink a few times. She ducks her head. Her chin-length highlights fall over her face. "She tells me I should consider cosmetology, but I like what I do. I don't care that there aren't too many women who work pipeline. I enjoy the great outdoors no matter the weather."

Sheri takes her in. Cheryl looks sturdy enough but Dani's a tiny little thing. "You two work pipeline?" Sheri pauses. "No offense, Dani, but I would've pegged you for a stewardess or someone who works in an office. Don't you worry about your nails when working pipeline?"

Dani giggles again. "Not really. They're easier to work in than you think. It's like a lot of things in life. You just have to get used to it is all."

Sheri glances down at her wedged boots. "Do you walk around in those on the job? I'd tip and twist an ankle, and it'd be all over for me."

She giggles some more. She's a real giggler. "No. I don't work in these shoes. We wear steel-toed boots."

"And hard hats," Cheryl adds.

"Yeah, there's really no point in doing your hair when you wear a hard hat," Dani muses. "I haven't found a hairstyle yet that holds up under a hard hat."

"So how long do you plan on staying?" Matt asks.

"Oh. Well, I don't know," Dani answers. "I guess we'll see."

"I've got to ask. How did you know you wanted to work pipeline?" Matt says.

Cheryl taps her toe. "Well, we both wanted to travel and see lots of places, but neither of us had the finances, so we figured we'd choose a job that let us do that."

Matt nods. "But isn't pipeline kind of spur-of-the-moment sometimes?"

"It is. We've learned to pack light. We're both sort of spontaneous so it works for us," Dani says with a smile that's all dimples.

The doorbell rings again. "Excuse me," Sheri says as she heads to the other room. She smiles when she sees an elderly lady walk through the front door. It's Mrs. Betts.

"Hello," Sheri calls out from across the room. "I'm Sheri."

Mrs. Betts adjusts her glasses and comes forward with her cane. "I remember, dear. My body might be old, but my gears are still grinding."

Sheri gives her a hug and takes her arm. "Please, come in. Would you like to sit down?" Sheri steers her toward Randall's big chair. The young man who came with her remains at the front door. Sheri turns back to him. "You can come in too."

"That's my grandson, Owen. He's going to his girl-friend's for dinner," Mrs. Betts announces. "Go on then, Owen. I'll call when I need a ride home."

"Bye, Grandma," he answers and walks out, leaving the front door wide open.

Sheri helps Mrs. Betts into Randall's chair. She's so short that her legs don't reach the floor.

"Oh, my. This is such a soft chair. I just love it."

Sheri hears the door shut behind her.

"Who left the door wide open? They're letting all the heat out," Randall barks.

Sheri whips around to shut him up with her eyes.

"Who do you think?" Mrs. Betts calls out.

Randall's whole face lights up. "Sally. What a nice surprise. I didn't know you were coming." He ambles up beside Sheri and leans down so close that his shoulder bumps against hers. "Nice to see you."

Mrs. Betts points a finger at Sheri and then Randall. "It's nice to officially meet the girl I've heard so much about. You were right, son. She's a keeper. You'd better not let this one get away."

Sheri blushes from head to toe.

Randall flies to a standing position and stares straight at the kitchen as if that will make everyone in the room disappear.

"Right. Well, everyone's here now, so I'm just gonna bring supper out. We can all sit at the table," Sheri announces.

The kitchen doors fly open. Matt and the girls come out carrying dishes. "Did I hear someone say dinner?" Matt grins at Sheri. Randall's eyes narrow.

34

Randall sits at the table, fuming. He thinks to himself, *There's nothing like a seventy-five-year-old woman blurting things out like she doesn't own a hearing aid that works perfectly fine to make me want to fall through the floor.* She's a whole lot of conniving and not the least bit oblivious, but he's not about to kick his main food supply out of his home for trying to set him up with his houseguest, whose lips are the softest he's ever kissed.

Randall side-eyes Mrs. Betts, who knew exactly what she was doing when she sang Sheri's praises so loudly. The problem is they're all true. Still, there's more than one turkey at the table today. Matt knew exactly what he was doing when he shoved him into the chair next to Sheri's, but he's not complaining about holding her hand as she says a prayer of thanks for the meal and everyone there. Randall is just going to be grateful for this delicious meal and the fact that Shannon is at the other end of the table where she can't accidentally brush up against him all through the meal like she's done in the past. The woman is nothing but a thirsty opportunist.

The food is passed around. Before Randall knows it, he's forgotten all about his grudges against Matt and Mrs. Betts. He's enjoying himself more than he ever thought possible. Conversation flows along with the laughter. Dinner is delicious. He hasn't had food this good since he sat at his mother's table. He catches Sheri in the corner of his eye and realizes something. This is all because of her. It scares him half to death.

"So, Sheri, I hear you're going to be the new librarian," Shannon says from her end of the table.

"Yes, that's right," Sheri answers.

"Do you enjoy it?"

What a question, Randall thinks.

"Very much, yes," Sheri answers with a smile.

"Isn't it, like, boring?" Shannon's questions are innocent enough, but her snarky tone could scare off a small shark.

Randall is embarrassed for Shannon. He can't believe he forgot how much she loves her little digs that aren't exactly subtle, but Sheri invited her. She'll just have to endure Shannon.

"Not to me, no. It's fun trying to find books others will enjoy. It's fun climbing into imaginary worlds." Sheri's tone is even.

"If you say so." Shannon doesn't sound too convinced.

"What do you do?" Sheri replies.

"I'm a hairdresser," Shannon answers.

Sheri gives Randall an accusatory look, the kind that says he told her there weren't any decent hairdressers close by. He's not about to apologize because he told her the truth.

"That sounds fun," Sheri says.

"It is." Shannon looks down the table. "Randall, did you get a haircut? What happened to your beard?"

He slides his foot next to Sheri's beneath the table, feeling ornery. "I decided to try something new."

Sheri takes a sip of her water.

"Oh, well, it looks a bit amateur. You can come and see me anytime if you want an experienced hairstylist," Shannon says with no attempts at hiding being suggestive.

Sheri moves her foot away from Randall's so he scoots his chair closer to hers until their legs bump. "Thanks, but I'm good. A change is just what I needed."

Sheri's eyes fly to Matt, who sits across from her. She's more than ready to change the subject. Shannon and her obnoxious flirting are too much. "Hey, Matt. Did you know they have a log-splitting competition in this town?"

He grins. "No, I didn't. That sounds like fun."

"It is fun. They have a golden trophy and everything," Rick answers from the other end of the table.

"That sounds very cool," Cheryl adds.

"Yeah. We might just have to enter," Dani agrees.

"You wouldn't want to break a nail," Shannon sneers.

"This is true, but nails can be replaced. I like to try new things. Swinging an ax sounds like an adventure," Dani states before cracking a sly smile.

"Well, I'm not about to do a man's work. I wouldn't want to do anything that would jeopardize my real job. Everyone knows hairdressers have to be careful with their shoulders," Shannon says as she bats her eyelashes and ducks slyly to brush an invisible crumb from her dainty shoulder.

"That's good thinking, Shannon. It never hurts to be cautious," Sheri agrees.

"So is there a method to splitting logs?" Cheryl asks.

Rick and Bill nod in sync. Bill swallows his bite of food first. "There is, Cheryl, and it's important to know how to handle an ax. You'd hate to hack yourself. A gash from an ax can be pretty nasty."

Shannon visibly shivers. "Gross. Let's talk about something else."

"Well, this dinner was delicious, dear," Mrs. Betts says as her blue eyes zero in on Sheri. "With cooking skills like this, I can't believe you're not married."

Oh, boy. Here we go again. "I guess I just haven't found the right one," Sheri answers brightly.

"Well, you will, dear. I just know it." Mrs. Betts glances around the table slowly.

Bill and Rick stand up out of their chairs. "Well, that was a real good dinner, Sheri and Randall. Thanks for having us," Bill rattles off while backing away from the table.

Sheri looks all embarrassed. "Don't hurry off on account of me, guys. I'm not going to ask you for a proposal."

Her joke falls flat. If Randall wasn't so annoyed with the subject of marriage popping up around every corner whenever Sheri's in the vicinity, he might almost feel bad for her.

Matt clears his throat as Sheri turns away from everyone. "Who wants dessert? Those pies have been calling my name since I got here." He looks down the table. "Bill and

Rick? Bring your plates in the kitchen and I'll get you some to go if you need to leave."

Randall sees from the looks on their faces they want to leave, but they also want a piece of pie. Rick relents first. "Thanks, Matt. I'd love some."

Randall watches as Matt follows them into the kitchen, making him feel so inept. Why didn't he think of that? He turns toward Sheri, but she's not in her chair. Randall gets up to take his plate to the kitchen.

"Randall, be a dear and take my plate to the kitchen for me," Mrs. Betts requests.

"Of course. Would you like some dessert?"

"Pumpkin pie and whipped cream, please," she answers.

He steps into the kitchen. The three men look as guilty as a police lineup. "What's going on?" he asks.

"Nothing," they all say in unison.

"It doesn't look like nothing," Randall answers.

Matt steps closer to him. "If you must know, I was just talking with them about the house project, Randall. That's all. Calm down."

Randall looks at Rick and Bill, two people he doesn't want to be indebted to, before he looks back at Matt. "I thought you said you had family members who could do this."

He exhales. "I do, but there's no harm in asking if it'll save everyone airfare money. Not to mention, where will they all stay?"

Randall pinches the top of his nose. "Fine."

"I've gotta say I'm a little offended," Rick says as he stares Randall down.

"Excuse me," Randall replies.

"You know I built my house, right? And my family is full of talent, Randall. They can give those Mennonites in the Lower 48 a run for their money when it comes to contract work."

Randall had no idea. "I didn't think of them. I'm sorry."

"I'm just saying if there's money to be had and a job needs done, I'd like to be considered," Rick answers.

"I don't want her to find out, okay?" Randall says as he gestures behind him with his thumb and leans in at the same time.

Bill sniffs. "Why not? You're doing her a huge favor. She might want to thank you for it." He raises his eyebrows.

Randall jams a pointer finger in his direction. "This isn't about *that*, Bill, and that's exactly why I don't want her to know. I'm not after that."

"Then what are you after?" Rick answers quietly.

Sucker punch. "I don't know," Randall admits.

Bill and Rick look at each other and laugh. "Oh, this is going to be fun," Rick says first.

Bill nods his head up and down. "Yep." Bill turns to Randall. "Just remember, the farther you run away, the more ground you'll have to cover when you return."

As usual, he makes no sense. "Whatever, Bill." Randall turns to the dessert table. "I'm here to get a piece of pumpkin pie for Mrs. Betts."

Matt snaps his fingers. "I'm on it." He scoops a piece of pie out before heading to the fridge. He pulls out the whipped cream and slaps a dab on it. He holds it out like a gift. "There you go." He throws a hand on his hip. "Now kindly leave the room so we can go back to talking shop. The less you know, the better."

Randall catches Bill and Rick's smirky faces still pointed

in his direction. He ducks his head and walks out. Why does everything that has to do with Sheri chase him out of his own home?

35

To Sheri's relief, the rest of dinner passes without too many bumps. That comment Mrs. Betts made about her being a keeper was mortifying, and the only reason Sheri can forgive her is because she's seventy-five years old. If you can't speak your mind when you're seventy-five, when can you?

Matt, ever the gentleman, stays behind to help pick up. "Thanks, Matt. You didn't have to do that," Sheri says.

He grins. "Hey, I'm just here for some leftovers. You got any to spare?"

She nods. "Of course."

He clears his throat. "So Randall said you're entering the log-splitting contest."

She nods again. "That's right. I am."

"So do you care if I enter?" he asks in earnest.

Sheri almost laughs. "Of course not. Why would I care?"

"What if I beat you?" he asks.

"Then you win," she says with a grin. "But you gotta

beat Randall too. I hear he's been the champion for like three years running or something like that."

"Is that right?" Matt answers.

"Yep. That's right."

Matt washes the baking dishes with Sheri. "Well, it sounds like the Ax King needs to be dethroned."

Sheri giggles and sticks out a soapy hand to shake. Matt grabs a hold. "To dethroning the king," they declare together.

A throat clears behind them. Sheri would recognize that sound anywhere. She tries to drop her hand from Matt's grasp, but he holds tight as he gives her a wink and scoots closer.

"Oh hey, Randall," Matt says. He slowly releases her hand. "We're just cleaning up."

"Don't let me interrupt you," Randall growls from the doorway.

"Don't worry. We won't," Matt answers joyfully.

Sheri almost feels bad. Randall's been nothing but accommodating today. His footsteps get quieter and quieter as he walks away.

Sheri turns back to the dishes. "Was that really necessary?" she whispers in his direction.

Matt hip-bumps her and chuckles. "It was fun." Matt wraps up what's left of the apple and cherry pies as he gives Sheri another wink. "Brace yourself, Sheri," he says before he strides through the kitchen door.

Sheri thinks she should probably stay in the kitchen, but she's too curious. She follows Matt to the front door. Randall sits in his chair, which is just inches from the TV. He's so hyper focused he looks like he could crawl into the screen at any second except for when his eyes meet hers before he promptly looks away like he doesn't see her or Matt.

Matt's form fills the doorway. His back is to Randall. The grin he gives Sheri is full of mischief. "Thanks again for the pies," he says as he leans toward her. "I'll think of you every morning at breakfast time. Your cooking really hits the spot."

She knows at least half of what he's saying and doing is for show, but his words warm her heart. "You're welcome. It was so nice to meet you," she says as she resists the urge to lean away from his leaning in. She means every word. Matt is a kind, caring man, but he's nowhere near meeting someone new. He's still grieving his wife.

The door shuts, leaving only Randall, Sheri, and Jake, who stares at the table of food with naked longing. She walks over and grabs a big chunk of turkey. She tosses it to him. He catches it in the air.

"You and Matt get along well," Randall says.

"Yes, we do. He's a nice guy."

"And I'm not?" he protests.

"I never said that," she answers.

"You didn't have to," he responds.

"You want to help me take this food in the kitchen?" Sheri asks.

"No thanks."

Sheri fights the urge to point out that Matt would have helped. "All right, then." She hums as she carries the dishes one by one into the kitchen and eyeballs everything to see what she can combine to help it fit in the fridge better, but she thinks of Randall scrunched up in front of his TV and walks back out. "I'll just move this table so you can move your recliner back to where it goes."

He stands up. "You're not moving that table alone."

Sheri takes offense. "I can get it."

He frowns. "I won't be the reason you can't enter the log-splitting contest because you put your back out moving a table. Stop being so stubborn."

She rolls her eyes. "Fine." They turn the table sideways and fold it up before they cart it to the garage and lay it against the wall. Sheri feels his eyes on her. She remembers their kiss from that morning as much as she'd like to forget it. "Thank you for all of your help today. It means a lot to me."

"I don't want your thanks," he grumps.

She's so confused. "Then what do you want?"

His long legs eat up the space between them. "For you to stop chasing me."

Sheri thinks of Shannon and everything she said at dinner. "I'm not the one chasing you. How can you even say that?"

His eyes darken. It's like he doesn't hear anything she says as his eyes fall on her lips. "I want to stop wanting you, but I can't." His hand cups her jaw. His other hand is on her hip. "You feel so right in my arms. I don't understand." Their lips meet. He nudges her mouth open just a little. She lets him in.

Sheri knows exactly how he feels when he tells her he doesn't want to want her because she feels the same way. She tells herself it isn't wise to get so close to a man who isn't interested in marriage, but her lips melting beneath his hot kisses tell her something else.

The longer she's around him the more she realizes she could really fall for him. He's responsible. He's not easily swayed, except when it comes to who he kisses, except that's not true either. Shannon was throwing herself at him, and he wasn't the least bit tempted. Sheri feels foolish when she thinks of inviting women over to the house to meet him when she's ecstatic her little plan backfired. It seems the only woman Randall is interested in is her. She should really stop kissing him when he keeps insisting marriage is the last thing he wants, and she will. Eventually.

Randall is as close to Sheri as he can get. He can't help but notice every bit of her feels so perfect. All he can think of is her when they're all wrapped up in each other. He knows it's not fair of him to keep coming at her, but he can't seem to stop, just like he told her. What's he going to do?

Matt's a perfectly nice guy. Definitely too nice of a guy to have lost his wife at such a young age. Randall never thought he'd be the type to wish a widower ill, but that's exactly how he felt when he saw Matt talking to Sheri. The way they looked at each other with such ease made Randall want to rush her and kiss the crap out of her like he's doing right now.

He's got to get a grip. Seeing her with Matt might be the instigator in this hot kiss they're having, but it's not the only reason. Randall feels like he's going mad. He can't believe he's falling for someone he just met. He's got to get away, and he will soon enough. Right after he's done kissing her into oblivion. There's no need to rush.

She looks up to meet his gaze. "For the record, I'm not the one doing the chasing." She regrets her words as soon as she says them, but she can't take them back. She knows she has a bad habit of having to be right too much of the time, but darn it, she is right. He's the one who keeps kissing her. She gives him a tiny shove. "I've got to get all the chairs out here, and then I'm going to rearrange your fridge."

"Sure, why not? You've rearranged everything else I own," he barks at Sheri as she walks away.

"Is that you offering to carry chairs out with me?" she responds.

"No."

"Fine. Just stay out of my way. *Capiche*?" She raises an eyebrow in warning.

"Sure. I'll stay out of your way. In *my* home," he grumbles.

"Sounds fair to me," she replies. "Just call me the little red hen. I do it all. I don't need your help."

Randall opens his mouth again to respond, then clamps it shut for fear that she'll make him do something helpful if he keeps responding to her. He's all out of goodwill for Sheri.

36

Randall stares at Sheri as she walks away. *The nerve of that woman, accusing me of chasing her,* he thinks to himself as he decides that's the last time he follows his instincts with her. He shakes his head and waits for his anger to leave him. He knew exactly what Sheri was doing, flirting with Matt in the kitchen to make him jealous, and darned it if it didn't work. That's the last time that woman gets the better of him.

Sheri can hold hands with whomever she wants to. She's just not doing it in his house, he decides. He stomps back inside and drags his recliner across the floor. It makes the worst sound. Randall feels ridiculous and prays he didn't scratch the floor with his little temper tantrum.

"I'm watching my game," he says into the empty space.

"Fine by me." Her voice comes from the kitchen. She makes quick work of moving the chairs back to the garage. "Randall."

"Yeah."

"Can I throw out your expired food?"

"Sure."

"All of it?" she prompts.

He sighs. *She's exhausting.* "I just said fine. Just do it already."

"All right, but you won't have anything left but Thanksgiving dinner," she warns.

"I'll just make do with Mrs. Bett's canning. It'll be fine," he yells.

Many *thunks* and whispers later, Sheri's footsteps fill his ears. She plops down on the couch to the left of him. It rests against the back wall. "If you sit at the other end, you can see the TV," he tells her.

She sits catty-corner to him. Her head is parallel to the side of the flat-screen TV. "I don't want to see the TV." She curls up on the end of the couch and closes her eyes. "Put a fork in me. I'm done." She closes her eyes.

A half hour goes by. She's curled up, sawing logs. He walks over and covers her with a blanket. She turns over on her side, away from him. He can't help but admire her backside a little too long.

"Stop staring," she mutters.

His face turns red. "I wasn't," he argues.

"Then stop doing what you weren't doing," she mutters.

He turns back to the TV with a grin. "Got it." He glances over at Jake, the traitor, who lies on the floor beside the couch. "I see how it is, Jake. You love her more. Fine. I won't forget this when she moves out."

Jake lays his head on his paws as if to say he doesn't care. Randall can't help but agree with him. He'd prefer her company to his most of the time too. He chews on his lip and thinks of ways to get her out of his home so he can have some semblance of normalcy and peace of mind.

His phone goes off. It's been a few days since he's gone on a fire run. He glances at his pager. It reads "10-33." He searches his brain and texts Scott, the semi-retired fireman.

RANDALL:

What's a 10-33?

SCOTT:

"Emergency. What're you doing using codes? We don't do that.

Randall laughs to himself.

RANDALL:

I didn't use the code. It was Max. You know he's old school.

SCOTT:

What're you doing talking to me? It's an emergency! Gear up and get your ass down there.

RANDALL:

Fine. I'm going already.

He texts Scott one last time before jumping up out of his chair, muttering all the way. "That's not good. It could be anything."

He rushes over and shakes Sheri's shoulder. "There's an emergency. I've got to go."

He runs to his room to suit up in his gear. Seconds later, he turns to leave. Sheri grabs him by the collar and jerks him forward. Her kiss is gentle but firm. "You be careful," she says before she takes a step back, like she doesn't know what happened. He knows just how she feels.

"I will," Randall answers. For the first time in his life, he's not the only person he takes out the door to face the fire.

He lifts his walkie-talkie to his lips to talk to Max. "10-69, 10-76. This is Randall reporting."

"What's your 10-76?" Max responds.

"Two minutes," he answers.

He arrives at the firehouse and finds Scott waiting there with dark-eyed Bill. "It's out at the pipelines. A man fell into a pit, and it's filling up," Scott explains.

"We've gotta move," they say together.

Randall's stomach tightens. It must be bad if they both showed up to help.

He doesn't think twice when he calls Sheri. "We're headed out to the pipeline. Can you reach out to Cheryl and Dani and ask them to meet us out there? It's probably one of their coworkers."

"I'm on it," Sheri answers.

Minutes later, they're on-site. The three men hop off the truck and start out on foot. A man waves his hands at them. "Hey, I'm Chase. Be careful. The ground is slippery and unsteady. You need to be as light as possible. It can't take much weight."

Randall glances over at Scott and Bill, then down at himself. "Shoot. We don't have any lightweights out here. Hold up, Bill."

They stare at each other and then back at the site.

"Don't even think about it, Randall. You're not any lighter than me," Bill grumps.

"It's filling up. We've got to get him out," Randall yells over all the noise.

"Yes, I agree, but it won't do any good if we cause it to all cave in," Scott replies. "We need a solid plan."

"I'm light. I'm going in," Dani announces from behind them.

"Not without an anchor," Scott orders.

"What have you got? We don't have much time," Dani yells.

"What good is losing two people on the job?" Cheryl answers as she slips an arm through Dani's. She's not about to let go.

Bill's already some distance behind them.

"I've got the flat hose." Randall runs back to Bill and grabs a hold of the hose to help him drag it toward Dani. Scott gets a hold of the end. "We're going to wrap this around your waist and tie it tight to secure it."

Cheryl hugs her tight. "You've got this, Dani."

Dani's tiny form walks across the frozen ground, which slowly turns to mud beneath her feet, a fact that can't be denied as she starts to slip and slide. Somehow she keeps herself upright until she goes over the edge. They all wait on solid ground in anxious anticipation. Randall has no idea how long to wait. He texts Sheri.

RANDALL:

Please pray.

She dings him right back.

SHERI:

Already praying.

He can't help but smile.

Twenty-seven long minutes later, Randall feels a tugging on the hose. "Pull," he yells at Bill and Scott. They all start pulling. Just when he thinks they're getting nowhere, he sees two mud-covered faces. They pull and tug and tug and pull until eventually everyone is back on safe ground. The three men rush the two of them, who lay on the frozen ground exhausted. They help them stumble back to where Cheryl waits.

"We'll take them by truck to the hospital. You can meet us there," Randall says to Cheryl.

"You've got it," she says, but her eyes are on Dani.

37

Sheri waits at the house, although it drives her crazy. Her mind races with worry. What if Randall gets seriously hurt? What if someone else is hurt? How does she really feel about him? What if he never finds out?

"What is happening?" she mutters to herself as she paces back and forth.

Her phone goes off.

RANDALL:

Got them both. They're going to be fine.
They're at the hospital.

Her eyes read the text twice. She sheds a few tears.

"Thank you, Lord," she whispers to the empty house.

SHERI:

Thanks for letting me know.

"I'll be a while," Randall answers which is just as well.

She's not ready to see him, not after imagining him being buried alive and never coming home.

Sheri decides it's a good time to take Jake outside. She needs to walk. The backyard is spacious, but she needs a bigger distraction than pacing. She needs it ASAP. She texts Randall.

SHERI:

> If you have a key, I'd like to go to the library to take a look sometime soon.

RANDALL:

> Sounds good. As soon as I can get over there, we'll do it.

Sheri does a few more laps with Jake around the yard before she heads back inside to lie down on the couch to nap. She wakes to someone wrapping her in a blanket.

"What time is it?" she asks Randall, who leans over her.

"It's about three thirty in the morning," he answers in an amused tone. "Ready to go to the library?"

"No. Go to bed, Randall. I swear."

"You going to sleep on the couch all night?" he asks.

"Maybe."

"You'll be sore in the morning," he insists.

Why won't he be quiet?

"Fine. Take me to bed," she grumbles.

His arm slips through hers and he jerks her off the couch. She follows behind him quietly.

"This isn't the kitchen," she mumbles.

"You can't sleep in the kitchen."

"I can't go with you in there," she says as she stands outside his bedroom.

"I'll behave myself," he answers.

"No, you won't," she argues.

"It's late. I need my sleep. Just come on," he urges.

Her knee bumps into the other one as she tries to remain upright. Her eyelids droop with the rest of her that rests against his chest. "Fine," she says as she wanders over to fall down on his bed. It's so much softer than hers, but she's not about to tell him that. She turns over on her side with her back to him. Seconds later, he's curled up along the back of her. She tries to scoot away.

"You scoot any more and you're going to fall off the side of my bed," Randall warns.

Reluctantly, she molds herself into his form. She can't help but notice how right it feels. She tells herself not to get too used to it. Randall's not the marrying kind, or so he's told her more than once. She closes her eyes and goes to sleep.

———

Sheri wakes up by herself. *Did Randall get another call?* she wonders. She didn't hear his pager go off. She smells something in the kitchen. She goes to get up.

"Don't you move a muscle," Randall says from the doorway to his room. He carries some sort of platter. "I brought you breakfast in bed."

She can't help but smile. She's never had breakfast in bed. "Thank you." She smiles at the single flower beside her smaller plate. "Thank you for the flower."

He looks embarrassed. "I stole it from your vase. It's actually from Matt."

She smiles up at him. "I love it."

He points at the plate. "It's French toast. That's one of the few breakfast items I know how to cook." He sits down beside her.

"Where's your breakfast?" she asks. She looks worried.

"I'll eat mine later." He squeezes her knee. "Take a bite."

She tries to ignore what her hair must look like or the fact that she has morning breath. Not to mention she has the urge to pee. She cuts off a tiny piece and dips it in the syrup before she takes a bite, chews, and swallows. "It's delicious. Thank you. I just need to..." She gestures awkwardly.

"Oh, yeah. Sure. Go ahead."

She hops out of bed and runs for the nearest bathroom. Once she's relieved, she glances in the mirror as she washes her hands with soap and water. Her hair sticks out all over. Her eyeliner covers way too much of her face. She breathes into her hand. "Ugh." She squeezes a bit of toothpaste on her finger and starts on her teeth and tongue. She wipes at the stray eyeliner to remove it. She pats her wild hair down the best she can.

She opens the door and hurries back to the bedroom only to find Randall eating her breakfast. "What are you doing?"

He grins. "I didn't know if you were coming back. I hate to waste a hot breakfast."

She snatches her plate back. "That's mine. Go make your own."

He picks up her coffee cup from the end table and takes a sip before setting it down. "I must say, you look pretty good in my bed." He leans in to kiss her. She all but jams a bite of French toast in his face.

"You think you're pretty smooth, don't you?" She lays

down her plate and stands up. She's furious. He's determined to have more fun than she'd like. "This isn't happening between us. I won't allow it. If you want a good time, call Shannon. I know she's got your number." She walks out with her dignity barely intact. A commitment is the last thing on his mind, and it's the only thing she'll consider. She wishes he'd quit chasing her because he's wearing her down.

38

Randall's phone goes off. He catches the number. It's his cousin, Jan, who is totally team Sheri. He shuts his bedroom door and opens FaceTime because she'll just keep calling if he doesn't pick up.

"Hey. What's up?" he answers as he takes a bite of cold, soggy French toast, which feels just about right after Sheri stomped out of his room.

"Not much here. What's up with you? Why do you look so dejected?" She slams her dough on the counter noisily. "Are you having woman troubles?"

"I don't know. We had a nice Thanksgiving dinner. Everyone visited and had a good time. I got called to a rescue, and everyone came out all right. I got back to the house in the early hours. We slept together, and then this morning, she stomps out of my room after rejecting my breakfast-in-bed offer." He twitches a little. "I kind of put myself out there," he mutters.

"You slept together?" Jan's so loud.

"Keep your voice down, and no, we didn't sleep together. Not how it sounds."

She grins even bigger. "Oh, you cuddled. Ahh, that's sweet. So you have feelings for this woman, and you don't know what to do about them."

Randall hates her teasing tone. "Everything comes back to marriage with this woman. Always. It's maddening."

"Because she doesn't want to be a roll in the hay for you. Is that what's got you all riled up?"

"Don't make me sound like a jerk, Jan. You're my cousin."

Jan is front and center. Her blue eyes flash. "I'm also a woman. It sounds to me like she's asking you to respect her."

"I don't disrespect her." *This is dumb.* "You know what, I'm not having this conversation with you. I don't have to explain myself to you—or Sheri. She thinks she can move into my house, demand a ring from me, and the rest of my life. Well, she can just think again. No woman is going to tie me down. I'm just going to hang back, keep my distance, and stay busy. She can find out how much fun life is without me. So how about that?"

"And vice versa," Jan answers in a satisfied tone that he's not sure he likes.

"Yeah," he agrees. "Wait a minute. What?"

"You can find out how much fun life is without her," Jan says with a grin.

"Oh, I can't wait. It'll be a blast," he responds, much cockier and surer than he feels. He texts Rick and Bill.

RANDALL:

How soon can you guys start on this
house job with me?

BILL:

Like yesterday. It's been too quiet. We
need a project.

RANDALL:

Great. I'll get a hold of Matt.

"Bye, Randall. I can tell your mind is somewhere else," Jan taunts.

He looks back at Jan, who's way too smug. "Bye, Jan."

He shuts his phone screen down. "Time to get to work." Randall pulls on some clothes and marches out of his bedroom.

"Oh, good. You're going out. Could you drop me off at the library, please?" Sheri's all dressed up to go out. Her bright blue eyes stare into his.

"Sure." He wants to ask how she's getting in without his key, which she hasn't mentioned since she stomped out of his room this morning, but he refuses to ask for information she's not offering.

They walk out to the truck. She climbs in and checks her phone before texting. He backs down the driveway. Minutes later, they're at the library. Bertie waits outside. Sheri gives him a small smile. "Thank you for the ride. I hate to keep her waiting. It's too cold for someone her age."

She hops out of his truck and walks away without a backward glance. Randall pulls away from the curb as they head inside. Anger and other emotions he doesn't understand fill him at the feeling of being dismissed. He heads to

Sheri's falling-down, fairy-tale house, ready to knock out a few walls.

Randall is happy to see that Rick, Bill, and Matt are already there. He heads up the walk with them. He slips through the window just like before so he can unlock the front door from the inside. They walk through the entire house together. Randall is embarrassed at how many details Matt rattles off that he didn't catch. There's a lot to be done.

"Does she have any ideas on how she wants this house to turn out?" Matt asks.

"I think she just wants it livable, and of course, she's on a budget," Randall replies.

"How are you going to get payment from her without her knowing?" Rick asks.

He coughs. "I'm not."

Bill shoots an incredulous look at Randall. "Are you tellin' me you're payin' for the remodeling?"

Matt smacks Bill's chest. "What's it matter to you what he does with his money, Bill? Everyone knows houses are an investment."

Randall breathes a little easier now that he doesn't have to explain something he doesn't understand to Bill and Rick. Randall has no idea why he's fixing up her house, but he's going with getting her out of his house as soon as possible.

"She, um, mentioned something about a fairy-tale house," Randall gets out between gritted teeth as he stares at the ground. He's not about to look at Bill and Rick, who make no attempts to hold in their laughter.

Matt nudges him. "I've done a little work on a project

like this with my family before. It's actually pretty cool. She's going to love it."

Randall grabs a hold of Matt's encouraging words and ignores Bill and Rick.

"That sounds kind of girly," Bill says.

Matt's head pops up. He stares Bill down. "It's going to be tough. It requires some thinking outside the box. Do you think you can do it?" he challenges.

"What's so challenging about building some sort of dollhouse?" Bill argues.

"You want to get paid or not?" Matt says.

"Yeah. I want to get paid," Bill pouts.

Rick's smirk quickly disappears at the mention of money. He steps up. "Hey, uh, Matt. I think I can give you some pointers too."

"Fine. But first, shut up and listen," Matt answers, and so they do.

Randall can't believe his luck. Who knew he'd find Matt, the house-flipping genius, in this tiny Alaska town? As much as Sheri frustrates him, he can't wait to see her face when this house is done, just like he can't wait to see how little Miss Opinionated likes it when she has to eat some crow just to give him a proper thank-you.

39

Sheri and Bertie hit it off from the beginning. Sheri thinks Bertie is the sweetest woman. Sheri notices her circulation is a few decades old, but that can easily be remedied. Bertie has a good heart, and she's not afraid to speak her mind—two things Sheri loves.

"I didn't stay in this job for the money. I don't need it. I just want something to do. I need a routine," Bertie says.

"Would you like to work with me?" Sheri asks.

"Strictly on a volunteer basis," Bertie says with fire in her eyes. She leans toward Sheri. "I know another way you can make money," Bertie says in a sneaky tone.

"Oh." Sheri's more than a little worried. She can't imagine what Bertie's about to say.

Bertie chuckles. "It's no secret this job won't pay the rent or the mortgage, and I've always believed a woman should be allowed to make her own way if that's what she wants to do."

Sheri grins. "I think I love you, Bertie. What is the job?"

Bertie sits down at the table. "There are a number of people in the community who aren't getting any younger but would like to stay in their homes. All they need is a little help with housekeeping and maybe some help with their medications."

"What do you mean? I don't have any sort of training for that."

"You can take a CMA class online since you live in a remote area. If you do that, you can pack people's medications for them and get paid to do it. And anyone can help clean homes. They just have to be able-bodied and put in the time," Bertie answers.

The longer Sheri thinks about it, the more she warms to the idea. "Thanks, Bertie."

Bertie reaches over and lays a wrinkled hand on Sheri's. "You're a good egg, Sheri. This town needs all the good eggs it can get." She looks around the library. "Now, this library needs a major overhaul, and something tells me you're just the girl for it."

Sheri smiles down at her. "You don't mind?"

Bertie shakes her head back and forth. "Heavens, no. I just don't have the energy or creativity to think of new things. Anything we can do to get more patrons is fine by me."

Sheri looks around. "There's a lot to change, and it'll take time and money, but I like challenges."

Bertie taps her nose. "My grandson plays on the high school football team. You'd be surprised what those boys would do for restaurant pizza and ice cream."

Sheri laughs. "I like the way you think." She taps the table with the pencil. "First things first. I'm going through the books and having a book sale. That could be a good fundraiser. Whatever books are left over from the book sale could go to a detention center or the Senior Center. Anywhere people can use them."

"Sounds good to me," Bertie says.

The afternoon flies by as the two women fill boxes with books. Sheri's fingers dance and her heart thrills as she skims over the spines, checking out the inside covers.

"We've got a ton of grant money," Bertie says out of the blue.

"Really?" Sheri answers, thinking Bertie's going to tell her some number in the hundreds.

"Yes. Like tens of thousands," Bertie says in a tone that suggests she's reading a grocery list.

Sheri fights her excitement. "Are you sure, Bertie?"

"Yes. It's carried over for a few years. I didn't know what to spend it on."

"Is there a deadline?" Sheri asks worriedly, knowing grant money almost always has a deadline.

"I'm not sure," Bertie answers.

"Who's your treasurer?" Sheri asks with no small amount of impatience. If grant money isn't spent, it can be taken away.

"Mrs. Betts."

Sheri can't help but giggle. "You two women run this town," Sheri teases her with a wink.

"I don't know about that, but we help out where we can." Bertie smiles brightly back at Sheri with a twinkle in her eye.

"Do you happen to know her phone number?" Sheri asks.

"It should be written over there by the computer." Bertie points.

Sheri opens a big ledger by the computer that's covered with dust. "Bertie."

"Yes."

"Do you use this computer?"

"I prefer the ledger," Bertie answers, all prim and proper.

"All right." Sheri digs around in the black book and finds Mrs. Bett's number. She gives her a call. Mrs. Betts answers on the fifth ring.

"Bertie, this better be good. I was in bed watching my stories," Mrs. Betts scolds.

"Hello, Mrs. Betts. This is Sheri again. I'm going to be the new librarian." Sheri can't fight the excitement she feels.

"Oh, dear. That's just wonderful."

"Thank you. Bertie and I are down here at the library, and we were wondering how much is in the library account right now and if there is a deadline on when we have to spend the money."

"Give me a second, dear. I'll get you that answer. I'm just going to lay the phone down."

Minutes go by. Sheri thinks she's been forgotten, but she waits. "We have to spend thirty-five by five p.m. tomorrow."

"Thirty-five hundred," Sheri answers, thinking she can do that easily. Money doesn't go as far as one would think, and she has a lot of improvements in mind.

"No, dear. Thirty-five thousand."

Sheri can hardly believe her ears, but her feet are dancing. "Right. Does the library have a company card? Or does this have to be done by check?"

Mrs. Betts laughs. "We're old, dear, but we're not that

old. We have a company card. You get me the orders, and I'll take care of the rest. I'll call the bank first thing tomorrow, so they know what's coming."

Sheri can't help but grin. "Sounds good to me, Mrs. Betts. Thanks so much," she gushes. She hangs up the phone with a huge grin. Sheri loves spending other people's money. Especially for a good cause. "All right, Bertie. We've got thirty-five thousand dollars to spend by tomorrow evening."

"Oh, dear. I'm glad I brought my sweet tea. It's going to be a long night," Bertie says with a big smile that's full of promise.

Sheri nods her head. "Yes, it is."

Sheri snags the ledger and goes straight to the back page. "I'm using a page for our expense report," Sheri says as she tears out a page to write on.

"Good idea."

"So, I'm thinking bean bags for the kids' room and a few big area rugs. We're going to need paint for all the walls." Sheri stops. "Can we pay the kids for their work from the grant money?"

Bertie nods. "As long as you can provide receipts to prove it, yes."

Sheri taps her pencil and nods her head. "O-kay. We're going to need a new computer system, a Wi-Fi router, a few more computers, some new tables, some partition furniture, some native Alaskan art, and seasonal art projects for children."

"That's quite a list, Sheri," Bertie answers.

"Oh, we're just getting started, Bertie," Sheri says with a grin. "We'll be ready when we have the open house. Just you wait and see."

A tear rolls down Bertie's cheek. "Sheri, you are a godsend. You couldn't have come at a better time."

Sheri smiles back at her. "It's a God thing all around, that's for sure."

"How'd you end up in Alaska?" Bertie asks.

Sheri giggles. "Well, I have a best friend named Jenni," she says and then proceeds to Bertie about how everything came about. Bertie's a great listener.

"Darn that scoundrel, Jerry. Though I can't say I'm sorry you're here." She studies Sheri. "Just give Randall a little time and space. If he's anything like my Henry was, he just needs a little time to come to his senses."

Sheri shifts in her seat beneath Bertie's knowing gaze. "Randall can do what he wants," she mutters. "I need to get through the big things on this expense report so I can get to my favorite part."

"What's that?"

Sheri's eyes light up. She can't help it. "Ordering books."

Bertie laughs. "You really are a true librarian."

Sheri nods her head. "Yes. Well, I grew up an only child. Our house was pretty quiet, but I didn't mind. I've always been a reader. I enjoy it more than watching TV. There's nothing like climbing into a good book."

Bertie taps the table. "The only trouble with too much reading is if we're not careful we forget the joys of social interaction and the necessity of it. Sometimes it's easier to be alone, but what's easiest isn't always what's best."

Sheri sighs as she thinks of Randall and the hurt feelings they've caused one another. "You're probably right about that."

Four hours later, they're up to $34,500.00. Sheri

glances over at Bertie who looks tired. Sheri feels bad. "I'd say it's time for a break. How'd you like some leftover Thanksgiving dinner?"

"Oh, I wouldn't want to impose," Bertie answers with longing in her voice.

Sheri waves her off. "It wouldn't be an imposition. Didn't you just say it's better not to eat alone?"

Bertie laughs. "All right. You don't have to twist my arm. I'd love to." She taps the table. "If you look in that drawer by the computer, you should find the spare key to the library."

Sheri tugs it open and takes out the key. She walks over and checks it in the door. "We're in business."

Bertie gets up slowly from the table and walks to the front door. "Don't forget to turn out the lights," she says.

Sheri rushes around the building with her phone light on. "Got 'em."

40

Randall is digging into his supper when the front door opens and Bertie steps inside. He's more than embarrassed to be caught sitting in his recliner in his long underwear, but he's not getting up now.

Sheri's face flames as if Randall is sitting there naked. She rushes around from behind Bertie and grabs an afghan. Then she snatches his plate.

"That's my food," he says.

Sheri tosses the blanket on him. "Cover up, Randall. You've got company."

He flattens the blanket while he glares up at her. "Bertie's your company," he growls. He's exhausted after spending a whole day in that fire trap of a house. It was for Sheri's benefit even though she doesn't know, which he tries to remind himself, but it's a little hard when she's glaring at him for relaxing in his own home. "Give me back my plate," he grumbles.

Sheri has a murderous glint in her eye. For half a second, he thinks he might be wearing his food. She lowers her hand. "Go ahead. Take it," she says in a saccharine-sweet voice.

Randall reaches for it, still wondering what she's going to do.

"Quit tormenting the man, Sheri, and let him have his dinner," Bertie barks from somewhere behind her.

He gazes up at Sheri, filled with satisfaction. "May I please have my supper?" he says.

"Sure." She lowers the plate before dropping it an inch or two from his lap. The edge of the plate hits him just right, and he coughs.

"Thanks," he groans.

"You're not welcome," she says beneath her breath before she marches past him. "Bertie, I've got just about everything from Thanksgiving Day. I hope you like turkey and potatoes," Sheri sings.

"It all sounds good, Sheri, so long as you don't drop it in my lap too."

Bertie's a little saucy, Randall thinks, but he breathes easy. He's mostly relieved to find he's off her neighborhood-watch naughty list since Sheri put up the Christmas tree.

"I wouldn't do that to you, Bertie," Sheri fires right back.

Seconds later, they're back. Sheri looks less than happy to follow Bertie to the couch. "Thanks for letting me sit out here, Sheri. It's more fun watching the games with others," Bertie crows.

Sheri's scowl slowly disappears. "Sure. I'm happy to," she answers as she hugs the corner of the couch that doesn't allow her to see the TV.

They sit in silence, watching the game. Randall glances

over at Bertie. "So what were you girls up to today?"

"Spending thirty-five thousand dollars," Bertie answers without missing a beat. Her eyes sparkle and shine.

He glances over at Sheri. "Is that right?" he asks.

Sheri nods her head. "Yep. The library has grant money, and some of it has a deadline. It has to be spent by tomorrow or else we lose it."

"So what are you going to do with all that money?"

Sheri taps her toe on the side of the couch while she ignores Jake staring at her food. "Bertie and I decided the library can use an overhaul; we're going to change things around."

Randall laughs at her response, thinking that's all she's done since she moved into his life.

"What's so funny, Randall?"

"Nothing, Sheri. I'm sure you'll be great at it. Shaking things up is your specialty."

Bertie giggles. "Change isn't always a bad thing, Randall." She raises a finger. "You know, Sheri, there's a library van if you don't want to rely on anyone for transportation. You could just drive it."

Fear seizes Randall, and it's ridiculous. He knows he should be happy Sheri won't have to borrow his truck anymore, so why does it bother him so much? "That van's been sitting forever. I'm not sure it's safe to drive," he interjects.

Sheri's eyes narrow. "I'll just have someone check it out. We have the funds to pay for repairs."

Bertie nods her head. "Bill is a mechanic. I'll give him a call first thing tomorrow." She gives Randall a wink. "Bill's wife, Sandy, is a big fan of the library. He'll be happy to."

He glances between the two women. He's not so sure

their friendship is a good thing. "So what are you going to do with all of your free time, Bertie?"

Bertie smiles over at him. "I'm still going to be working at the library, Randall. I just won't get paid."

"That doesn't seem right," he answers.

"It wasn't about the pay. I don't need it. I just want to be useful," Bertie answers.

Now he feels bad. "Bertie and I have lots of plans to bring more patrons into the library. It's going to be great," Sheri answers.

He thinks of Sheri's house project. "Well, it sounds like you've got a project to keep you plenty busy."

Sheri looks a little sneaky. "I have a few projects going to keep me busy, yes."

Bertie stands up. "I expect I'll get on home now."

Sheri gives him a hard look. He starts moving. "Give me a second, Bertie, and I'll follow you home," he suggests.

Bertie giggles. "It's been a long time since a young man followed me home. I'll take it."

He lays his plate down and gathers his afghan around him before he stands up. He shuffles to his bedroom door in his long underwear, feeling like an idiot in his own home, but that's not a new feeling when Sheri's around.

41

Sheri can't help but feel like the days fly by. She's absolutely thrilled with the library's transformation thanks to the grant money, Mrs. Betts, and all her connections. Sheri couldn't be more pleased with how it all turned out. All the books she ordered had arrived, and it's been so much fun dispersing them around the room in all the "New Release" sections she made to display them.

She meanders through the separate sections of adult, YA, and children's books. She couldn't be happier with the pictures Marck painted on the walls. Marck is the local art teacher and an amazing artist.

The Chase Charger football boys did a tremendous job of moving her shelves around and reshelving all the books in record time for the price of plenty of pizza, ice cream, and some spending money. Bertie certainly knows her community.

Cody checked the van over thoroughly. A few parts were replaced, and he was paid for his labor. Marck also repainted the outside of the book van. Randall teased Sheri a little about driving the library van around town, but she doesn't care. If being a quirky librarian is the thing she's known for, she doesn't mind a bit.

It's the end of another day. Sheri's getting ready to close up shop when the bells ring over the door. She peeks around the computer and spies Randall. He hasn't been in the library since everything changed.

He looks all around. "Wow. It's so different."

The tone of his voice makes her feel so proud. "Is it good different?" she asks.

"Yeah. I think I might actually want to come in here," he replies.

She laughs at his answer. "I take it you didn't spend much time in libraries growing up."

He shakes his head. "Not exactly." His eyes meet hers. "I was all boy. Anything that involved mud and dirt and possibly getting hurt, you could count me in."

She giggles. "Sounds about right."

He approaches her desk. "You want to give me a tour?"

How can one question sound so loaded? she wonders.

"Sure." She steps out from behind her desk. He snags her hand. She wants to let go, but she can't. "Well, as you can tell, you entered through the kid's section," she says as they take in all the different colors on the walls.

"Aha, that's why it was so bright and colorful," he observes.

"Yes."

She walks forward and enters the miniature maze. "So this is the young adult section, which is why we have a few computers tucked into corners with the fun furniture." She points to the corners. "And then we have the Zen feeling going on here with like a rug and pillows that they can sit on and such. You know how teenagers prefer the floor half the time anyway."

He nods his head with approval. "This is all very well thought out."

She bristles. "That's my job."

He raises her hand to his lips and kisses her knuckles. "It was a compliment."

She turns away and gives his hand a tug to keep him moving. "So back here is the adult section. We have westerns, mysteries, and nonfiction." She rocks back on her heels and waves her arms. "And that's about it."

Randall looks around. "Doesn't this place have a second floor?"

It's her favorite place in the library, which she isn't ready to share. "Yes."

"Where is it?"

"Let go of my hand," she says.

"If I have to," he says with a dramatic sigh.

She walks to the very back and opens the pale pink door that has "As You Wish" written on it in silver, sparkly cursive. She heads up the narrow staircase. "Am I mistaken, or is there a red carpet painted on these stairs?" he asks.

She smiles. "You are not mistaken."

"What is this?" he asks.

She reaches the top and ducks a little to walk beneath the arched ceilings until she gets to the middle. "This is the romance section." Something changes on his face. She knows exactly why she didn't want to bring him up here.

"Is it?" he asks in a flirty tone of voice.

She avoids looking him in the eye. "Yes, and now you've seen it." She goes to walk past him. "It's more for us women," she mumbles.

His arm wraps around her. He tugs her close. "Did you miss me, Sheri? Because I've missed you." His hot breath falls on her lips.

She can't help but wonder how hard it was for him to admit that. Knowing where things are headed, she tries to cut it off as she leans away from him enough to look up. "There's no mistletoe up here. You can't use that flimsy excuse."

He grins down at her. There's no deterring what he's after. She should be more annoyed, but she's too anxious about what happens next. "What's your excuse for not answering my question?"

She glares up at him. "Yeah, I've missed you, but next time I'll use a fryin' pan. That ought to solve my problem," she growls.

He throws back his head with laughter. "You are some kind of woman." His hands run up and down her arms, muddling her thoughts of resistance. "What am I going to do with you?" he whispers.

"Let me go," she whispers back.

"I don't know if I can," he says in a rugged voice that threatens to sweep her up if she's not careful.

She holds his gaze. "You can't keep what you don't want," she offers as she steps a little closer, knowing how sweet of a kiss is waiting for her.

"I want to stay away from you. Believe me, I've tried." He sounds like he's hurting, and it hurts her too.

She lays a hand on his cheek. "I don't know what to say. I think we want different things."

His eyes burn hotter than she thought they could. "Do we?"

He lowers his lips to hers, and she is lost. The bookshelf

digs into her back, but she hardly feels it as she clings to him. Seconds go by. It feels like forever.

"Hello," Matt's voice comes between them. She turns sideways to escape his grasp.

"Just a second, Matt," Sheri answers as Randall releases the back of her wrinkled shirt from being bunched up in his hand. He jams his hands in his pockets.

What am I doing? he thinks to himself.

She starts down the stairs. Matt looks confused. "Oh, hey, Sheri. I thought Randall was here. I saw his truck out front, so I just thought—"

"Matt," Randall grumps from behind her.

Recognition shows on Matt's face. Sheri blushes from head to toe. "I was just leaving," she says before she turns back to Randall. "Do you mind following me out? I need to lock up."

"Whatever you say," he growls as he marches past her and Matt. The door slams in front of them.

"Don't be too hard on him," Matt says as he walks backward toward the front door with a telling grin.

"Why does everyone keep saying that? I'm not doing anything," she argues.

Matt's only response to her question is to shut the door quietly. She hurries after him, turning her back to flip the lock with the key.

"Darn Randall and his sweet words and kissing lips. Now every time I walk up those steps, I'm going to think of him," she whispers to herself.

42

Randall is still in shock, thinking if someone told him a library would throw him right back to high school, making him feel like some hormonal teenage boy, he would have called them crazy. But that's exactly what happened when Sheri led him up those stairs to the romance section. Everything in that room screamed feminine frills at him: the pink walls, the red-carpeted stairs, and the antique white chairs hidden in the corners. It all got to him. So fast, so hard, and so bad.

Then, to top it off, there she stood in the middle of it with her win-me-over eyes and those lips that beg for his kiss. He knows she's never acted this way with any other guy. Just like he knows no other girl has ever made him feel half of what she does. The worst part is she doesn't even do it on purpose.

She's wearing him down, and he doesn't know what to do about it. Staying away from her doesn't do anything but make him want to be closer. This whole experiment is backfiring on him. Big time. He's got to get her out of his house.

He rolls past her library van as he pulls into the garage. He heads inside. He's hungry and it's supper time. He starts when he spies her sitting on the couch. Lately, she's been holing up in her room, and he tells himself it's better that way.

"There's plenty of soup in the Crock-Pot, and there's bread in the oven," she says.

"I could kiss you right now," he burst out.

"You already did," she answers with a tiny smirk.

This is a new response, he thinks. *At least she didn't mention marriage or commitment about something as small as a kiss.*

"So I did," he answers before he walks to the kitchen to get his supper. He scoops up some soup and walks back out. "So what have you been doing down there in your room?" he asks.

"I'm taking an online class," she answers.

This surprises him. "Oh?"

"Yes. Bertie suggested I take a CMA class to become a certified med aide so I can help out the elderly around town who would pay for a little housekeeping and some help with packing their meds on a weekly or monthly basis," she answers.

"That sounds like a plan," he offers.

"It's better than becoming an exotic dancer," she says dryly.

He chokes a little on his soup. "This is true" is all he can think to say.

"If I have two jobs, maybe I'll be able to save up money to fix up the house I bought," she suggests.

He nods his head and ducks to avoid her gaze. "Yeah, maybe."

"Do you not agree?" she asks in earnest. "Do you think that house is just going to be one big money pit?"

He hopes not. "I, um... Well, there's no hurry. I mean, you're welcome to stay here as long as you need."

She shakes her head. "I know you believe that, but we can't live together. Not if you can't keep your distance. And we don't know where our relationship is going or if we even have one."

He can't believe she's putting it all on him. "You kissed me back."

She lays her spoon down. "You think I don't realize that? I'm just saying I'm not the one chasing you. You're chasing me. And you need to stop."

He knows he shouldn't be so smug about her reaction. "It wouldn't work so well if you didn't like being pursued," he answers before he takes a bite of his soup.

"I didn't ask for it. So don't act like I did," she says while she stares into her soup bowl.

He takes another bite of soup. "Maybe you shouldn't be such a good cook or such a good listener. And maybe you shouldn't wear that flowery perfume you wear and be so happy all the time," he grumps at her. He doesn't like being called out.

She gets up off the couch. "If it bothers you so much, stop eating my food. I made it to be nice."

"Then stop being so nice," he yells at her.

She bustles around in the kitchen. She's retreating, and it's just as well. He can't believe she's letting him have the last word. He must really be getting to her. He smiles at the thought.

There are footsteps behind him. Nope. "If you don't like my humming, plug your ears. And if you don't like my perfume, then stuff cotton balls up your nose. I'm me, Randall. I can't be anyone else," she declares.

He sets his bowl of soup down beside the lamp and steps into her space. He lays a hand against her throat to feel her pulse jump beneath his fingertips. "I wouldn't want you to be anyone else," he whispers as he traces her bottom lip with his thumb.

43

Sheri turns and walks away from Randall as he stares after her. Her frustrations get to her. Only he could tell her the sweetest things she's ever heard and tick her off in the process. He's so maddening. She marches downstairs and FaceTimes Jenni.

"Hey, girl."

Sheri's heart rate slows at the sound of her best friend's voice. "Hey."

"How's your med class coming?"

She smiles. "It's coming. It's nice to have something to focus on."

"Besides the man upstairs," Jenni answers in the way that only a best friend can.

"Exactly."

"What are you going to do?"

She sighs. "I'm counting the days until that New Year's Ball. I'm going to find my Prince Charming. I just know it," she says with all the enthusiasm she can muster. "It has to work."

"Just give him time. He might surprise you," Jenni encourages, and Sheri swears it's like everyone is talking to each other about her and Randall.

"Well, he has 'til Christmas," she grumbles.

"To do what exactly? You can't possibly expect a marriage proposal in less than two months," Jenni counters.

She frowns. "I guess not, but is it too much to expect some sort of grand romantic gesture? Or just, like, an admission of his feelings for me? I need something to give me hope that I'm not just a bit of fun for him."

"Did you tell him that?" Jenni asks with excitement in her tone.

"No. I'm not about to give him an ultimatum," she says, feeling all insecure.

"You expect him to read your mind? He's a man. Trust me. You have to spell things out for them," Jenni states.

She thinks of all their romantic exchanges. "I've given him a piece of my mind, Jenni. Many times."

"Well, then I guess he's been told," Jenni answers as she grimaces before pushing back on her tummy with her hand. "I just know I've got a soccer player in here," she grunts out.

Sheri feels so selfish. "I'm sorry. I've been talking about me for far too long. Are you ready for Christmas?"

"Just about. I think I've got all my shopping done," Jenni says, setting off alarm bells in Sheri's head. She's been so busy with the library and Alaska, she hasn't gotten anything to send to Jenni for Christmas.

"I'm sorry, Jenni, but I've got to go," she blurts.

Jenni laughs. "Brain fart?"

Sheri hates that word, and Jenni knows it. "Yes."

"Love you, sister."

Sheri smiles back at her. "Love you too."

She ends the call and races up the stairs to find Randall sitting in his recliner. "Hey," she says breathlessly.

"What?" he answers her as he stares at the TV.

"I need you to take me Christmas shopping, please," she requests.

He turns in his chair. "I hate shopping."

"Please," she says, hating every minute of it.

"Why?"

"Because I totally spaced, okay? Every year I shop for my best friend, Jenni, and I waited too long to get it done online this year. The presents will never get there by Christmas time. I feel just awful about it." She fights the urge to cry.

"Okay, fine. Don't start crying about Christmas shopping. Seriously."

She wipes a tear from her eye. "I'm sorry. It's just not like me to forget," she says as she stares at the lit-up Christmas tree.

"Don't beat yourself up. You've been very busy," he responds. He gets out of his chair. "Speaking of which, don't forget the log-splitting contest is this coming weekend."

"One week before Christmas?"

"Yep. The Winter Festival is always a week before Christmas. It's tradition. It brings in more tourism that way because families visiting for Christmas usually attend." He gives her a kind smile. "Believe it or not, it makes for some pretty great memories."

She considers this. "That actually makes sense." She

feels bad for asking him to haul her out of town. "Are you sure you don't mind taking me shopping?"

"I said I would, didn't I?" he grumps.

"Yes, you did."

"Then I will. Be ready to leave at 6:00 a.m."

She blinks. "Are you serious?"

"Yes. We're about three hours from Fairbanks."

She's immediately on her phone, googling Fairbanks shopping. Her heart skips a beat. She forgot how much she loves window shopping.

"So they've got like craft stores and clothing stores. Ooh! They have a Barnes and Noble," she squeals.

"Yep," he answers dryly, but there's a smile on his face.

She holds out a hand for him to high-five. He doesn't. She closes her hand into a fist and does a little dance. "I'm so excited. This is going to be so much fun," she exclaims.

"Oh, joy," he answers in a tone that is anything but joyous, but she doesn't care. She's going shopping!

She rushes downstairs and digs through her clothes to decide what to wear. She snags her favorite boots, the ones with the heel. "What am I thinking? We're going to be walking around." She puts them back and goes for her blue tennis shoes that sparkle, which makes her think of her sparkly sweater.

She scurries to the bathroom to wipe down her face and pat it dry before applying her mask. She lays down on her bed and holds her phone above her head to stare up at the websites of the places she's going tomorrow.

"Knock, knock."

She starts as she hears footsteps enter her room. She fights the urge to sit up. Her mask might fall off.

"I can't sit up. I have a mask on," she says as if that is an acceptable answer.

"Can I wear one too?" he teases.

"If you really want to," she says before letting out a giggle.

"I do," he declares in earnest.

"They're in the bathroom in the middle of all my girly stuff," she answers.

Minutes later, he walks out with a mask dangling between two fingers. He sits on the edge of her bed. "Scoot over," he says. She wiggles to the left. "How do I put this on?" he asks.

She turns just slightly to look at him. "You've got it turned around." He adjusts it. "Now just lay it on your face."

He closes his eyes and lays it on his face. "It's cold," he says.

"It's supposed to be," she answers.

"What does it do?"

She rolls her eyes. "It softens my skin."

He chuckles. "So that's where you get your baby-soft skin and your natural glow? From a box?"

She elbows his ribs. "Just be glad God made me with thick skin. You're not being very nice."

He nudges her back. "I'm only hard on people I really like." His hands lace together on his chest. "So what are we searching for tomorrow?"

"I'll know it when I see it."

"Who are you buying for?"

She turns toward him. "I told you, already. Jenni and her family."

His finger traces her upper arm. "Just Jenni's family." She feels like he's searching for information.

"Are you buying me a Christmas present, Randall?" she says with a hint of warning.

"Maybe."

"I don't know what to buy you," she answers.

He chuckles. "I guess you'll figure it out." He goes to sit up. She grabs his arm. "You can't move. The mask isn't done yet."

"How long is this going to take?" he growls.

"Ten minutes," she answers, even though it's usually five.

"I have to lay here for ten minutes," he groans.

"Yep."

He turns toward her, and she turns toward him. He pulls on both sides of his mask to hold it on his face as he leans in to touch his forehead to hers. "You look like an avocado," he whispers.

She laughs. "So do you," she whispers back. He closes his eyes, and she does too. She feels him scoot closer and closer until they're flush against each other from head to toe. Minutes later, he moves just a little.

"Can I remove my mask?" he whispers.

"Yes."

He does, and so does she. He leans in and kisses her. He pulls back. "Your face is slimy."

She giggles. "So is yours. You have to wash your face with warm water. Come on," she says as she heads back to the bathroom and drops her mask in the trash can. He does the same. She wets two washcloths in the sink with hot water. She hands him one before she leans into the mirror to wash her face. He stands behind her but leans around one side to wash his face. It isn't wise, but she turns to face him.

"Do you feel refreshed for our trip tomorrow?" she asks.

He cups her face in his hands before lowering his lips to meet hers. "I'm ready to go."

His words have a double meaning, which she mostly ignores. "I'm tired. 5:00 a.m. is going to come early," she says, as a reminder.

He looks confused. "I said six."

She nods. "I know, but I need time to get ready."

"You kicking me out of your bed, Sheri?" he says in a flirty tone.

"I never invited you into it," she answers quietly.

"Touché." He kisses her softly. "Good night," he whispers into her ear, turning her insides to mush. He walks out of her bathroom without another word.

"Good night," she whispers as he reaches the top of her stairs. It'll be a long time before she gets any sleep.

44

Randall wakes up at 5:40 a.m. and hops in the shower. He's dressed and in the kitchen by 5:55. She looks slightly annoyed but holds up a cup with a lid.

"I got your coffee ready. Here's your breakfast." She holds up a Ziplock baggie. "I toasted a bagel for you. It has cream cheese."

"How thoughtful of you," he grumbles.

Her face falls a little. "Did you change your mind? I think I can get there on my own." Her voice cracks, and he feels bad.

"No. I said I'm going, and I am."

She walks up beside him and snakes an arm through his before stashing two cups of coffee between her other arm and her side. She lifts her face toward his. "Kiss me, darling, and take me shopping," she says all dramatically.

He wakes right up. He doesn't need to be told twice. He leans down and plants one on her. His bagel hits the floor as her hand grabs onto his waist. He sings inside before he pulls away. "Fairbanks, here we come," he says.

STEALING THE GLASS SLIPPER

"Mm-hmm," she answers.

"You dropped your bagel," he muses.

She blinks. "It's your bagel," she says as she squats down to pick it up.

"Come on, lady. This train's leaving the station," he calls from the door to the garage.

"I'm coming." She hurries across the room.

"I'm sorry, Jake. You've got to stay home." Lumbering Jake answers Randall with a snort before heading back to his dog bed. Randall turns to Sheri. "Has he been ou—"

She covers his mouth with the Ziplock bag. "Shhh. Yes, I already took him. Don't say that word."

He can't believe he's smiling while being silenced with plastic at six o'clock in the morning. She shuts the door, and they climb into the truck. The garage door opens.

She glances at her watch. "It's 6:07."

He raises an eyebrow. "And?"

"Just making a note of the time," she chides.

They drive along and sip their coffee. She rattles the bag. "Do you want your bagel?"

He looks over at her. "Did you already eat?"

She nods. "Yep. I'm usually hungry before my feet hit the floor."

"I'm sorry, but I'm not hungry yet," he answers.

"Okay."

The inside of the truck is as quiet as the drive into the city. Right before they get to their destination, sunshine comes in through the window. Her bright green sweater sparkles. "You're wearing a very sparkly sweater."

She grins. "Yep. It matches my sparkly tennis shoes."

He glances at her feet on the floor. "So it does. Where are we going first?"

"I thought I'd go to the bookstore first because it opens first."

"But it's across town," he notes.

Her chin juts just a little. "Nothing else is open."

"It will be by the time we get over there. Do you really want to go Christmas shopping at a bookstore?"

"Would I ask to go there if I didn't want to?" she growls.

"Fine. I'll take you to a bookstore for Christmas shopping."

"Thank you." She bites the words off as they come out of her mouth. He thinks it hardly sounds like a thank-you.

Twenty minutes and many stoplights later, they arrive at Barnes and Noble. She's out of the truck as soon as he puts it in park. He can't help but grin. She is serious about her shopping.

He hops out of the truck and moseys up to the store entrance. *What on earth could be so exciting about a bookstore?* he wonders as he scans the bookstore for Sheri, who isn't hard to find in her bright green sparkly sweater. She stands in the middle of the puzzle section with a black mesh bag over her shoulder. She drops a puzzle in.

"Are you going to follow me around the bookstore?" she asks, making him feel like a scolded schoolboy.

"I guess not." He turns and walks away.

Elvis Presley belts out "Blue Christmas" from the store speakers, and this makes him smile. He wanders over to the calendar section. He hears a big sigh from the other side. "I couldn't see you," he says to a wall of calendars.

"Fine" floats over the tops of pictures of dogs and wolves. He continues his perusal. His gaze stops on a modern-day Cinderella calendar. He stuffs it in the side of his jacket and takes the long way to the front, where he pulls it out in front of the black-haired cashier. His eyes are so dark Randall can't see his pupils. He thinks the guy is a little young to have such a whimsical handlebar mustache. It makes him want to call him Pepé, and he can't believe the clerk has the nerve to give *him* a funny look.

He leans forward. "I'm trying to hide this from someone," he whispers.

The cashier's face lights up like he just woke up. "Security," he says into the microphone.

"Here. I have money."

The desk clerk eyes the bills on the counter. "That's not enough," he barks as he leans back and scans the room. "Sir. Stay right here."

Randall pockets the cash. "Don't be ridiculous. I'm not a threat. Take my credit card. Please," he begs, feeling rather desperate.

He lays his badge on the counter. "I'm not crazy, sir. I'm a fireman," Randall says, even as he realizes he's probably making things worse. He studies the cashier. Between his huge frown and his wide eyes, Randall guesses he's not hearing a word he just said.

The cashier pats Randall's badge. "Sure. I believe you," he answers in a nervous tone that tells Randall he doesn't believe a word from his mouth.

"Just give me my calendar and my credit card, and I'll be out of your mustache—I mean, hair." Randall stuffs his badge back in his pocket. He snatches his card from his fingertips and the plastic bag he holds in the other. "Thank you, sir," he manages as he hurries away, but not before he notices him giving a nod to someone in the store. He follows his gaze and sees the security guard.

So much for purchasing something for Sheri on the down-low. He sighs as he walks out.

He tries not to act like a thief as the security guard trails him. No alarms go off when he passes through the detectors posted in front of the exit doors. He steps outside. The guard keeps coming. He takes a deep breath as he turns to the guard. "Look, sir. I'm with a woman. I was trying to buy her a Christmas present without her knowing. That's it."

The guard smiles at him like he's stupid. "I just wanted to say, sir, thank you for your civic duty."

He blinks. "Excuse me?"

"As a fireman."

"Oh." He exhales. "You're welcome." He relaxes a hair at the security guard's friendly smile.

"Youth these days. They don't pick up on anything subtle. You know what I'm sayin'," the old man tries once more.

Randall nods his head. "Yes. I was just trying to tell him I didn't want anyone to see what I was doing."

The old guard throws his head back and laughs. "Trying to shop with the missus is a headache and a half, but that's marriage. You take the good days with the bad ones."

He wants to correct him, but he doesn't. They're having such a nice conversation.

"I hear ya," he says instead.

The man gets all serious. "Well, I'd better get back to it." He slaps him on the back. "Hope the rest of your day gets better."

"I'm sure it will," he assures him before heading to the truck and hopping in.

His phone goes off. He's missed three phone calls from Sheri. *Uh-oh*, he thinks. "Hello."

"Where are you?"

"I'm in the truck."

"How was I supposed to know that?" she demands.

"You know now," he says as he braces himself for more.

"This is true," she answers right before she hangs up.

"Well, that was anti-climactic," he mutters as he quickly stuffs the calendar beneath his front seat before he hops out to cut her off. She's almost to the truck. "Here, let me get that," he says with as much chivalry as he can muster.

"Where you going to put it?"

"In the lockbox." He points to the box that sits in the truck bed.

"Does it have a lock?" she asks.

"Yes." Randall hops up in the back of the truck and rolls through his keys before finding the tiny one. He uses it to open the padlock. He opens the lid and lays her things inside. "There," he says before he puts the padlock back on and locks it shut. He hops back down, and they climb in the front of the truck. "Now where to?" he asks.

"I think I saw a plaza that had a boutique and a craft store, and then the mall is just a few blocks from there," she answers.

"Where are we eating lunch?"

"I thought I'd just grab something at the plaza. I need most of my time for shopping if you don't mind," she answers.

"All right," he says. Although he does mind—a whole lot. Lunch was about the only thing he was looking forward to.

45

Randall pulls up to the boutique, and Sheri hops out. She just knows she can find a few things for Jenni and her daughter inside. She rushes inside to begin her search for the perfect Christmas present. She's not there but five minutes, and she sees it: a sparkling, siren-red, strapless dress hangs on the back wall. The top is covered in sequins. The belt around the middle is made of glittering silver. The bottom half is layer upon layer of sparkly lace with tulle over a satin skirt. She can't take her eyes off it. It's the perfect ball gown.

A lady approaches. "Do you want to try it on?" she asks.

She shakes her head. "It's probably not my size," she answers, and she wants to cry. She chastises herself for being ridiculous. It is, after all, just a dress.

"Nonsense, darlin'. You never know unless you try." The lady speaks with such high hopes, Sheri can't help but get a little excited. The lady loops an arm through Sheri's. "Come on. Let's give it a try. I just have this feelin'."

She follows the lady to the back of the store. The saleswoman uses a long pole to lift it from the rack. She holds her breath as the dress floats down toward her. Sheri's hand reaches for the hanger. She carries it back to the dressing room. It takes her a minute or two to strip down. She steps into the dress and tugs it up around her top. She reaches back to zip it up, but she can't get it all the way up. "Hello," she calls out.

"Let me help."

She almost shrieks out loud at the sound of Randall's baritone voice right outside her dressing room door. "What are you doing? You're not supposed to be back here. It's a lady's dressing room," she whisper-shouts at him.

A pair of eyes peek over the top of the door. She gives him a drop-dead look, which he pointedly ignores. "There's no sign that says I can't be. Come out already. I want to see you better."

She is so angry. She can't believe he snuck into the women's fitting room. She can't believe he peeked over her door. She also really wants to know if the dress fits. She turns the knob and the door falls open. "Fine," she says as she scoots across the floor toward him. She whips around and sucks it in. "Hurry up and zip it."

His warm breath hits her back. "You could say please," he whispers near her ear.

"Please," she says, but she feels like she's asking for something else.

"That's better." His knuckles brush against her skin as he tugs the zipper up.

She walks toward the center mirror and steps up on the little platform. She can't stop staring. She can't believe it fits. She twirls in front of the three mirrors.

"Are you going to get it, then?" he says, interrupting her

twirling.

She glances down at the price tag. "Not today. I'll have to come back for it another day."

"That's too bad. It looks real nice."

She smiles at her reflection in the mirror. "It's just the dress I need for the New Year's Ball."

"Where you'll meet your prince," he answers in a flat tone.

"Exactly," she sings.

"Well, we can't have you missing that." His quiet voice is devoid of any emotion.

She hears his words, kind of, but she's mostly stuck on the dress. She takes one last long look before she walks back to him. "Time to return to reality," she says as she faces him. She spins around once more. "Unzip me, please."

"As you wish," he whispers against her neck, before laying his lips just there. She shivers a little before she shrugs him off.

"Come on, Randall. Quit playing around." She hates the plea in her voice.

He unzips her. "Why do you think I'm playin' around?" he mutters at her back, but she doesn't answer. She's not up to having another conversation about commitment with him, especially when she's Christmas shopping. And she's not having it in a dressing room either.

"Thanks for helping me with my dress," she calls out from behind the closed door as the dress falls around her and she steps back into her ordinary life.

She leaves the dress on the hanger in the dressing room before she snatches up her purse and walks out. She scans the store for good deals but doesn't see any. She's too distracted by the dress. Sheri knows it's silly, but she can't stay there any longer, or she's going to go and buy that dress, and that's not what she's there for.

She hurries out the front door. She stops a few doors down and texts Randall.

SHERI:

I found a sale in another store. I'll be back soon.

Fortunately for her, there's more than one boutique in the plaza. She forces herself to slow down and go through everything. She finds some souvenirs specific to Alaska to purchase, including a coffee cup. Buying souvenir coffee cups to places they've traveled is something Jenni and she have always done. Naturally, Jenni's bought more than Sheri, but that's all right.

She finds a framed print or two of places in Alaska that are on sale. She spots a wooden willow tree angel that's wearing fireman's gear. She can hardly believe it. She throws that in her mesh shopping bag. She had no idea what to get him. She thinks she found the perfect thing.

She finds some grilling sauce for Justin that has Alaska written on the label. Just before she's done shopping, she spots a glass slipper. Thinking it's perfect for the romance section in the library, she adds it to her shopping bag. She checks out up front and steps outside just in time to almost run into Randall.

"You're already done," he asks with a voice so full of hope.

She hates to burst his bubble, but she still has Christmas shopping to do. She drags her foot back and forth a little on the sidewalk. "I'm done here," she says as she looks off to the side.

"Do you have time for lunch?" he asks in an unexpectant tone, but Sheri notes it's the second or third time he's asked about lunch.

"Sure," she answers, thinking it's the least she can do after he drove her all the way to the city.

"What would you like? There's Thai food. There's Italian," he offers.

"I like Italian."

"Italian it is." They walk back to the truck. He follows her to her side of the truck. "Let me get your door."

She can't help but notice she feels like she's on a date, but she does kind of have her hands full. "Thank you."

"Lunch in a restaurant," he muses. "It's safe to say this is a date," he says, confirming her keen observation. He takes the bags from her hands and climbs up in the back of the truck to put them in the lockbox.

She feels tricked, but it's not a bad feeling. "If I'd known we were on a date, I would have dressed nicer," she protests.

"What's wrong with what you have on?" He looks at her from above in the truck bed.

"I'm wearing tennis shoes."

"They sparkle," he suggests.

"I don't wear tennis shoes on a date."

"Well, you might need them. You tend to enjoy running away from me," he says with an ornery grin.

"Don't make me run away, then," she argues.

"I'll try not to." He hops down to the ground and grabs a hold of her truck door that's half open. "Watch your toes," he says before he shuts the truck door.

Sheri giggles a little to herself. She can't believe she's on a date. It's been so long.

46

Randall glances over at Sheri in her sparkling sweater, but all he can see is that red dress that fits her just a little too perfectly. It's not like she needed to accentuate her womanly figure more than every sweater she wears does. Not that she wears snug sweaters. There's just no hiding her figure.

But that dress sure did her a few favors. He never knew a few freckles on a shoulder could just about push him over the edge. Not to mention the way that stray curl of hers danced over her collarbone. He gets the shivers just thinking about it. He wanted so badly to brush it out of the way just to feel her skin beneath his fingertips that he had to place his lips on her neck for half a second.

"There's no way you're wearing that killer red dress to a ball. I don't want anyone else seeing all that flawless skin on display," he murmurs.

"Excuse me?" Sheri demands.

"Did I say that out loud?" he groans. He glances in her direction. By the look on her face, he knows he did.

"You missed your turn." Her tone is sharp and cutting. He's annoyed with himself for missing an entire parking lot and for being scolded.

"I know that," he answers louder than he intended. "I'm just going to go in the backside of the building. It'll be fine," he says a little quieter. He takes another look in her direction. She looks stricken. "I'm sorry. I didn't mean to yell," he says. "My mind was somewhere else."

"Clearly," she snaps.

"It's just...that dress really got me going."

There, think about that, Sheri. That's what you get for flaunting your beauty in my face, he thinks but does not say.

She lifts her chin. "I told you not to come back there," she announces as if that will erase the image forever stuck in his memory of her looking like a curvy Christmas queen.

He pulls into the parking lot and puts the truck in park. He turns to face her. "I'm sorry I yelled at you. Do you forgive me?"

"Yes," she says in a manner that tells him she does because she has to and not because she wants to, which doesn't make him feel any better.

She opens the door and climbs out. He practically jogs to get in front of her so he can open the next door, which she marches through with not so much as a thank-you or a smile. He frets while he tries to think his way out of being in the doghouse. They wait to be seated, but he may as well be by himself. She heads for the nearest corner opposite of him to sit and wait. The look on her face tells him to back off.

The waiter asks him for a number. "Two," he answers as he points in her direction. "Bar or a booth?" he asks.

"Which is quicker?" he asks.

"You can come to the bar now," the waiter suggests.

"I'll take it," he says.

He waits for her to walk in front of him, but she refuses, and so he follows along behind the waiter. They climb up on the barstools to wait.

"Can I get you a drink?" the bartender asks.

"I'll take a beer," he says before he turns to her. "What would you like?"

"A virgin frozen strawberry margarita," she replies.

The bartender gives her a measured look. Randall says nothing.

"I wanted a booth," she says.

"You should have said something," he mutters.

"I'm saying it now," she demands.

He sighs. "Well, now is a little too late."

He whips two menus from the wall beside him and hands one to her. "The faster you order, the faster this date will be over," he says between gritted teeth and regretting the very moment they set foot inside together.

Her lip quivers. "Fine."

He scans the menu until he finds the lasagna. "Are you ready to order?"

She glares at him over her menu. "I just sat down."

"Tell me when you are ready, then," he says as gently as possible, though he's seconds away from storming out the nearest exit.

"Don't worry. I will. Otherwise, I may not get to eat," she snaps.

The same waiter happens by. He grabs a hold of his arm. "Hey, sir. If a booth opens, is there any chance we can have one? My date just informed me she'd rather have a booth than the bar."

The waiter gives him a dirty look. "I'll do my best."

"Thanks." He forces a smile. Between Sheri being hacked off at him for not getting her a booth and the waiter staring him down for making a simple request, he's regretting this whole date idea.

The bartender approaches. "Can I take your order?"

"Um, yes. I'd like the lasagna please." He turns to her. "What would you like?"

She drags her eyes from the menu. "If I have to order now, I guess I'll have the smallest sample platter, please."

"Got it." The bartender flips the menus shut and walks away. He sips his beer.

"She didn't bring my drink," she says.

"I'm sure she will."

"You got yours right away," she says with a pout.

"Yeah, 'cause it's in a bottle."

Minutes drag by. He feels her giving him looks, like she's waiting for something, but what that is, he has no idea, and he's past the point of trying to figure it out. Her drink finally shows up, along with their food.

They're at least halfway done when the waiter returns. "I have a booth now."

He has no clue what to do. "That'd be great," he answers. He grabs his beer and his plate. "Come on. Let's go."

She stares him down. "I can't carry all this."

He lays down his plate and crams his beer between his elbow and his side. He grabs her drink and transfers it to his hand before he grabs up his plate again. "All right. Let's go."

He follows along behind the waiter and ignores the

looks of the other diners. They sit down in the booth. She glares at him.

"What'd I do now? You wanted a booth. We have a booth," he says as he scoots her drink in front of her plate.

She leans back in the booth. "Is this how you are on all your dates?"

He snorts. "Most of my dates aren't this demanding."

She sniffs. "So now I'm demanding."

He takes a deep breath and exhales slowly. "I apologized for yelling at you. If you didn't want to come in here with me you should have said so instead of hugging the back wall like I was going to attack you in public."

She looks a little sorry. "I don't like being yelled at for a mistake you made. I won't tolerate it."

He leans forward from his side of the table. "I already told you I missed my turn because you make me nervous. I can't keep my head around you. Isn't that enough of an explanation?"

She slides to the end of the booth. "Maybe I should leave, then."

"No. I don't want you to leave," he answers. "Please sit down and enjoy your meal." She scoots back in the booth and takes a bite of her food.

"How is it?"

"It's fine," she says, and that's the last word he gets from her during the entire meal. He can't believe he misses her yakking, but he feels so shut out.

"Where are we headed to next?" he asks as they walk out to the truck.

"I thought I'd go to the big craft store if that's not too much to ask."

"Count me out," he jokes.

"I didn't say you had to go in," she all but snarls.

"You know what? I'll just not say anything," he responds in kind.

"Fine by me," she retorts.

"You could do the same," he says before immediately wishing he could keep his mouth shut.

"And hope you know when you miss your next turn? I don't think so," she responds.

He holds his tongue and decides he will count to a thousand if he has to, but he's not saying one more word. Fortunately for him, the craft store's sign is big and bright, and it breaks through the mess of red that he sees. No one makes him as mad as Sheri.

He flips on his turn signal and whips into the parking lot. He drives her straight by the front door. "Why don't you hop out?"

She looks worried. "Where you going?"

"Not far. Just text me when you're done."

"Fine."

Randall waits until her hand is on the store door before he drives off. He knows where he's going. He's going to get that dress, which thankfully doesn't take long. He heads back down the highway but stops when he spots a giant Christmas tree. "That's just the thing she would love," he muses. He pulls into the parking lot and gets out. It reads, "Come join us for caroling at 5:30 p.m."

He notes the time on his watch. It's already 2:30. Surely, he can keep her in town for another three hours.

47

Sheri is thoroughly annoyed that she's in one of her most favorite places in the world, the craft aisle, and all she can think of is Randall, who tries her patience faster than anyone she knows.

There are times she thinks she could really fall for him, like when he brings out a table from the garage for company he didn't want on Thanksgiving Day, or when he takes her face in his hands so gentle and kind and lays the softest of kisses on her lips, making her feel like a fragile flower. She smiles at the thought, but then she frowns when she recalls the other side of him, the side that has to have the last word, the side that yells at her when all she was trying to do was let him know he missed a turn.

She pushes her cart through the craft store, trying to focus on what she's after, waiting for a craft idea to come to her, but her focus remains on him. "That's it! I've got to make him something for letting me stay as his houseguest. That'll get him out of my head," she says as she notices the lady a little ways down moving quickly away.

She clamps her mouth shut and keeps her thoughts inside her head. She decides to make him a wreath, but it will be like a manly wreath. She warms to the idea as she walks along. It will have tools, fishing lures, and whatever else she can find that screams male, because he is all these things and more.

There's a lot to this arts and crafts store, but she knows what she's looking for. Two hours later, she's fairly satisfied she's covered every inch of the store with her eye for bargains. She wheels a mostly full cart to the front of the store and texts Randall.

SHERI:

Checking out at the craft store.

RANDALL:

You're still in the same store?

SHERI:

I got stuck in the button aisle. 😊

RANDALL:

That doesn't even deserve an answer.

She shoves her phone in her pocket when she realizes she's holding up the checkout line. "Are you ready?" The clerk raises an eyebrow.

"Yes, please," she says.

Fifteen minutes later, she wheels her cart of treasures through the automatic doors to the waiting area behind the glass windows. She spies his truck parked near the exit. She walks toward him and tries to ignore her butterflies when she sees his gloved hand sticking out of his cracked window. She spies his charcoal gray Carhart stocking hat.

He turns in her direction and gives her a brown-eyed wink. "Looks like you bought out the store."

She shrugs. "Maybe."

He climbs out of his truck. "I'll hop up there and you can hand me your bags."

"All right."

It takes a few seconds to get the lock open. He reaches down. "Hand me a bag." It doesn't take long for him to load all six bags in the lockbox. He snaps it shut and puts the padlock back in place. "Where to now?"

"I think I might be done," she says with surprise.

He looks worried. "I, um, found a store I think you might enjoy."

"Oh, yeah?"

"Yeah. You want to give it a try?" She can't believe he's asking her to go to another store or how worried he looks while he waits for her to answer.

"Sure."

His grin is so disarming. Sheri wants to say more to make him relax. "Thanks for today," she says before she clears her throat. "All of it."

"You'd better get in the truck before you catch cold" is his reply, and so she does.

"So how did you find this store?" she asks.

He turns to her with a sheepish grin. "I took a few wrong turns."

She grins and ducks her head to the side. "You don't say."

It isn't long before they pull up to a tiny storefront. The awning is bright red. The door has a snow-covered green Christmas tree painted on it. She loves it. A few golden bells lie at the foot of the tree. She opens the frosted glass door and steps inside. Every inch of the walls is covered in ornaments from the ceiling to the floor, and that's just the beginning. Scattered throughout the store are trees of all colors, shapes, and sizes, covered with more ornaments.

She finds a St. Bernard beneath a tree and picks it up to show him. "Look here. It's Jake."

His hand covers hers. "Yes, it sure is."

She resumes her searching through all the ornaments, and that's when she spots one of Sophia Loren and Walter Matthau staring each other down, like in *Grumpier Old Men*. She snatches it up. "Look, Randall. It's us."

He laughs out loud. "That's perfect."

They walk through the entire store. She ends up buying more ornaments than she planned, but each discovery is more exciting than the last. She discovers the perfect cheese-head ornament for Justin, who is a huge Green Bay Packers fan. She buys a pile-of-books ornament for Bertie, the librarian. There's a sparkly green ornament shaped like a dollar sign for Mrs. Betts, the accountant. He buys her a mason jar ornament since she's his canner.

They check out and step outside. He glances at his watch. "Oh, shoot. We've got to go now." He grabs her elbow and tugs her toward the truck.

"What's the big hurry?" She wrenches her elbow from his grasp. "I can get in the truck myself."

He yanks open her door and shoves her inside. "I know, but this is the best part of our date, trust me. You're going to love it."

He sounds so eager to please that she can't stay mad at him. She moves her feet right before he slams the door shut.

He races around to the other side and hops in. They

start down the road. "Where was it? Where was it?" he mutters as his eyes scan the sides of the street.

A tall, lit-up Christmas tree catches her eye. "Oh, goodness. Look at that tree."

He grins and turns on his blinker. "You found what I was looking for." They wait for traffic and turn into a parking lot. "Wait for me," he says right before he gets out and comes around to open her door.

She climbs out and walks toward the carolers who surround the tree. Her heart swells with joy.

He links his arm through hers and pulls her close. "I thought you'd enjoy some singing tonight," he whispers in her ear.

They step into the crowd. Sheri sings along with the girl next to her, who shares her music sheet. She lets herself get lost in memories of Christmas past as she stares up at the star at the top of the tree and the tinsel drizzling off the branches, reminding her of her childhood days with Mom and Dad and all the fun they had decorating the tree each year. Dad would always get out the ladder so she could climb to the very top to put the star on each year.

Tears of joy roll down her cheeks as her eyes roam over the rosy cheeks of the little ones standing in the front row. Their eyes shine bright. They sing unabashedly with their whole beings, and their songs fill the night sky. Colorful hats and scarves adorn the harmonious crowd of merry carolers. It's a perfect night.

48

Someone in the crowd calls out "last song" and they all join hands as they sing "Silent Night." Even Randall sings along. Sheri takes his hand on the way back to the truck parked in the corner of the lot. He opens the door, and she crawls in.

"Thanks for the perfect end to a date, Randall," she says with a small smile, but there's a tremble in her voice.

He pulls up beneath a light in the parking lot to put it in park. He's not sure how he feels when he sees the tears running down her cheeks. It shakes him up inside more than he thought it would.

"I'm sorry for taking you here. I thought you would like it. The last thing I want do is make you cry," he says in a gravelly voice heavy with emotion.

"I know," she says as she wipes at her tears, but they just keep coming. "I loved every second of it. Honest," she says as she turns away from him to stare out the window. "It just brought back a lot of memories. That's all."

"So you're not sad," he says. "I mean, I didn't make you sad?"

She shakes her head. "I'm not sad. I'm sentimental. These are happy tears," she says.

"Oh." He closes her door as quietly as he can, thinking he'll never understand women.

He walks slowly to the other side and hops in. They stare out the front windshield at the Christmas tree for a few seconds. "I love Christmas time." She all but sighs the words.

He snorts. "I guess. It seems like all everybody does is worry about how to buy the perfect gift and not go broke."

She laughs a little. "It can feel that way. But Christmas is the season of giving, and I love to give. It's so fun making someone smile."

He looks over at her. "Are you ready to go home? I imagine Jake is about to bust."

Worry is written all over her face. "Oh, dear. Will he be all right?"

He nods. "Yeah. If he absolutely has to get out, he can."

"How's that?"

He taps a finger on the steering wheel. "There's a dog door in the laundry room where he sleeps."

She doesn't answer. She looks lost in thought.

"What you thinking about over there?"

She undoes her seat belt and scoots up next to him. She puts on the middle seat belt and lays her head on his shoulder. "I'm thinking about the red dress." She sounds so sad that he almost starts laughing, but he doesn't dare.

He throws an arm around her and pats her shoulder instead. "Oh, honey. It's just a dress."

She buries her nose in his shirt a little. "I know," she whimpers against his sleeve.

He reaches out and turns on the radio. "Feliz Navidad" pours out of it. She reaches out to turn the station, but he stops her. "Leave it," he says.

She turns to look at him. "You don't like Christmas music on the radio."

He shrugs. "You like it."

She leans back in the seat but she sits up a little straighter. "I don't want you to be miserable for the next three hours."

"I won't be. It's fine. Really. Please don't make this *a thing*," he pleads.

Her little nose lifts. "What does that mean?" she responds, her voice hardening.

"It means nothing, okay? Forget whatever I said. Please. I just want to enjoy the ride home. Play whatever music you like." He's backpedaling so fast that he's surprised his chain doesn't fall off. As it is, his pride went out the window at mile marker 337, which was a wink in his high beams.

She shrugs his arm from her shoulder and turns on him. "Did you like any of the Christmas songs we sang tonight?"

He chews on his lip. "I liked singing with you."

"That's not what I asked."

His thumb taps faster on the steering wheel. His mind spins as fast as his tires as he tries to think of the right answer. "Would you feel better if I lied to you about enjoying singing Christmas songs, or would you feel better if I tried to like one because you do, even though they're not my favorite?"

"What do you like to sing?" she challenges.

He grits his teeth. "Maybe I don't like singing in crowds. Maybe I prefer singing by myself, okay?"

She exhales slowly and snuggles into him once more, and he fights the urge to get away from her. "I'm sorry. I really enjoyed tonight."

"For how long" goes off in his head like a siren, but he doesn't say that either. "I'll take what I can get," he says as he wraps his arm around her once again for a side hug.

They ride along in the dark, listening to Christmas songs, and he finds himself humming along with her.

49

Randall shakes Sheri. "We're home," he growls in her face.

She lifts her head from his shoulder. "I'm so sorry. Why didn't you wake me?"

He reaches out and turns down the radio that's blaring a Christmas song. "I figured you were tired. Besides, your terrible Christmas music kept me awake."

She scoots across the seat toward the door. "At least let me get my bags out."

He grabs her hand and gives it a tug. "Don't you worry about that. Just go inside. There's no point in both of us being cold. I'll get it after I pull into the garage."

She thinks he's hiding something because he's talking awfully fast, but she's too tired to argue. "Okay, thanks." She goes to get out.

"Where are you going? Why don't you wait to walk through the garage into the house?" he grumps.

She leans against the door. "I'm sorry. I thought you told me we were home." She closes her eyes again.

Seconds later, he gives her a nudge. "Now you can get out."

She stumbles through the garage and up into the house. Jake greets her. "Hey, Jakey," she says as she leans over to pet him. His big tail wags back and forth.

"Excuse me," Randall says.

She moves to the side. He walks by with a bunch of bags, which he lays on the island in the middle of the kitchen. She can't wait to dig into everything. He stops mid-step and gives her a look. "Don't even think of wrapping these presents tonight. You've got the Winter Festival tomorrow. It's going to be a full day."

She smacks her forehead. "Oh, yeah. I've got to meet Bertie at the library first thing. We're having contests for the kids."

He wrinkles his nose. "Don't tell me...more gingerbread houses. I thought your secret frosting was just between us."

She giggles. "Ha, ha. Very funny. No, we're not doing gingerbread houses. We're frosting sugar cookies."

He wipes a hand across his forehead. "Phew." He throws a hand on his hip. "Well, don't forget: the berry cobbler contest is at eleven, the dog sled races start at one, and the golden ax contest is at three. There will be vendors set up all over too, but those are the three main events. Don't forget to register for your assigned number for the log-splitting contest. You can't compete without one."

She looks longingly at her shopping bags. She really wanted to get started on everything tonight while the ideas were fresh in her mind, but he's right. She won't be worth anything if she doesn't get some sleep. "I'll just take them downstairs, and then I'll leave them alone," she says as she stares at them.

"Hold up a minute. There's a few more in the truck."

He heads back outside. She sits down on a kitchen barstool to wait. It isn't long before he's back again.

"That's the end of it," he says as he lays more bags on the floor at her feet.

"Thanks."

He grins down at her. "You sure know how to shut down a store."

She glances up at him. "I found the sales. I didn't break the bank."

He shakes his head in disbelief. "If you say so."

She starts draping plastic shopping bags over her wrists. She somehow manages to get them all on both arms. She heads for the steps.

"Don't let your haul haul you down the stairs," he calls out.

"You're so funny," she yells back at him right as she almost trips over the last two steps. She grips the railing and whispers a prayer of thanks that she didn't face plant or twist an ankle.

She walks far enough into the room to set all her bags down before she kicks off her shoes and sheds her sweater. Her T-shirt clings to her. She's full of static. She changes into some jammy pants and a hoodie before she gets rid of her bra.

"Ah, I'm finally home," she says as she flops down in bed. She yanks some covers over her head and closes her eyes. She tosses and turns just a little. She smells Randall as she lays her cheek on the empty pillow beside her. She holds it close as she drifts off to dream.

———

Sheri's alarm wakes her up, and she turns it off. She'd love to sleep a few more hours, but then she thinks of Bertie. She can't leave her in a lurch at the library with all that sugar and a bunch of children. She hops out of bed, showers in ten, and steps into her favorite pair of black jeggings. She tugs on a bright red cotton tee. It's super soft. She loves it. She reaches for the green plaid flannel and throws it on next. She buttons it three-fourths of the way up. She snags her red-and-white striped fuzzy Christmas socks and pulls them over her cold feet. They're so cozy and warm. Lastly, she steps into her Timberlands. She does a few arm stretches and decides she's as ready as she's going to be for some serious ax swinging later on.

She grabs her red stocking hat on the way up the steps. She steps into the kitchen. He spins around with a grin on his face. "I warmed up your van for you."

"Thank you," she answers.

He holds up a thermos. "And I made you some hot apple cider with a cinnamon stick. I added a little honey too. It's good for sore throats, or whatever, from the cold."

"Gee, you sure went to a lot of trouble for one day." She doesn't know what to say; she didn't do anything for him.

"I did it for you," he offers.

"And I said thank you," she answers again, feeling inadequate. She points up at the kitchen clock. "I'd better get going. I don't want Bertie to wait on me." She reaches for the apple cider, but he holds it up high. She doesn't know what he's playing at, but she's got no patience for games. "You going to give it to me or not?"

"May I have a thank-you kiss?" he asks.

She grips his chin with her hand and stands on tiptoe to kiss his cheek. "There. Please give me my apple cider." He lowers his hand. She takes the cup from him. "Thanks," she says. He doesn't answer, and so she turns to walk away.

He smacks her on the butt. "See you on the field, champ. Bring your ax," he growls.

She rubs her offended bum. "That hurt."

"Walk it off," he says, as bossy as a coach.

"Fine. I will," she responds.

"That's more like it," he says.

"I know," she calls out as she opens the front outside door.

"So do I," he yells across the house as he shuts the heavy inside door behind her.

"Darn man can't keep his mouth shut," Sheri says to no one but the frosty air that hits her in the face. She clamps her mouth shut and practices breathing through her nose to keep her throat from getting potential frostbite. "If Randall and his incessant need to have the last word doesn't do me in, these Alaskan winters might," she grumps as she climbs into her warm van.

50

"Sheesh. That woman can try the patience of a saint." His words fill up the quiet kitchen. He gives a little whistle. "Come on, Jake. Let's go check out the town." He snags Jake's Christmas lei. The kids love it when they see Jake plodding along with the bright red wreath around his neck, and Jake's a good sport about it.

Despite his better judgment, Randall heads straight for the library, telling himself it's on the way to everything else. He hops out of the truck and goes around to open the door for Jake. Her van pulls up beside him.

"Are you following me?" She doesn't exactly sound pleased.

The library door flies open. "Oh, good. You're both here. I could use a little help," Bertie scolds.

He forgets all about Sheri and her grumpies as he heads toward Bertie. "Morning, Bertie. How are you?"

"I'm freezing cold, you dimwit. Get inside. You're letting all the warm air out." He walks past her. Sheri's close behind. "I need an adult at each table, and there are three tables and three of us, so it's just right." Bertie holds her cell phone out like it's a prize. "Did you see the event on the Whova?"

"What's that now," he answers, though he's almost afraid to ask. He never knows what Bertie's going to say.

"It's an app, ya nut. You download it for free, and it tells you everything about what's happening today. It's quite handy. It's an all-in-one platform. Any picture I take will automatically be shared on the site for this event, and any vendor here will have their information on the site too."

"I gave you your Christmas tree, Bertie. That's all you're getting from me." Randall can't resist putting his two cents in.

He glances at Bertie to see if she heard him. "Now, Randall. This app is user-friendly, and it allows you to interact with everyone at the event today instantaneously. It's simply wonderful." Bertie's eyes sparkle and shine.

He nods his head, which is all he's capable of doing when Bertie starts making suggestions, a thing she does quite often. "I'll, um, think about it." He pauses. "What is it I'm doing again?"

She smacks his arm. "You're frosting cookies with little children, Randall. You ought to fit right in."

He stops walking. "Wait a minute. You want me to man a table full of children, cookies, and frosting?"

Bertie smiles up at him. "That's right. All you have to do is be sure they don't poke each other in the eye with a table knife, and make sure no one eats all the frosting. We don't want any double-dippers, especially with their fingers."

"I'll do my best, Bertie," he replies.

Bertie eyes Jake. "Is Jake going to be a problem?"

He looks down at Jake laying on the floor. "Define problem."

"Will he be eating cookies off the tables? I don't have a lot of extras." Bertie's eyes flash with warning.

He breathes a sigh of relief. "He doesn't eat what isn't offered to him."

She gives him a nod. "He can stay."

Great, Randall thinks when he realizes he has no excuse to leave. "Well, I guess I'll wing it."

Bertie's at his elbow, which she clutches onto. "You'll do better than that, mister. You've got to keep an eye on everyone at your table. Make sure they all know they get one cookie to decorate and that they have to share the frosting. And *no* food wars. I won't have cookies flying across the room. This *is* a library."

He gives Sheri a look of warning over Bertie's head. "Did you hear that? Bertie says you can't throw cookies at me."

She rolls her eyes. "Like I would do that. I think I know how to behave like an adult, unlike some people I know." She gives him the stink eye.

As if cued, a bunch of children come scurrying in the front door. Bertie claps her hands. They all stop, like magic. "All right. Now you all know the rules. Repeat after me." She puts her hands to her eyes like glasses. "Look."

They mimic her movements. "Look," they all say.

She cups a hand to one ear. "Listen."

They do the same. "Listen."

She raises a pointer finger. "Be patient and wait your turn."

They raise their tiny fingers. "Be patient and wait your turn."

She claps her hands again. "Very good. Now, who's ready to frost a Christmas cookie?"

All their hands raise at once, but Randall gives them credit. They're all quiet.

Bertie points to the far wall. "Everybody line up." She walks along, numbering them from one to three. "All the ones go with Randall."

He raises his hand and one finger.

"All the twos follow Sheri."

She raises her hand with two fingers.

"All the threes follow me."

"I'm a three," a blonde-haired girl shrieks and jumps up and down, clapping her hands.

Randall hovers over his table. He watches seven hands dip popsicle sticks into three cups of frosting all at the same time. It is a daunting task.

"Oh, I almost forgot," Bertie calls out. "Once you have your cookie frosted, there are candy beads to decorate with too, but you must use toothpicks and run through the hole in the middle to pick them up to put them on your cookie so you don't get your fingers in the frosting," she says with a wink.

It isn't long until Randall spies a bunch of pink tongues hanging out to different sides of their mouths as the children try to get the toothpick in the itty-bitty hole. *Kudos to Bertie for being so clever,* he thinks. He was wondering how she was going to stretch frosting-a-single-cookie out. Everyone uses a good half hour for decorating.

"Okay. Now comes the moment of truth. Each table will be judged for the best cookie," Bertie announces.

Bertie, Sheri, and Randall circle the tables like dessert experts. Sheri comments here and there on color, bead choice, and design, getting lots of little smiles. Randall has no idea what he's doing, so he adds a little here and there to Sheri's comments. Eventually, Bertie and Sheri come to a conclusion for each table, and the winners are announced. Bertie hands out three five-dollar bills. It's hard for him to watch the rest of them not receive any reward. He feels kind of cruel. They all worked so hard.

"And now, you may *all* eat your cookies," Bertie says as she throws her hands in the air.

A collective "yay" rings through the library. They're all smiles as they pick up their cookies, the contest part forgotten. Randall decides Christmas isn't so bad after all.

51

Sheri can't believe how Randall just jumped right in and helped with the cookie contest. At first she was annoyed that he followed her to the library. But she couldn't help but notice he's a natural with children, even if he likes to pretend that he's not. She saw the look on his face when there were some sad faces from those who didn't win. Randall was definitely sympathizing with them. And then when they all ate their cookies, she swore Randall's face was happy as the rest of them, and he didn't even get a cookie.

They help Bertie clean up as much as they can before she shoos them out the door. "Go on now. Go enjoy the Winter Festival. Let me have my peace and quiet."

He puts a hand on the small of Sheri's back to get her to go outside, and she leans away from him. She can't take all this closeness. Not when she's got the New Year's Eve ball in her mind and she has no idea where their relationship is going.

"Where are we going?" she asks.

He shrugs. "I was on my way to the cobbler-eating contest."

"Lead the way," she says, and they walk down the sidewalk in silence. She can't help but feel cheery at the number of people milling around. She sees a number of Christmas sweaters. It's all so festive.

"Hey, guys." She turns at the sound of Matt's voice.

"Hey, Matt," she says with a smile.

"Where you going?"

"To the cobbler-eating contest. You want to go?" she invites him. The three of them walk along. Randall acts more sullen with every step.

"The contest sounds like fun." Matt's words break the awkward silence.

"It isn't really," Randall grumps.

Sheri nudges him playfully to try to lighten things up, but he backs away from her. "You're the one who suggested it," she teases.

"You don't have to go." He's acting so wounded. Sheri can't believe how childish he's being.

"I want to. I wouldn't want to miss out on any part of the festival." Sheri forces a brightness to her tone, even though Randall's doing his best to stomp out any Christmas cheer.

"Suit yourself," he states.

They approach the community building. Randall opens the door. They head inside, and he walks behind them. She doesn't turn around to check.

She spies the sign for the contest on the outside of a set of double doors. "Come on, Matt. It's in here," she says before she pulls on the handle.

They step inside. It's already dark. She finds a few

chairs, and they sit down. It's like an old theater. There's a stage up front, and the contestants sit at a long table. They wear wide, white bibs. They sit under the spotlight.

A man walks on stage. "You all know the rules. No using your hands. You are to eat as much cobbler as you can in fifteen minutes. You will not be brought a new dish of cobbler until your current dish is empty."

She counts six contestants. One of them is Cheryl. The other five are men of different ages, heights, and weights. Six kids carry out one pie plate a piece.

"When the bell rings, you may start. When the bell rings again, you have to stop." The man turns away from the audience to face the contestants. "Are you all ready?"

The contestants nod. The man raises a big bell and gives it a ring.

Faces fly into the cobbler, and soon everyone's face is covered in dark purple filling of some sort. She can't decide if it's fascinating or grotesque. The minutes drag by. She looks off to the side a few times. She buries her face in Matt's shoulder while they laugh silently together, because she can't watch. It's disturbing, especially when a young man in the middle leans over and barfs all over the floor. She almost loses it, but she has to stay to see who wins. She's committed.

Thankfully, not long after that, the bell rings a second time. Cheryl did a pretty good job of putting away four and a half pie pans of cobbler, but the little bald man at the end is the clear winner. He has eight empty pans. He stands up. Purple cobbler filling drips from his chin. He raises his hand in the air. The man in the microphone stands off to the side, holding out his microphone. "This is your sixth year as

Cobbler Gobbler Champion. Do you think you'll be back next year?"

"Yes. I just love Alaskan berry cobbler," the tiny man announces while purple goo drips on the table.

"Thanks, Glenn." The announcer hands him another pie. "Here is your reward, a family-sized berry cobbler along with a coupon for all-you-can-eat berry cobbler for one year at The Cobbler Cafe. Don't eat that all in one setting now," he jokes.

Glenn laughs. "I could, you know."

"I've had enough of this." She hears Randall's voice behind her. She and Matt follow him out of the auditorium.

"What's next?" she asks.

"I thought I'd get some food to eat," Matt says.

"That sounds good," she answers. She turns to Randall. "Are you hungry?"

He snorts. "After watching all that up onstage? Not really."

She takes a page from Randall's book. "Suit yourself."

He takes her by the elbow. "Can I talk to you?"

She nods. "Of course."

"Alone."

"Now?" *What is going on?* she wonders.

"Yes."

She turns to Matt. "Excuse me for a second, please."

Matt smiles knowingly at her and Randall. "Sure."

She lets Randall drag her into a small side hallway. "What is wrong with you?" she whisper-shouts at him.

"Did yesterday mean anything to you?" he demands.

She's so confused. "Of course, it did. It was very nice. What's that got to do with anything?"

"Then why are you running around with Matt today and shoving your face in *his* jacket?"

She fights the urge to laugh out loud. "You are unbelievable. Matt is my friend. I can walk around with him if I want to. If he were a woman, you wouldn't care a whit."

"Of course not," he says in disbelief.

"Then what's the problem?" she demands.

He stares at the floor. "I thought you liked me."

She lays a hand on his arm. "I do like you."

"Then why do you pull away from me?" he pouts.

She scoffs. "You really have to ask me that? It's you who can't decide how you feel about me," she says a little too loudly, but she's past the point of caring.

"I don't know. All I know is I don't want to see you going around with other guys."

She steps closer to him and gets in his face. He makes her so angry. "Randall."

"Yeah," he answers as his brown eyes meet hers.

"You're a grown man, and I'm a grown woman. When you decide if you want a *real* relationship that means something, let me know. A few kisses here and there were fun, but I'm worth more than just a good time. I'm not going to sit around waiting for you to make up your mind. I don't have time for that." With that, she spins on her heel and marches out to meet Matt. "Come on, Matt. Let's go have some lunch. I've worked up an appetite."

52

Randall feels a little shell-shocked after Sheri dressed him down. When that feeling passes, he's just angry. He sits in his truck, fuming. "If she thinks she can coerce me into walking her down the aisle, she's got another thing coming. I don't know who she thinks she is, accusing me of not being a grown man. I have a job, and it's an honorable one. I save lives. I don't need a boring librarian who hangs out with books all day telling me how to live my life." He speaks into his hands with his head ducked, feeling like an idiot. "Forget her and Matt. I'm not sitting in my truck pining over a woman."

He hops out and heads in the opposite direction of Sheri and Matt, who happily chat with their heads together as they head off to a hot dog stand to spread more Christmas cheer. Well, bah humbug on them, Randall decides. He's going for some nachos and a funnel cake. He'll just wait for Sheri to come along and scold him about eating too much sugar and salt, as he's sure she's bound to do. The woman never keeps her opinions to herself. He shakes his head as if to clear it of all thoughts of Sheri.

Halfway through his nachos and funnel cake, he wishes he hadn't combined the two, and she's nowhere to be found. He thinks his plan may have backfired. Big time. He glances at his watch. "Dang it." He sees it's about ten minutes before the dog sled race starts. He always sees the beginning, but he doesn't think he's going to this year. "Darn Sheri and her confusing ways. This is all her fault," he mutters and clamps his mouth shut when a kid standing beside him gives him a funny look.

He hears the sound of the gun in the distance. He runs off the path before the dog sleds come around the corner, racing by where he just stood. He spies her off in the distance in her bright red hat and boots. She's jumping up and down, clapping her hands. She clutches onto Matt. *The traitor.* He said he was grieving, but from where Randall stands, Matt looks like he's doing pretty well. Randall immediately feels bad for his terrible thoughts.

"I'm sorry," he mutters to no one in particular.

He takes another bite of funnel cake and feels a bit ridiculous while he looks on at Matt and Sheri, who are twenty feet away. All he has to do is walk over to them, but he refuses. They look like they're having all kinds of fun by themselves, he reasons. Matt says something, and Sheri throws her head back with laughter. She says something to him, and he leans over to the side and laughs into his hand. Randall decides he may as well have stayed home, and he knows one thing: he's showing no mercy, and he's winning that log-splitting contest. He doesn't care if he won the previous three years before. He's winning again.

Seventeen minutes later, the dogs return at full speed,

and a team crosses the finish line. Everyone claps and cheers for the dogs; but Randall can't take his eyes off Sheri, who is right in there with them. She whips out her phone and takes a few pictures of the dogs from a distance. She leans into Matt and takes a selfie with him. His chest hurts when he realizes she's never taken a selfie with him. He turns away and heads toward the area where the logs are. He can't believe how much it hurt to see her taking that picture with Matt.

He doesn't know what all this means. All he knows is he doesn't like it. He looks down at his watch. There's a whole hour before the next contest. He looks at Matt and Sheri once more. He's had all he can take of their friendship and decides to go home. He's not standing around like a fool watching her walk all over town with another guy, even if they are just friends, which he finds hard to believe because no man could be just friends with her for long. It's just not possible. Her hugs are too warm. Her kisses are too soft and sweet. Her laugh is so perfect.

He reaches down to pet Jake, his loyal companion. "Come on, Jake. Let's go home."

Jake whines in response, but he shuffles down the walk beside Randall.

He closes his house door and sits down in his recliner. He stares at the TV, but it gives him no joy. He looks over at his Christmas tree and pictures her standing beside it, smiling and humming as she hangs up ornaments. He gets up and goes to the kitchen, but she's there too, standing at the sink, washing dishes, and doing her little chore dance. He recalls her cooking his breakfast at the stove, yakking away with that silly smile on her face.

He heads toward Jake's crate, but she's there too,

leaning over Jake and crooning as she scratches his ears. He can't bring himself to touch her doorknob and open her door for fear the scent of her perfume will float right up his nose. She's been here less than a month, and she's imprinted on every inch of his home. He can't believe what he's doing when he FaceTimes Jan.

"Yo, home girl," Jan calls out. Her face falls immediately. "Oh, it's you."

"Who did you think it was?" Randall asks.

"Sheri. Duh."

"But this is my phone," he answers, almost in a panic at the thought that Sheri's taken over everything.

"I know, but you hardly ever FaceTime me. I FaceTime you, and you answer reluctantly," Jan says with forced brightness. "So what's up? Tell Momma Jan everything."

He gets the shivers. "Call yourself momma one more time and we're done talking. For like a year."

Jan laughs. "Fine. What's up, cousin?"

He sighs. "I'm having trouble."

"Woman troubles," Jan asks, but it's not really a question.

"How'd you know?"

She shrugs. "Why else would you call me for help?"

He looks off to the side. "Who said I need help?"

Jan's nose is on the screen again. "Do you need my help or not?"

He tries to cover the screen with his hand. "What I don't need is your gigantic schnoz filling up my screen."

She takes a step back. "Sorry." She tilts her head to the side. "Hey, aren't you supposed to be at the Winter Festival today?"

He fidgets. "How'd you know that?"

She rolls her eyes. "I have your town's event calendar on my laptop. Don't act all surprised. You guys have like four main events every year. They're not that hard to remember."

He plops down on a barstool. "You ever going to come to one?"

She snorts. "Yeah right. The only thing I'd come up there for is your wedding day."

He feels like he's suffocating. He tugs at his collar.

She laughs. "Geez, cousin. Grow a pair. Are you that afraid of settling down?"

"I'm not afraid, Jan. I'm just not ready," he says. "There are things I don't know about her."

Jan itches her nose with the back of her oven-mitted hand. "Like what? If she's a serial killer?"

His eyes widen. "No. Why would you say that? You've got to stop watching those true crime shows."

Jan rolls her eyes. "If you want to hold onto her, you'd better get ready—and quick. I'm pretty sure she's not going to settle for anything less."

He sighs. "I know, Jan. I know all about the ball and that she's looking for commitment, but I don't know if I can marry her. All I know is I don't want her with anyone else."

Jan snorts again. "That hardly seems fair. Do you realize how crazy you sound? I mean, what if a girl told you that she didn't want to be exclusive with you or whatever, but she didn't want you dating anyone else? How would you feel?"

He doesn't like Jan turning the tables on him so fast. "What are you saying?"

She slams her dough into the counter. "Brace yourself, cous-in, 'cause I'm going all Aunt Mona on your butt."

He's officially afraid. Aunt Mona doesn't mess around. "What?" he answers.

She raises her hand. "I say this, Randall, with all the love in my heart for you that I can possibly have. Either propose to her soon, or leave the poor girl alone."

He sputters at the thought. "I can't. That's crazy. I mean, we've only known each other since right before Thanksgiving."

She laughs out loud. "I hate to tell you, cousin, but you ain't getting any younger, and neither is she."

"She's four years older than me." He pauses. "Is that weird?"

She laughs out loud. "Are you serious? First of all, women in general outlive men by seven years. Secondly, men marry younger women all the time. *Much* younger women. So, no. I don't think it matters." She raises a hand. "But now that you mention age, like I said, the two of you aren't getting any younger. Who knows how much time you have left? The real question is, who do you want to spend it with, and how do you want to spend it?"

He stares at the screen. "Thanks, cousin. For a baker, Jan, you sure have a lot of wisdom."

She gives him a wink. "I should be thanking you. You're preparing me for raising a teenage son."

"That's just great, Jan. Thanks for comparing me to a hormonal teenage boy."

She laughs again. "If you don't like my analogy, do something about it."

"I'd better go. I've got a log to split," he says to the back of her as she stands at her counter, slamming away.

Jan whips around. "That's disgusting. I don't need to hear about your bowel habits. I get enough of that from my toddler."

He almost laughs. "It's not an expression or whatever, Jan. It's a real contest. Surely, you've heard of it before. I've been the winner three years in a row."

She giggles. "You split logs."

He nods. "With an ax."

"And you win a prize for that."

He nods again. "Yep."

She crosses her arms on her chest. "I thought people who live in Alaska are like survivalists."

"That's a fair statement."

"Why do you get a medal for surviving?" She raises an eyebrow.

"That's a great question. I don't know."

She raises her eyebrows. "Fair enough." She waves a hand at the camera. "Don't let me make you late for your contest. Go. Chop away."

He does a tabletop dance with his hands. "Wish me luck."

"Or you could let some other poor sucker win," she mutters.

"In the spirit of eternal competitiveness, no I cannot do that," he answers.

She raises her hands in the air. "Fine, but it might be the only thing you win, and you can't really hug an ax in the middle of the night, or at least it won't hug you back."

"You're saying I should let her win? She'll totally know," he answers.

"Which makes it all the more romantic."

"I'm *not* bringing romance into an ax-swinging contest," he growls.

"Randall James Graham, if you don't want my advice, don't call me." Jan's mom voice is back.

"Fair enough," he says right before he hangs up. "If a girl's going to pout about losing a friendly competition, she doesn't deserve to win," he mutters just as he thinks of the way he's acting about possibly losing her to another guy. "Shoot," he mutters to no one. He checks his watch again. He's got five minutes to spare. He can't be late. He runs out to the truck. "Dang it. You're going to make me late, and you're not even here," he grumps at the open air.

53

Everyone is in their designated areas and Randall is nowhere to be found. Sheri can't believe he's skipping out on this contest. The man can sure put on a pout.

"I'm here, I'm here," he bellows from somewhere behind her.

She turns to see him jog up the path.

"Don't run with your ax, Randall," Bob hollers from his wheelchair. He points a long index finger. "Ax safety is part of the contest. Start walking or you're disqualified."

Randall slows to a walk a few feet away. "I'm walking, Bob." He huffs and puffs in the circle beside hers. "Carry on, Bob."

Bob clears his throat. "As I was saying before I was so rudely interrupted, each person must adhere to all the rules of the log-splitting contest."

"What about being late?" Sheri pops off before leaning around to stick her tongue out at Randall.

"I hope that sharp tongue of yours becomes a popsicle

and cracks right down the middle," Randall growls as he steps into his circle.

She gasps dramatically. "Randall Graham, what a thing to say!"

He gives her a glare before turning back to Bob. "The rules clearly state one is not late if they arrive before the rules have all been read."

Bob bobs his head up and down. "It's a good thing you know the rules since you didn't get to hear most of them."

"Don't you worry, Bob. I downloaded them all through Bertie's Whova app. You might want to get on board with that," Randall spouts.

"You did no such thing. You're just trying to get my goat. There's no need to fuel the fire between Bertie and me."

That statement catches Sheri's attention. *What is Bob talking about?*

Bob looks at Sheri and then Randall again. "If nothing else, you could take a lesson from a seasoned bachelor and an old spinster like Bertie. Some things aren't worth fighting over. By the time I figured that out, she wouldn't have anything to do with me."

Sheri blushes from head to toe. She can't believe Bob is in on this plot to get her together with Randall. She wishes they'd all stop it. Randall is going to think she's been talking about him to people, and that's the last thing she's been doing.

"Bob..." Randall says with no small amount of warning in his voice.

"Yes."

"Just read the dang rules so we can get this thing going."

Bob licks a finger and turns his page. "Rule number seven: no sharing axes. Rule number eight: if you chop off any part of your body, you are out of the contest. Rule number nine: if any piece of wood embeds itself in any part of your body, you are out of the contest. Rule number ten: no giving advice to your neighbor. Rule number eleven: no stealing your neighbor's logs. Rule number twelve: there's no right or wrong way to split a log. Rule number thirteen: everyone have fun. Rule number fourteen: you can't stop rules on the number thirteen. That'd be bad luck."

Sheri exhales slowly and decides if she hears one more rule about axes and body parts, she doesn't know if she'll stay. Remaining bodily intact is worth more to her than winning people over. She's still not sure about all this, but then the bell rings.

She hears cracks all around—reminders to get busy. She lines up her log and takes a swing. She dings the corner of the log, and the vibration goes all the way up to her shoulder. The log rolls off to the side. She feels so defeated.

She puts the log in place again and centers her focus. She tries to go back to the day in the woods when she was by herself. "One log at a time," she mouths and resolves to not leave her circle without splitting at least one. She takes a deep breath and lets the ax fall, and it works. She fights the urge to do a celebratory dance over the two logs that lie in front of her.

She nudges them off to the side like it's no big deal and lays down another. She takes a deep breath and does it all over again. Before too long she falls into a comfortable rhythm, and she's feeling pretty good. She ignores the ache in her shoulders and the handle cutting into her palms.

She's pretty sure she has fluid-filled blisters. The bell rings, and she lays down the ax with relief.

She looks over at Randall's pile of logs. His face is red, but other than that, he's not even breathing hard. *What a show off*, she thinks as he gives her a gloating grin. She turns away from him to walk over to Cheryl. A whistle blows.

"Get back in your circle and keep your number attached to your person, or you will be disqualified," Bob barks at her as he wheels his way down the sidewalk, scribbling away on his clipboard.

"Good job," Randall says from behind Sheri.

She doesn't look at him. He's going to be all braggy, which is worse than his childish pouting from earlier. Sheri stands with her back to him, jamming her gloved hands in her pockets to wait to be excused by Bob, who is nothing but thorough. This is ridiculous. It's freezing cold, and it's obvious she's not even close to winning. Her pile of logs looks rather meager compared to Randall's and the guy on the other side of him. She fidgets and squirms inside her coveralls. She peeks at her watch, noting it's been like ten minutes, and Bob has only judged one person. She removes her number and drops it in the circle of logs. She's leaving.

54

Randall watches Sheri abandon her post. He can't believe she's being so impatient. Sure, Bob's a bit of a slow poke, but everyone knows that. He feels torn. If he leaves, he has no chance of winning, but that guy on the other side of Sheri with his sizable pile of logs looks like he could give him a run for his money, and Randall hates to lose.

He turns to watch her walk down the alley toward the house. Jake trails after her like a traitor. Randall starts after her but stops when he almost trips on a log on the edge of his circle. He can't believe he almost lost the contest on account of Sheri. He turns around and looks the other way while he waits impatiently for Bob to finish his judging. He plops down on the stump inside his circle.

Forty-five minutes later, Bob taps his clipboard. "First of all, I'd like to note we have two women in the contest this year, and that is an exciting turn of events. I've always said every man *and* woman is welcome to enter the contest. Secondly, after careful consideration and much admiration for all of your hard work, it is my pleasure to announce that the winner of this year's log-splitting contest is...Randall Graham." Bob looks over at him. "Please step forward and collect your golden ax, Mr. Graham."

He supposes he should keep his mouth shut, but he can't help it. "Permission to leave my circle, Bob," he says with a smirk.

Bob scowls. "Permission granted, Randall. Come and get it," he challenges.

He takes a giant step out of his circle and approaches Bob. He holds up the golden ax with both hands on the handle.

"Please note the proper way to hold an ax," Bob calls out as Randall takes the ax from him and steps quickly away, swinging it just a little as he goes. "You're going to nick your knee," Bob warns.

He does a spin turn. "It's gold-plated, Bob. Calm down. It's not good for your blood pressure."

"I take metoprolol," Bob calls after his retreating form.

"Good to know," Randall hollers.

"Where you going? The ceremony isn't over," Bob scolds.

He turns and waves his ax above his head. "It's over for me, Bob." He slowly turns around once more and heads for home. He trudges down the sidewalk, feeling more unsure with every step. He's walked this same sidewalk too many times to count, but this time feels different. He has no idea what waits at the end. He only knows he's about done fighting whatever it is he thinks he can't give up. Bob's words of warning keep running through his mind, mostly because it's too easy for him to imagine growing old all alone. He knows he can be stubborn and difficult. It's part of who he is, but for the first time, he contemplates wanting to have everything his way if it means living all alone. Forever.

He stops in his tracks. He feels as if a light bulb just lit up his brain. "I don't want to be alone," he says aloud before he quickens his step.

———

He steps inside his front door. He's ready to dump all his pride at Sheri's feet and make some sort of commitment to being in a mature relationship, whatever that means. *It's awfully quiet,* he thinks. His breath hitches when he sees a red envelope on his table with his name on it. His feet feel like lead as he walks toward it. He can't help but smile when he sees the construction paper Christmas tree glued to the front of it. He opens the card.

My dear friend Randall,

I'll never forget the kindness you've shown me over the holidays. Despite your grumpy ways, you have the true Christmas spirit, and I am indebted to you.

You'll always be the man who I watched the Northern Lights with, the man who taught me about wildlife safety, how to swing an ax, and so much more. I don't know what my next step is, but I know one thing: whenever I think of Alaska, I'll think of you.

For reasons I think we both understand, I can't be your houseguest a day longer. There's just too much Alaskan mistletoe magic between us for me to handle.

I'm still holding out for that glass slipper. I owe it to

myself to give the New Year's Ball a chance. With that in mind, I'm moving out.

Please let me go.

From one kindred spirit to another,

-Sheri

He reads her words again as he sits in his recliner. He didn't know his heart could physically ache inside his chest, but that's what's happening.

He jumps up. "I have to go find her," he blurts out, making Jake jump a little. He sits back down. "She said not to. What does this mean? Does she want me to come after her, or does she really mean she doesn't want to see me?" He looks over at Jake, who stares up at him with sad eyes. "This is madness, Jake."

He drops the card and heads to the basement, looking for some sort of clue on what to do. He sees that her bed is made and her slippers are gone. He shoves the bathroom door open and scans her sink. It's bare. There's no perfume, no facial cleanser. There's no pile of makeup. His heart sinks. *She's really gone.*

55

Sheri walks between the library van and Bertie's front door, thinking that she never thought she'd be hiding out from the man she just might love or that she'd be roommates with a seventy-five-year-old woman, but this is her life now. She has nowhere else to go except the library, and she was all prepared to sleep over there, but when Bertie saw her walk in with her laundry basket full of clothes and her bathroom stuff minutes ago, she shook a finger at Sheri.

"Oh, no. You're not camping out in my library," Bertie declared.

Sheri's lip quivered, and tears rolled down her cheeks. "I can't stay with him, Bertie. He doesn't love me." She bit her lip before she commenced to bawling.

"Now, now, dear. You just come on home with me. I insist." Bertie gave her a pat on her shoulder as they walked outside. "You mark my words, Sheri. By Christmas time, that foolish man will come looking for you if he knows what's good for him."

Sheri isn't about to argue with Bertie, but she knew what she wrote. Sheri thought to herself, *He's not coming for me. Not when he's so set on being a bachelor.*

She raises her chin. "I don't care if he does or doesn't. I'm getting ready for the New Year's Ball. It's time for new beginnings. It can only get better from here," she says with a resolution she doesn't feel.

"Yes, dear. That's the spirit," Bertie says, but Sheri could tell she was just being agreeable. Bertie doesn't believe a word she said any more than Sheri does. "Darn men and their darn stubbornness. They never know when to quit," Bertie mutters.

Sheri nods in absolute agreement. "Yes, Bertie. You are so right."

Bertie raises a finger. "They need grit and determination to survive Alaska, this is true, but sometimes they take it too far."

Sheri tosses her laundry basket in the back of the library van and climbs in the driver's side seat. "I'll just follow you home if that's all right."

Bertie slaps the side of her van door and gives her a wink. "Try to keep up."

Minutes later, Sheri arrives at Bertie's house, parking her library van on the side of the street so she can unload, which she just finished doing.

Sheri makes her last trip inside. Bertie sits on her couch, knitting away. Sheri recalls something Bob said. "So what happened with you and Bob if you don't mind me asking?"

Bertie looks up from her knitting with a steely eye. "I mind you asking." She gives Sheri a kind smile as if to soften her words. "It's not much, but it's home sweet home, and you're welcome to share it with me," Bertie says brightly.

Sheri smiles back at her. "Thank you, Bertie."

"Don't thank me yet, girl. Living with me ain't free," Bertie says with a wink.

Sheri stands up straight, squaring her shoulders. "I'm not afraid of hard work."

"That's good," Bertie says as her needles click against each other.

Sheri looks out the window. "Is that Matt out there shoveling your walk?"

Bertie grins. "Yes. He's such a dear. He shovels my walk, and I do some cooking for him." Bertie taps her toe. "Why don't you stick your head out the door and ask him to eat with us tonight?"

Sheri shrugs. "Okay." She goes to the front door and opens it just enough to stick her head out like Bertie said. "Hey, Matt. You coming over for supper tonight?"

He stops his shoveling to give her a big smile. "Wouldn't miss it." He makes a face. "What are you doing here?"

Sheri swallows hard. "I'm staying here for a few days."

Matt gives her a knowing grin. "Had enough of Scrooge, have you? I don't blame you."

"He's not that bad, Matt. We just have different opinions about everything." Her eyes water, and she takes a deep breath.

Matt looks like he feels bad. "Hey, have you been by your house lately?"

She shivers at the thought. "Heck, no. That thing's a firetrap. I wouldn't dream of staying there."

A look of confusion crosses his face. "But I thought..."

Bertie clears her throat from behind Sheri, and she startles. She didn't realize Bertie got off the couch. "Keep shoveling, Matt. Sheri and I will have supper ready in no time at all."

He ducks his head. "You got it, Bertie."

Sheri walks behind Bertie with a basket, feeling like she missed something between Bertie and Matt.

The kitchen door swings open. Sheri can't believe she didn't smell anything before. "Bertie, what is that? It smells delicious."

Bertie turns with a wink. "I'm making my special meatloaf and potatoes. I can't tell you the recipe. It's a family secret."

Sheri sniffs the air once more. "I can't wait to try it. It smells heavenly."

Bertie snorts. "I wouldn't go that far, but thank you." She gives Sheri a little shove, and they leave the kitchen and walk through a few rooms. "Now, you can put your things in that spare room down the hallway. I think the oven and the Crock-Pot's about done cooking supper."

Sheri walks into the room with a bed by the window and sets down her basket of clothes. She sits on the edge of the bed. She can't believe how much she misses Randall already. She feels a little crazy. She sits in the dark for five minutes before Bertie pops her head in. "Hey, go tell Matt it's supper time."

Happy to have something to do besides sit and sulk, Sheri calls to Matt out in the yard. They walk into Bertie's kitchen together. Sheri smiles at the three plates set out.

"Fill up your plates and come sit down," Bertie instructs, and they don't hesitate. Then Bertie holds out two hands.

"Lord, we thank you for this food and this time together. Please bless this food to our bodies, and please help Randall come to his senses about this wonderful woman sitting beside me. Amen."

Sheri rolls her eyes. "Bertie, prayer isn't for your matchmaking."

Matt chuckles. "I don't know. Poor Randall needs all the help he can get."

Bertie shakes her head. "I've known that rascal since he was in diapers. He's as hardheaded as they come." She takes Sheri's hand. "But he's got a good heart, and his head is in the right place. Most of the time."

Sheri tries to be patient but she doesn't want to hear any more about the man she's trying so hard to forget. "Enough about Randall. I'm trying to eat while I still have an appetite." Sheri manages a joke, even though she wants to cry at the mention of his name.

Bertie gives her a sad smile. "Seeing you two sit here got me to thinking. I'd like to go to Fairbanks tomorrow, and I thought it'd be a good place for you to pick out a dress for that New Year's dance you're going to."

Sheri can't help but smile. "That'd be perfect. There's a red dress that I should have bought, but I didn't. I'm going to this time." She turns to Matt. "How about it? Are you up for a trip to the city?"

"Sure. Why not."

The rest of the night passes quickly which is good because Sheri's about done. Between the ax contest and the emotional rollercoaster Randall put her through, she's exhausted.

Sheri is up first thing in the morning, and so is Bertie, who is unusually quiet at the breakfast table. There's a knock at the door. "I bet that's Matt. Will you be a dear and let him in?"

Sheri walks over to unlock it. "Morning, Matt."

He gives her a nod. "Morning. Are you girls ready to go?"

Bertie walks into the room slower than they've ever seen her move. "My arthritis is really getting to me today. I think I'm going to have to stay home. You two run along and have your fun."

Sheri feels a little set up, but she really wants that dress. She walks toward the front door with Matt and practically shoves him onto the front porch. "If you want to stay home, I totally get it. We don't have to go. I think Bertie's pulling a fast one on us," she whispers.

He chuckles. "I know she is, but I was kind of looking forward to getting out of town."

Bertie hobbles over to peer out the front door. "You two take my car. I insist. That way I won't worry about you being out on the roads."

Matt takes the keys from her hand. "So long as you let me fill 'er up with gas."

"I won't say no to that," Bertie says as she holds out a piece of paper that moves with the wind. "Oh, could you two get these items, please? There are just some things I can't get around here."

"Sure, Bertie. We'd be happy to," Sheri says as she snatches the paper from Bertie's two fingers. "Is there anything else I can do for you while I'm out?" She must sound less than accommodating because Bertie gives her a look right back.

"No more than what I'm doing for you—and just for a

few days. I like my privacy. You're going to have to face Randall sometime you know."

Sheri thinks of her letter. "No, I don't. I said all I need to say."

"One-sided conversations don't solve anything," Bertie answers.

"Come on, Matt. Let's go," Sheri begs.

56

It's the night before Christmas, and Randall is sitting alone in his house. He feels so dejected that he doesn't even turn on his Christmas tree lights. Sheri's been gone for a week, and he's been a stubborn fool. He's avoided the library like the plague because it's obvious she doesn't want to see him, a fact he knows to be true because he heard through the grapevine she's been running around with Matt since she moved out.

Randall's work on her house is the only thing that's been a success. It's almost done despite Rick's entire family coming down with the flu ten days ago. The illness lasted seven days, and it took them another three days to fully recover. Bill had a family emergency, and he's been gone for the past six days. Randall's been the primary worker, and he's done a lot. It turns out remodeling is the perfect distraction for a wounded heart.

He feels like a beaten man, a feeling he's never felt before. He's not sure what to do about the fact that his pride is officially gone. He stares at her snow boot in the corner, the one that lies beside his golden ax. Sheri's bright red, satin-and-lace dress, with all its layers, hangs off his coatrack, just in case she decides to come back. He knows he should probably move all of it, but what he can't bring himself to do it. He knows no one will be stopping by, not anymore. She's gone. No one will come to see him on Christmas Eve. He turns off his lamp and hunkers down in his recliner. He feels like Scrooge, but he doesn't care. Christmas can go on without him just like so many years before, but this year he doesn't want it to. Now that he's met Sheri, he knows what he's missing.

Randall is just about to sleep when Jake lets out a low woof. His heart skips a beat, and hope rises in his chest. He can't help but wonder if she came back for him. He sits up to stare at his front door, and that's when he sees the candles. There are candles outside every window of his house. He wonders what is going on. He slips on his boots and walks softly across the room to open his front door. There's a small crowd outside. His eyes search for her, but she's nowhere to be seen.

A throat clears. Randall looks down. He sees the stern face of Bob, who sits up straight and true. "You don't deserve her," Bob growls as he shakes a telltale finger at Randall.

He frowns back at him. "I know that, Bob, but don't worry about it. She's not here."

He snorts. "I know that. Why do you think I'm here?"

He's had enough of this. "I have no idea!"

"We put out an APB on a woman driving a snowplow. We'll track her down for you. I guess it takes a village to find you your one true love," The dark-haired, brown-eyed officer calls out from the back with a telltale smirk on his face.

Randall blinks a few times. He can't believe what he's hearing. "Why is she in a snowplow?"

Matt steps up into the light. He's the last person Randall wants to see. "I guess she heard you were coming after her and she tried to get away."

His ears get stuck on the word *tried*. Why is Matt speaking in the past tense? "Is she okay? Did something happen?" Panic fills him.

Bob wags his finger from his wheelchair. "Nothing's happened yet. You want her back, don't ya?"

His eyes fly to the floor. "Well, yeah."

"You won't get her moping on your couch." Bob leans forward. "What'd you do to hurt her so bad?"

He looks at Bob and then at everyone closing in on him with their candle flames. "Why do you all think this is my fault?" he says in a quiet voice.

Bob snorts. "Because we know you."

He turns toward his front door and puts one hand on the handle. He doesn't owe anyone an explanation. He pulls it open, but something stops him: Sheri. Sheri is the reason everyone showed up for him. He turns to face them all again. "Sheri wants a commitment from me."

"Then why don't you give her one?" Bertie hollers out from the back.

He shakes his head. "I don't know if I know how. I've never done that," he answers.

"You're scared of falling, Randall, but it's too late. You already are. Anyone can see it." Bertie's on a roll.

He wants to hide from everyone's stare, but instead he stands there, feeling clueless as can be. "So what do I do?"

"Get in your fire truck and hunt her down," Scott, the semi-retired fireman, answers from somewhere in the back.

He itches the back of his neck. "But it's not an emergency, and that's your tax dollars I'm using."

Scott raises his hand in the air. "I make a motion that Randall use the fire truck to go after Sheri, the love of his life. All in favor, raise your right hand." Hands go up everywhere. "All opposed say, 'Aye.'"

57

"Aye," Sheri answers from the street in reply to Scott's call. She can't believe the crowd of people standing on Randall's front lawn. He put up a Christmas tree, so it can't be the Christmas Carolers Committee, but they're all holding candles, so she's not sure.

"Sheri." She hears Bertie's voice before she sees her. "Sheri's here. It's a Christmas miracle."

She almost laughs. "I wouldn't exactly call it that, Bertie," she answers as she walks slowly forwards, feeling a little like Moses as the crowd parts. She stops at the bottom of the steps and looks up at Randall.

"What are you doing here?" Randall asks in a quiet voice.

She feels foolish. "I couldn't exactly let you spend the county tax dollars on my behalf," she says with a smile, "and I may have put the snowplow in a ditch. It just stopped on me."

"What did you do to my baby?" Jerry pops out of the crowd, getting in her face.

"No more than what you did to the house you sold me," she says right back at him.

Jerry has the sense to look a little repentant. "Fine. Where is she? Where did you leave my Jadis?"

She giggles. "You named your snowplow Jadis?"

"Yes, because she's the Queen of Winter, like in the *Chronicles of Narnia*."

Color me surprised, she thinks. *I didn't think Jerry would know that movie.*

She tugs the key from her jacket pocket. "If you say so. *Jadis* is pulled over on the side of the road about five blocks from here."

"Which way?" Jerry's face has worry written all over it.

She points away from Randall's house. "That way."

Jerry starts to walk away. "Did you leave her runnin'?"

She fights the urge to roll her eyes. "Jerry, I'm trying to give you the key, and I just told you it's out of gas. No, she's not running."

He exhales slowly. "Oh, good."

She slaps the key in his hand. "Don't lose it." She turns back to Randall. "So, have you got anything to say to me?"

"Why don't you step into the light so I can see you?" he counters.

She swallows her pride and walks up the steps to his front porch. She lays a hand on Bob's wheelchair and waits for his apology.

He gets a stubborn look on his face. "Welcome back, and for future reference, don't leave me a Christmas card as a proper goodbye."

Sheri bites her lip and vows she will not cry, at least not in front of Randall. "Well, if that's all you've got to say, I'll just be on my way." *That's all he's getting from her,* she decides. She turns to leave, but Bob snags her arm.

"You'd better stop right there, missy, before you pull me and my wheels down Randall's steps."

Sheri looks down at him. "Let go of me, Bob. Please."

"I can't, Sheri. Not until you two have said all you need to say. Randall has more to say. Don't you, Randall?" Bob prompts.

He clears his throat. "Will you please look at me, Sheri?"

Sheri slowly turns around and stares up at him while she wills her heart not to break all over again. She did enough crying in the snowplow, which might be why she ended up halfway in a ditch. "I'm sorry."

"I know that," Randall spits out.

She's not making this easy on him. She doesn't care if apologies are hard for him to make.

"Would you like to come inside where we can talk?" Randall says in a voice that tells her he's barely keeping his cool.

She shakes her head. "No. I'm staying right here."

He taps his toe. His fists ball up at his sides. "Fine. If that's what you want, then fine." He raises one hand in the air. "Just so you know, whatever is said out on this porch, don't say I didn't warn you, and never say I didn't try to bring you inside."

What on earth is he talking about? she wonders. She raises her nose a little. "Go ahead. I've got nothing to hide." A slow smirk forms on his face and darn it all to heck if she doesn't find it sexy as all get out.

"Wait just a minute. I'll be right back." With that, he spins on his heel and shuts his front door.

She goes over to the front porch swing and sits down. Minutes go by, and she has her doubts. *What if Randall's so mad at her for leaving that he doesn't come back out?* she wonders. *How long should I sit here waiting?*

The front door flies open, and Randall's back. He holds a long, tall cardboard box, and she thinks the messy bow wrapped around it is made out of an Ace wrap. He drops it on the porch with a thud. "What's all that?" she asks, not in the nicest tone.

He turns in her direction. "Why don't you come over here and find out?" he challenges.

She gives a non-committal shrug. "I'm comfortable where I am, but thanks."

He picks it all back up. "Fine. If you want to be the proverbial pain in my ass I know you to be, I'll come to you."

Bob coughs. "Language, Randall."

"I'm working on it, Bob, trust me, but this woman brings out the worst in me." Randall sets the box down in front of her and drops to one knee. He takes her hand and lays his lips on her knuckles. She melts a little inside. "If you're going to insist on being a Christmas princess, I'll do my best to be a Christmas Prince." He raises an eyebrow. "As you know, a true princess has the habit of leaving her prince a trail." His voice rings loud and clear, and the crowd answers with a few giggles and chuckles here and there. Sheri blushes clear down to her toes, but she's frozen with delicious anticipation. She can't wait to find out what's in the box.

He reaches in all slow-like and pulls out the red Christmas dress she found at the boutique. "Let the record show item one is a ball gown for my Christmas princess."

Her eyes narrow. "That's why Matt and I couldn't find it."

Randall's smile starts to disappear, and his face tightens, but then he slowly relaxes. "Just remember which prince bought it for you."

She stills like a deer in headlights. "I can't believe you bought it. I thought I'd never see it again."

He gives her hand a gentle squeeze before delving back into the box. He pulls out his golden ax. "Now, most princesses wear a golden tiara, but my princess lives in Alaska, and everyone knows a true Alaskan knows how to swing an ax." He holds the ax before her in open palms with his head down as if he is about to be knighted. "Do you accept this ax, Sheri, as a token of as much surrender as I can offer?" His voice is soft and low.

"Yes, I do," she answers in the same manner.

He raises his head with a smile. "Good, that's very good."

Her heart glows like a candle aflame. "Are you done?"

He shakes his head. "Not quite."

She buries her face in her hands. "Okay," she answers into her fingers.

He tips the box on its side and gives it a good shaking. Something moves inside. He pulls out a snow boot. "As you all know, Cinderella also had a glass slipper. I present to you, my darlin', an Alaskan glass slipper: a snow boot."

The crowd laughs out loud. He holds her boot high in the air. "Sheri and I were working in the shed on something when I cut my hand clean through my glove. She was in such a hurry to get me inside, she ran right out of her boot and left it behind in the yard." He smiles at her. She feels it all the way to her toes. "This crazy girl ran through the snow in her socks." He shakes his head. "That's when I knew she was a woman to love." His eyes meet Sheri's. "I'd be a fool not to fall for a woman who would run practically barefoot through the snow just for me." He slowly lowers the boot to the floor. "Do you want to try it on to see if it still fits?"

She kicks off her shoes and lowers her foot into the boot, but it gets stuck halfway down. She tries to keep going. Pain shoots through her big toe. She cramps all the way to her calf. She swallows hard. "My foot is stuck," she whimpers.

He pulls it out. "Hold still. I'm fixing it."

She grabs a hold of the boot and yanks it back toward her. "It fits, Randall. It's just a little tight."

He chuckles. She can't believe he's laughing at her at a time like this. Heat creeps up her neck.

"Relax, Sheri. There's no need to break your foot. If it doesn't fit, it doesn't fit," he tries to soothe her.

Sheri lays a hand on his shoulder and stands up while she shoves her foot into the boot. She stomps around a few more times, and her foot finally hits bottom. "See?" she shouts in triumph. "It fits!"

He falls back on his butt. He has a bemused expression on his face. "Well, then there's only one thing left to do." He reaches into his jacket pocket and pulls out a tiny box.

Her heart beats triple time. He opens the box and lifts it up. There's an oval-shaped green gemstone nestled between tiny diamonds attached to a gold ring.

"Sheri Mallo, will you date me, and only me, for the unforeseeable future?" he asks.

"And move back into his house," Bertie hollers.

Sheri is struck dumb. She can't believe what is happening. "But...it's green," is all she can think to say.

"Excuse me," he says in a tone that tells her that's the last answer he expected to hear.

"The stone on the ring. It's green," she says, feeling more ridiculous by the second for ruining his romantic gesture.

"It's jade, Sheri. Jade is the gemstone of Alaska. Do you not like it?" He sounds so eager to please. She feels terrible.

She reaches out to touch it. "I love it. Thank you," she says.

He blinks. "You didn't answer me." Her finger stops moving, but it rests on the ring stone, that's so smooth.

"Yes, I did," she says absentmindedly, as she feels a bit overwhelmed.

"No, you didn't," he insists.

She sighs. "I know I did."

He snaps the box shut on her beautiful ring, and she moves her fingers just in time. "I asked you to commit to me, and you didn't answer my question," he says quietly.

"I have a ball to go to," she whispers.

"But that was before you met me," he insists.

"I have to give it a chance," Sheri says.

He frowns up at her. "You didn't say yes to my question."

She lays a hand on the golden ax beside him and glances down at the one snow boot. "Ask me again...after the ball."

He blinks. "You want me to ask you the same question after you go to the ball to find a husband." He shakes his head. "I don't think I can do that. It's now or never. I'm asking you now to make a decision about me."

A tear rolls down her cheek. "I can't answer you now and you know why." She leans in and gives him a kiss on the cheek. "I'll miss you," she whispers as she pulls away.

He holds in a yell as she walks awkwardly down the steps in her mismatched shoes, carrying his golden ax in one hand and the red dress in the other. He can't believe that after all that, she left him without a backward glance. He sits down at the top of his steps. The candle flames go out as if cued, and the crowd disperses.

Randall looks over at the man in the chair, who is speechless for once. "Well, Bob, I guess it's just me and you and Jake."

Bob chuckles. "Sorry, Randall. I've got to go. It's almost time for the Christmas Eve Scrabble tournament. I can't miss it. There are cash prizes."

He raises an eyebrow in surprise. "Where's that?"

Bob gives him a shove in the shoulder. "Online, son. You really gotta get out more." Bob taps the arm of his chair with his fingertips. "Be a good man and roll me down the ramp, would ya? It's a little slick."

58

Randall spends another long week alone. He can't believe how empty his house feels. It's been six long days since Sheri walked out of his life for the second time, and he can't believe all he wants is for her to come back. But he's done throwing himself at her ungrateful feet.

It's the day before the Christmas Ball, and he sits in his recliner, as usual, staring at the TV. There's a knocking at his door. Jake looks over at him, expectantly. "I don't want to answer, Jake. I'm not in the mood for company," Randall grumps.

The knocking gets louder.

"Go away," he yells.

The knocking continues, and then the knob turns.

He lets out a long sigh. "Come in already."

"Randall, what a nice surprise! We wondered if you would be home."

He cringes at the sweet sound of Mrs. Betts's voice. "Hey, Mrs. Betts," he answers to the dark hallway that leads to his main room.

He braces himself when Bertie peeks around the corner at him. "Randall James Graham, what are you doing here? You need to go after her."

"She went to the ball, Bertie. She doesn't want me. I offered her everything. You saw. You were there." He looks down at his lap. "She rejected me."

Bertie throws a hand on her blue-jeaned hip. "Yes, you did, Randall. There's no denying that, but she clearly wants a prince. If you want her back, you're going to have to go and get her."

He pulls on a string hanging off his jeans. "I'm not making a fool of myself anymore. I'm done with that. I'm fine by myself."

Mrs. Betts stares him down. "You don't look fine to me. You look like a man wishing for something he's not willing to work for."

His chin flies up. "I did! I worked harder for that woman than I've ever worked for anyone." He's out of his chair and pacing. "She doesn't want me, and that's that."

"Well, I've never known you to give up so easily. Clearly, she's not for you," Bertie needles him as she settles into his couch, and Mrs. Betts is right beside her. Bertie gives Mrs. Betts a nudge, and she nods her head in agreeance.

"That's right, Bertie. I wasn't too sure they fit together either."

"She's perfect for me, just like I'm perfect for her! We're both overly opinionated, and we have to have the last word, and she's a woman I respect. We see eye to eye most of the time, and she doesn't take any crap from me either." Randall shakes his finger in their faces. He's shocked to see them smiling up at him with knowing grins. "You two tricked me," he grumbles.

Bertie nods her head. "Do you believe your own words or not?"

He stomps his foot. "Of course, I do." He stops talking and glares at her again. "Stop doing that."

Mrs. Betts looks as serious as he's ever seen her. "Put your money where your mouth is, son, and go get her."

He frowns. "I can't. I have nothing to wear. I have no ticket to that stupid ball, and it costs a thousand dollars."

Bertie reaches into her purse and pulls something out. "Here. Lucky for you we Bingo ladies are awful generous, and we want Sheri in our town to stay. She's a big-hearted lady. She's loyal to a fault, and she's kind and she's a keeper." She looks him up and down. "And we like you too," she says in a quieter voice. "We don't want you leaving town if she comes back with another man on her arm."

He has a moment of panic. "You really think she'd do that?"

Bertie doesn't blink as she stares him down. "She gave you fair warning."

He starts for the door before he looks down at his clothes. "What will I wear?"

"Oliver's a good friend of mine. He's got a tux shop nearby the ball. He'll get you looking sharp. If you start driving now, you'll be there by morning. You can go there first thing and get a tux and then go to the hotel for a nap before the ball. We'll watch your house while you're gone."

He runs back to the women. He leans over and gives them both an awkward hug. "Thanks for looking out for me."

Bertie pats him on the back. "Hey, that's what neighbors do. Now get going."

————

Randall stands by his truck in the parking lot. He eyes his ticket to the ball one more time. "Just go in before you lose your nerve," he says to himself. "Those women paid all this money for the ticket. You can't let them down."

He walks across the lot. His heart is in his chest. His feet feel like they're weighted down. He can't believe how nervous he is; more nervous than he ever was for any high school dance he ever attended. A huge Christmas tree is lit up outside. Giant metallic blue-and-silver ornaments lay at its base. He slows his walk as he watches other men and women wander inside, all dressed up in their formal wear. He feels so out of place. *It's been so long since he tried,* he realizes. He looks down at his trembling hand. "Don't back out now, Randall," he whispers to himself inside his head. "This might be your last shot."

He takes a deep breath and starts for the red carpet that leads inside. Bright lights blind him as he hands the ticket to the lady standing inside. She scans the barcode and gives it back. "There you go, sir."

He folds it in half and shoves it in his pocket before walking through the double doors. Randall is overwhelmed by the amount of people in the room mingling around. He searches the crowd for a red dress but doesn't see one. He heads for the bar for a beer and a snack.

"What can I get you?" The guy looks like he's sixteen.

"Are you old enough to be serving alcohol?" Randall asks.

"I'm here, aren't I?"

Randall leans on the bar. "I'd like a beer."

"We don't have that, sir."

Randall straightens up. "Then what do you have?"

"We have white claws or a glass of wine."

"I'll take a red wine, then."

"Which one?"

Randall is thoroughly irritated. "Any one will do. Do you have any snacks?"

The guy drops a protein bar in front of him. "Here you go, sir. It's full of protein, and it's low carb."

Randall snatches it up along with his wine. "Thanks."

The guy flashes him a smile. "Have a nice night. Come back any time."

Randall shakes his head as he walks away. "That's not likely," he grumbles. He finds a chair at a table in the farthest corner and plops down in it. A few women wander by, but he hardly looks up.

His eyes are glued to the front door. The music is loud, but he doesn't hear it. There are plenty of beautiful women in the room, but he doesn't see them. He's waiting for Sheri, and he's starting to doubt everything she said. He sips his red wine and nibbles at his protein bar, trying to make both of them last. He's not going back to that poor excuse for a bar that doesn't even serve a decent bottle of beer.

The night is almost over. Randall has lost all hope of seeing Sheri. He wants to leave, but he's been there all night and he's out of ideas. It's like he's stuck and he can't make himself get up out of the chair.

"Ladies and gentlemen, this night of magic is almost

over, so grab that special someone to share your first dance of many more to come."

Randall stares down at the table and sighs. "Oh, well. This won't be the first party I've shut down, but it'll be the last," he mutters.

A golden ax falls on the table in front of him, making him jump. His eyes take in a pair of bright red snow boots right before he looks at the hand that dropped the ax. He spots the green ring. He sits back in his chair.

"Dance with me," Sheri says as she extends her hand.

There are so many things he wants to tell her, so much he has to say. He takes her hand. "I thought you'd never ask."

He follows her to the dance floor. He takes her in his arms. They sway to Anne Murray's "Could I Have this Dance."

"I almost didn't come tonight," she whispers near his ear.

"I've been here a while," he answers.

She lays her head on his shoulder. "You have?"

He nods. "I have. I want points for that."

She giggles and clears her throat. "Sometimes it takes me a while to see what's important."

He chuckles, and his chest rumbles. "You and me both." He chuckles again. "I can't believe you brought that ax in here."

She giggles. "They almost didn't let me in. Their idea of a tiara and yours isn't quite the same."

Randall throws his head back with laughter. The other dancers give him a strange look. He straightens up. "Well, apparently they haven't met too many Alaskan princesses."

She snuggles into him. "A smart princess is always prepared."

"Preparation is important, but a prince is too." He speaks in a cautious voice. His breath hitches as he waits for an answer.

Sheri's hand sneaks to the back of his neck, and she draws him in for a sweet kiss. "Yes, finding the right prince has always been a dream of mine."

"And have you found him?" he whispers as he dares to hope now that she stands before him.

"Yes."

EPILOGUE

Six Months Later

S heri and Randall stand at the grand opening of their Airbnb, called "An Alaskan Fairy Tale." It was their labor of love. Bill and Scott stand at both ends of the long, red ribbon stretched out between them.

She gives him a wink. "Grab the ax handle, honey."

He is heated through. He can't believe how one little word from her lips hits him in the chest every time. He never thought he'd like being called honey. He stands beside her and lays a hand right above hers. They raise the golden ax and bring it down, cutting the ribbon in two.

She turns to him and kisses him in the middle of all their friends and neighbors. Her face glows with happiness as she wipes a tear from her cheek. "I can't believe this is happening."

He laughs. "Well, it is. Come on, follow me."

She walks across the circular stones that lead to the steps of her fairy-tale house. She looks out into the crowd until she finds Matt.

"Matt, come up here."

He jogs up to join them. She slips an arm around Matt's waist and the other around Randall's as she gives them both a squeeze. Bertie waves her hand from out in the yard. "Everyone say, 'golden ax.'"

Randall, Matt, and Sheri laugh as they say, "Golden ax."

Bertie snaps a few pictures with her phone. She gives a thumbs-up. "Perfect! These are going to look great on the landing page I'm creating. It's going to be great for tourism. I just know it." She holds up her phone again. "I got it on Whova too. It's the open house event."

Sheri heads down the stairs. She looks up at the golden axes that adorn the front of the house above the porch. She giggles as she remembers the day Randall suggested them as they sat together at his kitchen table, brainstorming after she recovered from finding out he'd spent his entire nest egg on remodeling her firetrap of a home.

"You want crossed axes to be our signature mark?" she asked him in disbelief.

He ducked his head in embarrassment. "Yes. They're... they're kind of like you and me."

She gave him a look before interrupting. "Did you just compare me to an ax, Randall Graham?"

He threw up his hands. "Hear me out. We clash and make a lot of noise, but used together the right way, we hold up under pressure, we work hard, and we get things done."

She giggled again. "Leave it to you, Randall, to get all philosophical about a blade attached to a wooden handle."

He leaned back in his chair, crossed his arms on his chest, and looked very pleased with himself. "I'm a lumberjack, and you love me all the more for it."

She blushed from head to toe. "So help me, I do."

"Sheri!"

She snaps out of her memory.

"Sheri, come inside," Bertie summons her from the top of the steps. "Come help me take some more pictures."

Sheri walks back up the steps. Randall throws an arm through hers. He looks down at her. "Did you ever imagine you'd be a librarian, a med aide, a housekeeper, and the co-owner of an Airbnb all at the same time?"

She looks down at her ring and back at Randall. "I'm not doing too bad for a girl in her forties." She gives him a nudge. "I might be a girl you want to hold on to."

He pats her hand. "I plan to, darlin'. Don't rush me." He taps her on the nose. "Good things come to those who wait." He gives her a wink. "Isn't that what you always say?"

Sheri lets out a long sigh. "Yes."

They walk along behind Bertie. "Any time you want to move up from the basement, you're more than welcome," he teases her.

"Not without your last name, I'm not," she says right back.

He stumble-trips, and he goes down.

She stops in her tracks. "Are you all right?"

He rights himself as he rises up on one knee. "Sheri Mallo, will you marry me?"

She blinks. She can hardly believe what is happening. "Do you mean it?"

"I asked, didn't I?"

355

"Yes," she whispers.

"Yes, I asked? Or yes, you will?" he can't believe how confused he is. A proposal is pretty straightforward.

"Yes, I will marry you," Sheri says as she takes his face in her hands and kisses him.

He stands to his feet. He takes a hold of her hand and leads her to the front door. "Hey!" he yells to the crowd standing outside. "You're all invited to a wedding. She said yes!"

They all clap their hands and cheer. "When is the big day?" Bill hollers out.

"Tonight. It's happening here. Tonight," he answers.

She blinks. "I don't have anything to wear. Who's going to marry us? How are we going to feed everyone?"

Bertie sneaks up behind them. "I've got it all planned out. He and I've been talking a little bit."

He looks all sheepish. "I thought you could wear that red dress of yours. It's my favorite." He fidgets. "I bought that tux after the dance. It's pressed and ready."

She feels a little left out. "And who's going to marry us?"

"I am," Matt says from behind them.

She stares at him. "You're not a minister."

Matt smiles. "No, but I'm ordained. I got a certificate online."

She looks at Randall. "I guess I'm ready to move out of your basement."

Randall laughs out loud. Matt looks at the two of them like they're a little crazy. "O-kay."

Bertie claps her hands, and everyone quiets. "Return tonight for Randall and Sheri's wedding celebration." She points to the sign hanging from the chain links. "An Alaskan fairy tale!"

The crowd around them cheers, but Sheri only sees Randall. "I can't believe you gave me my fairy-tale house."

He smiles down at her. "I can't believe you gave me your heart."

———

Don't miss out on your next favorite book!
Join the Melange Books mailing list at
www.melange-books.com/mail.html

THANK YOU FOR READING

———

Did you enjoy this book?

We invite you to leave a review at your favorite book site, such as Goodreads, Amazon, Barnes & Noble, etc.

DID YOU KNOW THAT LEAVING A REVIEW...

- Helps other readers find books they may enjoy.
- Gives you a chance to let your voice be heard.
- Gives authors recognition for their hard work.
- Doesn't have to be long. A sentence or two about why you liked the book will do.

ABOUT THE AUTHOR

I live in the beautiful Flint Hills of Kansas. I'm blessed to do two things I love- nursing and writing. I have wonderful family support including my husband, our son, daughter-in-law, and two daughters, as well as many friends who willingly give their input whenever it is requested. I'm thankful for the characters and stories as they come along, as well as the companies who publish them and readers who read them.

facebook.com/RachelAnneJonesAuthor

x.com/Jones1974Ra

instagram.com/diari197

tiktok.com/@idreamofdandelions

ALSO BY RACHEL ANNE JONES

With Satin Romance

A Joy-Filled Christmas

Pickles-N-Fries and Fireflies

Stealing the Glass Slipper

———

With Fire & Ice YA Books

__Novels__

Marmalade Uncapped

Essence of Emma

Lovestruck: Kisses, Lies & Oatmeal Cream Pies

__All Or Nothing Series__

Chasing Denver

Rough Terrain

A Firm Plateau

__Radioactive Series__

Love and Armageddon

House of Cinders

M.I.A.